Larry Buttrose was born in Adelaide, South Australia. He is a poet, playwright and travel writer. *Sweet Sentence* is his second novel. He lives on the far north coast of New South Wales.

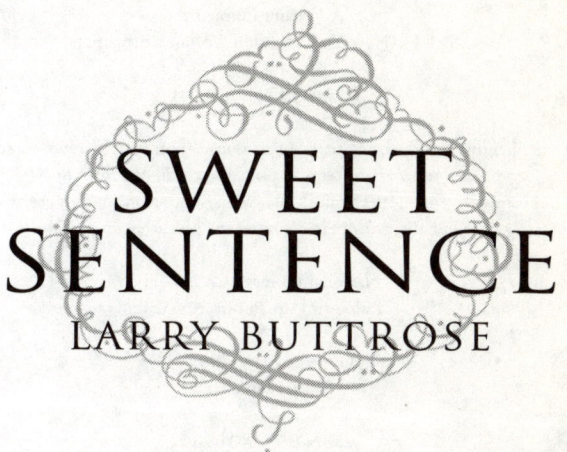

SWEET SENTENCE

LARRY BUTTROSE

SCRIBNER

SWEET SENTENCE
First published in Australia in 2001 by Scribner
an imprint of Simon & Schuster (Australia) Pty Limited
20 Barcoo Street, East Roseville NSW 2069

A Viacom Company
Sydney   New York   London   Toronto   Singapore

© Larry Buttrose 2001

All rights reserved. No part of this publication may be reproduced,
stored in a retrieval system, or transmitted, in any form or by any
means, electronic, mechanical, photocopying, recording or otherwise,
without the prior permission of the publisher in writing.

National Library of Australia
Cataloguing-in-Publication data:

Buttrose, Larry, 1952– .
Sweet sentence.

ISBN 0 7318 1090 2.

I. Title.

A823.3

Cover design by Yolande Gray Design
Cover image by Getty Images
Typeset by Asset Typesetting Pty Ltd in 11/15 Adobe Garamond
Printed in Australia by Griffin Press

Quote from *Poet of the 21st Century: Harry Hooton Collected Poems, poems
and prose introduced and selected by Sasha Soldatow*
reproduced with kind permission of HarperCollins Publishers.
Song lyrics for 'Hobo's Lullaby' by Goebel Reeves (© Sanga Music, Inc.)
reproduced with kind permission of Essex Music Australia Pty Ltd.

10 9 8 7 6 5 4 3 2 1

Acknowledgments

I gratefully acknowledge the generous assistance of the following people in the writing of this book: Kathryn Riding, Nalini Chettur, Sandy Aranha, Lori Silverbush, Walter Bisetto, Mardi Kendall, Ian Iveson, Julia Stiles, Heather Jamieson, Bridget Howard, Jody Lee, Angelo Loukakis, Rachel Skinner, and Peter and Victoria Thompson.

In memory of my uncle, Charles Buttrose

Depends on what you can give
and not what you can get.
– MAHATMA GANDHI

Neglected sign, Varanasi railway station

THE
MERRY
WIDOW

The moon made an entry onto a cloud-curtained stage, hushed with the first of night. The atmospheric conditions prevailing, the still, dense tropical air, or perhaps it was simply the curvature of the earth (her physics wasn't up to it), rendered it a flattened oblong, like a ball struck out of shape by a bat, and it was coloured the rich yellow of old butter. She sat on the sea wall and watched it, gradually inflating as it rose, assuming its customary roundness and leaching colour until it approached a creamy whiteness. Thus, as she witnessed it, all was right with the moon.

Out on the Bay, the waves were wind-chopped and came charging in, tumbling on top of each other like scrimmaging dogs. They crashed onto the piled up boulders and sprayed up a haze salted with dabs of brine that slicked the faces of the people on the esplanade. There was an immense number of these, so many that the police had blocked off traffic, and stood guard at their posts in their body-hugging lilac uniforms and red *kepi* caps. It always struck her as passing strange, policemen in lilac, but they acted like normal enough police, arrogantly fending off the taxis and rickshaws, and the stately chauffeur-driven Ambassadors of the wealthy, the drivers making at least a show of arguing to illustrate the status of their patron in the back seat. The entire mile or so of the esplanade remained vehicle-free, and the roadway and the concrete promenade above the waves became strollway, playground and open-air sitting room for the citizenry of all religions, castes and classes.

The crowd was thickest in front of the Gandhi statue that marked the esplanade's midpoint. A market had sprung up in the square of wasteland opposite, and people clustered around lantern-lit stalls where spiced delicacies fried in rows of big black woks. They ate their *samosas* where they stood, watching children climbing up the statue of the Mahatma and sliding down its support struts like the bannisters of the staircase of a great-uncle. Some badgered their parents for a rupee for a shooting gallery or toy stall. Street sellers cajoled with bright handfuls of balloons and bunches of tiny cane propellers that whirred loudly in the breeze.

Julia walked alone in the crowd, not knowing the occasion that had summoned it together, even if there was one beyond it being a Sunday evening and the weather fine. As she walked, she became aware of a pair of infants tagging along with her. They were poor, but dressed up for the night out. On another occasion they might have put out a hand for a rupee, but this was a night off for everyone, and they only laughed and chanted 'hello! hello!' She halted and looked down at them, a girl and a boy, grinning with sudden shyness and half-trying to conceal their faces. When she replied 'hello' they squealed and scurried back into their safe familial knot. She felt a momentary guilt at not having offered them a rupee or a piece of the sweet cashew-nut *burfi* in her pocket. But then, she thought, are all of our contacts with the very young here to be mediated by money or sweets?

She had ventured out to buy a bottle of water and a roll of toilet paper, utter neccessities and she needed both. So far the only places she had seen open on the esplanade sold pizzas, burgers and ice creams. In the end she had to walk all the way through the Ville Blanche to the foul-smelling canal that marked the border with the Ville Noire, where she remembered a day or two before seeing a row of stalls selling a cheapside allsorts of cigarettes and matches, toothpaste and sachets of hair shampoo. There she was at last able to find a bottle of water, and, after a farcical mime for the Tamil-speaking shopkeeper, a roll of toilet paper.

The route back took her past the entrance to the temple, where she paused to watch the resident elephant conferring the blessing of Ganesh onto pilgrims for a rupee, and was herself blessed with a delirious draught of jasmine from a stall selling flower garlands. A leper woman, white hair neatly parted and oiled, stretched up a lotus of finger-stumped twin palms, and Julia dropped in the two-rupee note she had been holding, her water change, like a boon from a passing god on a heavenly palanquin.

Dragged from the shallows of sleep by the cawing of crows, he awoke tangled in mosquito netting. He tried to recall his dreams, but they slipped away too swiftly, and soon he merely lay in his bed staring up at the ceiling beams, thinking of nothing. Through the French windows came the rattle of the dried leaves of the courtyard palms, an unpleasant clatter at this hour, at any. From below came the high-pitched voices of the *ayahs* making breakfast. They were piercing, and made Marco want to get up and go out right away. This was not to be achieved quite so readily, however, and some ten or fifteen minutes passed before he rose and proceeded to wash, to shave and dress. His delay in rising had been caused by him having no clear idea of what he might do on that morning, other than what he did on every other morning, which was to walk down the esplanade to breakfast at Le Cafe Blanc, and digest the *Hindu* and the *New Indian Express*. Reading the papers was something of a bloodsport here, and there was that to look forward to, as well as the half-read novel which was his siesta time reading, but beyond them lay a day unrevealed.

Julia found the morning fresh. Beyond the esplanade, waves broke in a choppy brown broth, while on the horizon a reticent sun was just emerging from a range of grey cloud banks. Returning indoors from her balcony, she squeezed a lime into a cupful of mineral water and drank it while brushing her hair in the wavy distortion of the dressing table mirror.

A bell sounded in the distance, a guest summoning morning

coffee. A minute or two later she heard the slow flip-flop of rubber on tile as one of the *ayahs* ascended the stairs in response. She heard the bolt of the room across the landing slide back and the voice of the male occupant accepting his daily order. He sounded English, though there was another tone in his accent, enticingly faint, the soft cadence of something European – Spanish or Italian perhaps. He had been in that same room, Room Ten, since her arrival in Pondicherry, but in that fortnight she had only seen him on one occasion, as he closed his door one evening. Then she had glimpsed an angular man with black hair neat cut and parted straight as the Red Sea. He stared fixedly out through gold-framed spectacles, his manner seemingly requesting she pay no closer attention, and she had obliged. There had been one other possible sighting, but that very fleeting, of him straight-backed, eyes directed forward, in the shadowy rear of an autorickshaw.

She pulled on the black cotton dress draped over the end of the bed, crossed the tiles and shot back the bolts of her double doors. She traversed the silent landing with the upstairs guest rooms running off it, and padded down the stairs. The Dining Room was small and austere, almost claustrophobic, with its half dozen tables and chairs, battered sideboard, and *de rigueur* framed portrait photographs of Sri Aurobindo and The Mother. It was always quiet early. Most of the guests tended to make their entrances later. Others preferred to eat in their rooms, or go out. The guests were a mixed bunch of Aurobindo devotees and budget travellers, mostly European and American. There was the occasional fellow Australian too. A nurse from Perth had recently stayed a day or two, a can-do type with a passion for rafting and bungee jumping. She was so outdoorsy that Julia couldn't help wondering what might have brought her to a place like Pondicherry, with its almost saintly streets and tempo of daily life evenly measured by the comings and goings of the Sri Aurobindo Ashram, and the Alliance Francaise with its *affaires culturelles*. But she often found herself wondering what the other guests were doing in Pondy, and in that old French house with stained walls, tepid showers and languid staff.

Some were there of course to 'find themselves'. On arrival they exchanged their jeans and T-shirts for robes of sacred white, and mooched their days about the Ashram. Others were most definitely travellers, on the beat down from Chennai towards Madurai, and the palmy beaches of Kerala. They studied their guidebooks at the breakfast table like manuals of warfare, determined never to pay a rupee more. There was also the occasional traveller who (Julia noted with a tiny thrill of pride) carried *The Hobo's Lullaby* guide to India. These were generally travellers broaching middle age, female and solo, who would come down one morning, pick at toast staring into space, and later be glimpsed down on the rocks watching the stick figures of the fishermen on their log boats out to sea. As evening came and the Rue Nehru shops busied, they might be seen flicking disinterestedly through the racks of dusty shirts on the street, or alone at a dining table. Any conversation with such women was strained and ended inconclusively, yielding not much more than that they worked in a dance academy in Oslo or did social work in Liverpool. When asked what they were doing in Pondicherry they would shrug as if to say 'I don't really know, what are you doing here?'

Julia peered around a corner into the kitchen, looking for Lakshmi. A girl in her teens, she always wore a hot pink sari. Perhaps it was her only one, yet it was always fresh and clean. Julia saw her rinsing dishes, doe-eyed at the sink.

'Good morning, Lakshmi. Is my washing ready yet please?'

The girl's eyes clouded, and so, indicating the dress she wore, Julia added: 'See, this dress isn't very clean. But you have another one like it, a green one, which I gave to you yesterday for washing. Is it ready yet, please?'

'Laundry. She's asking about laundry,' came a male voice from behind. 'You have to use the right word. Laundry. That's the one she knows.'

Suppressing a mild annoyance, Julia half turned to him and said: 'Thanks. Yes. I'd like my laundry please, Lakshmi.'

The girl gave an affirmative wobble of her head and stepped into a side room, returning with a bundle of washed and ironed clothing. Julia saw each item neatly tagged, her own dress near the bottom of the pile.

'Don't you just love how they tag everything,' the male voice said. 'All those annoying little holes in your clothes.'

Julia knew the girl wouldn't understand much of what he had said, and Lakshmi's response was another wobble of the head and a look down to the floor as she presented Julia with her dress.

'They just love to tag things, number things, anything and everything,' he continued. 'Haven't you seen them in the corner stores, how they even number stacks of banknotes? They're totally obsessed with numbers. No wonder they like cricket so much. It's all numbers.'

'Thank you, Lakshmi,' Julia said, turning to go, but finding the narrow doorway obstructed by the proprietor of the masculine voice. He was young and American from the fall of his fringe to the white of his sneakers. In between was a grey gym T-shirt and Levis, brown-eyed good looks and a casual awareness of it. Every pore exuded health. He smiled down with a gestured request for Julia to wait, and remained in her way.

'And that's my jeans there, Lakshmi,' he said. 'See, those Levis, just like these ones I'm wearing.'

He indicated his nub-fitting denims, and the girl's eyes went down to them and rested a moment. Her fingers flew through the pile of laundry and located his jeans, which she offered up on the upturned palms of both hands.

'*Nandri*,' he thanked her. Then he gave her a look, and kept looking with a stare of comic high seriousness that finally split apart in a grin. Flattered by the attention, Lakshmi burst into giggles, and ran back into the kitchen.

'Al-right! Clean jeans. Number one job of the day done.' He looked back at Julia. 'So, you having breakfast?'

'Not just yet, no.'

'Not hungry?'

'I've got some things to do upstairs first.'

'Should I maybe save you a place at the table?'

'I could be a few minutes. I wouldn't want to hold you up.'

'No problem. Order you coffee, tea?'

'Alright then, thank you. *Masala* chai, a pot.'

Back before her mirror she put the brush through her hair again. She approved of the strength in her face, verging as it did on the handsome, although sometimes she worried it wasn't quite pretty enough. For whom, and for what? That boy downstairs? She shrugged a reply to both unvoiced questions, uncapped her lip balm and peered deeper into the glass. Despite almost five weeks in the South Indian sun her facial skin remained pale and moist, from a determined regimen of a good French sun-block and broad-brimmed hat, and, on especially sunny days, her black cotton umbrella from MummyDaddy's emporium on Rue Nehru. Her eyes were brightened and the whites whitened by papaya juice and restful indolence, but the brightness only accentuated the indeterminacy of their colour. The irises mingled blue, green and yellow, and some murky tones between, into a colour politely called hazel, but which was only that by default, having failed to fix itself into any major chromatic key. The nose had a patrician straightness she suspected might be the touchstone to the rest of her. The lips were somewhat ascetic, and at home at this time she might have applied a coating of red lipstick. Here they were resting, too. Her hair had once been blonde but now tended mousy, straight and fine into limp, and she kept it athletically short. Her fingers found the lipstick, and started twisting the stick up towards the light. But again she stopped. For him? Who was she kidding?

His name was Josh, and over a breakfast of *dosais* and *pooris*, and the conversational pots of coffee and chai that followed, he explained that he was a medical student on time off from his studies, travelling through India. He was appalled by the money excesses of the American health system, and had vowed never to be a part of it. Upon graduation he would dedicate himself to the people of the Third World, travel from one country to another, wherever the need was greatest, giving his services to the poor. His quest was to wage a 'one man medical crusade', which he readily admitted was hopelessly quixotic, although it might not remain so if other young doctors came to join him in the work. He had been in India for a month, up in Calcutta, where he had rendered his first voluntary service to the sick and destitute, working with Mother Teresa's order. He said it had been a moving and beautiful experience binding the lesions of lepers, teaching the orphans, sponge-bathing the ravaged bodies of the afflicted in their beds. It was work he felt everyone should volunteer for, even if just for a few weeks, as it was so badly needed, and it repaid by making you know what it is to be fully human: a humbling experience.

Julia said she always found it truly impressive that people could give so much of themselves for people they did not even know. When he baulked at the phrase 'truly impressive', embarrassed, she hastened to add that she knew of course he had not told her his story in any way to impress her, but that his ideals and aspirations, and the volunteer work he had rendered already, were really that, 'truly impressive', in a human sense. For instance, she herself could not imagine doing it.

His broad brow puckered. 'Why not?'

'I just couldn't.'

'No,' he said, with a tympanic little laugh. 'You don't get away with it that easily. Why do you say that?'

'I'm not a doctor, to begin with.'

'Neither am I, yet. Not for another whole year. But you don't even need any medical experience. The Mother Teresa people are happy with any skills you can bring. And everyone brings some kind of skill. What do you do back home in Australia?'

'I'm a publisher.'

'Publisher? You mean, like, a book publisher, or newspaper publisher, or …?'

'Books. I … and my husband … publish travel guidebooks.'

'You mean like *Apropos, Blitzer, Vamoose* kind of thing?'

'Yes. Only we're a bit more specialised. Boutique, I believe the term is. For people who travelled with *Solo Soles* in their twenties and are now into their forties. Who want less budget bed and board and more sightseeing, and car hires, and palaces converted into hotels, and …'

'Shopping?'

'Yes,' she admitted, tilting her face forward to sip, so that he almost missed her candid smile. 'Our readers shop.'

'What are your books called?'

'*The Hobo's Lullaby*. And you probably haven't seen them because they're niche-marketed. For people who travel who still mentally cast themselves as young, but who are … are …'

'Old?'

'Old-*er*.'

He broke off a piece of the papery *poori* and cupped it to spoon up some of the pool of fluorescent yellow vegetable *masala* which had been poured into its centre. She sipped her tea. It was very gingery and cardamomy, almost to her taste, though contrary to her request the kitchen had sweetened it, so much that it was syrupy in the mouth.

'So what are you doing here – distribution deals or something?' he asked.

'No, I'm updating our current India guide.'

He cupped his hand beneath his chin. 'How do you mean?'

'I travel around, check up on hotel and restaurant prices, how they've changed, and see what new places have opened up. There's always lots of new shops, like Lakki here in Pondy for instance.'

'You mean that air-conditioned mall-type place in Mission Street? But it's horrible. I mean, it's not, like, you know, very *Indian*.'

'No, it's part of the new India, I think.'

He broke off another contemplative wafer of *poori*. He was a big man, and his young hands were large. They looked somehow too large to be eating a *poori*.

'Updating a whole guidebook. Wow.'

'Oh, I'm not doing it alone. There's a team of us on it, in different parts of the country.'

He looked up into her eyes. His were brown as *gulab jamun* balls in syrup, glistening in the smooth of his cheeks. 'Ever considered throwing it all in, for something more meaningful? Like going and working for Mother Teresa's people, or something like that? Something that might mean *something*, however tiny and insignificant, in this stupid fucking world ...?'

He had spoken with a restrained but incremental passion, climaxing almost theatrically on the *stupid fucking world*. The passion was fine and permissible in a young man, but she had discerned something else, an underlying bitterness almost, the source of which she could not even intuit, and that was nowhere near as measured. And he had allowed himself to be outspoken with someone so recently met and little known, and been implicitly critical, she felt, because he was young and goodlooking, educated and self-possessed, the idealised silhouette of the younger man. And she was the older woman.

'No,' she said. 'I haven't.'

She looked down at his hand, which she had felt fasten onto her wrist in the full flush of his declaration. His eyes followed hers down, and he mustered a shucks grin. 'Oh, sorry.' He removed the hand and placed it on the table in front of him.

'My commitments keep me very busy,' she said. 'I'm sure you understand.' She got up and strapped on her money belt.

'Well, thanks for sharing breakfast with me.'

'It was my pleasure. Please, let me get this.' She took out a hundred-rupee note and placed it by her steel cup and saucer.

'Oh, no, please ...'

'I insist,' she replied. 'Well, I must be off. Bye.' And she walked out before he could say another word.

Passing through the foyer towards the main entrance, Julia saw the Manager in his office with several men, official looking types in business shirts with pens clipped in breast pockets.

They were standing around what looked like architectural plans, in the middle of a discussion approaching argument.

Kingston Chance sat in one of his trademark dark suits in the foyer in a cane armchair, leafing long-nailed through the pages of a back-issue of *India Today*. As she passed by, his eyes contacted hers and rolled ironically in the direction of the meeting in the office.

'Wanted to tear this place down for years, haven't they. But they never will, not without the big *baksheesh* to the appropriate people. These walls will outlive us all.'

She smiled, and stepped over the threshold into the courtyard garden. It was cool from overnight rain, fragrant with fallen frangipani. She walked down the path and through the gateway, crossed the road onto the promenade by the seafront, and laid a course for the Gandhi statue.

Kingston Chance was in Room Seven, right next to hers. No-one knew exactly how long he had lived in the Sea View, but it was said to be a number of years. South African, he was a man of military set, heavy browed and jowled, English accent acute, formal of voice and retiring of habit. He was usually reticent to speak, unless it was at breakfast (he was for some reason at his most outgoing first thing in the day), when he might expand on some particularity of the city-state of Pondicherry, its French colonial history, its architecture, the cavalcade of souls that had passed down its streets. He was said to be writing a book about the place, but no-one had ever seen him with pen in hand, or heard the tap of a keyboard from behind his door. His avowed passion was books, and he read 'entirely promiscuously'. He had let it be known he had an ex-wife in Mumbai, where he had been in business of some unstated kind, before turning up suitcase (and not much more) in hand at the Sea View. He resided alone in his room, walled in with hardbacks stacked in tin-plate cases from floor to ceiling, and was never sighted after noon.

Mildred was also on the first floor, in Room Nine. A statuesque Canadian approaching the tail end of middle age, she retained almost masculine good looks. Her voice was deep and well-articulated. In company she had the stillness of an accomplished actor, and ended any conversation with a look in the eye and a firm handshake. She had been in Pondicherry for several weeks, trying to find out all she could about Aurobindo and the Ashram, but couldn't say exactly why. She and Julia had talked once or twice, each exchange turning into a virtual workshop on Julia's 'continuing to operate on the mere relationship level', her 'addiction to emotion' and 'resistance to meaningful search in life-terms'. She was gracious enough, but a bit difficult too, and Julia tended to avoid her.

The twice-glimpsed man in Ten had the biggest and best fitted out room in the place, enormous, with high ceilings and a balcony overlooking the sea. Mildred coveted it, for among other reasons having been told The Mother used to meditate on the balcony. But the man had politely refused to budge, saying he was well established. Julia had sought more detail about him, but Mildred had not been able to provide much more than she already knew, beyond the opinion that his furnishing was minimal and in good taste, and his name: Mr Manzini.

Josh was in Room Eight, and Julia herself in Six. This accounted for all the upstairs rooms. Downstairs, in Room Four, there was an elderly couple from Delhi on an extended holiday. The word was that the man had been a 'freedom fighter' with Gandhi and Nehru, and had capped the illustrious political career that followed Independence – he had risen to the top ranks of the Congress Party – with a governorship in one of the northern states. His wife was demure, but possessed of a wry eye. Both spoke English with the cultured accent of the Indian elite, and when friends came to visit, as they occasionally did, they would take tea and snacks on the cane settees and armchairs in the Sitting Room and chat the afternoon away.

The room beside theirs, Room Five, was in the paint-peeling poorest condition of all in the guesthouse. It was occupied by a Dane called Britt, a gynaecologist, recently qualified and still setting up her practice in Copenhagen. A short-statured blonde lesbian, she got around in the all-white of the devotee. Like Mildred she had come to Pondicherry because of the Ashram, though in her case the search had been sparked by absent-mindedly flicking through a friend's coffee table book about India, noticing a tiny reference to Aurobindo, and suffering a fainting fit upon reading his name.

The only remaining room was number Three. It was occupied – all the rooms always were, with a pathetic string of hopefuls on the doorstep every day – but Julia had never seen by whom. It was said a man lived alone in there, but if so he was even more discreet in his comings and goings than Mr Manzini. There was no Room Two, or One. No-one knew why, or if they had once existed, what had happened to them.

Julia did not know the name of the Manager. No-one, guest or staff, ever called him anything but 'Manager'. Kingston had once mentioned that he was from Goa, was unmarried, and that his *grand passion* was collecting French antiques. It was a good thing that something interested him, because the day-to-day running of the guesthouse little did. This was done by Guru, a petite, ever-smiling Tamil with a face of mix'n'matched parts. He was head (and only) waiter, chief steward and cleaner, in-house wrangler and wangler. There was also Vishnu, the security man, with a clipped moustache and martial bearing to accompany his khaki uniform, but Kingston scoffed he was 'really a pussycat'. And there were the *ayahs*, poor women and girls from the villages beyond the Pondicherry limits, who cooked, swept, and cleaned the floors on their hands and knees. Their eyes were almost always downcast. Only Lakshmi engaged with the guests, even laughed with them.

Walking on towards the Gandhi statue, Julia regretted that she had not gone up to her room before venturing out, as the day was clear and sunny and she had neither hat nor umbrella. But to go back inside would be to chance running into the young American, and she did not want to risk that. She felt that she had handled him just about right, and made a clean exit. To encounter him again would require a new attitude, one that took into account that they were now acquaintances, with a history of sorts, and she had not yet formulated a final opinion on him.

Meditating thus, she found she had come to a halt on the street, with the first *rickshawallahs* coming her way honking their klaxons and calling out offers to take her out to Auroville for 'the tour', all asking after her 'programme' for the day – when the truth was she had none, she had just gotten out of the guesthouse Dining Room and away from that young man, and that was as far as it went for her. She had no idea of what she would do next.

She resumed walking, as much to put some distance between the rickshaw touts and herself, muttering 'no thank you' and continuously shaking her head, picking up her pace towards the statue of the Mahatma. Her eye scanned down the esplanade, and the long row of French colonial buildings abutting the ocean. The wind and sea had weathered many of the facades like the faces of old people, pale and spotted, discoloured in patches, bits collapsing in. Others had been given a tuck and lift, with the original features painted back in. The best renovated buildings usually belonged to the Ashram, as exemplified by the Sri Aurobindo Press. It had been entirely made over, replastered and painted, the outer walls daubed the distinctive grey of the Ashram, the shutters a tranquil sea blue. It always looked serene and organised within those gates, where softly humming presses stamped out the books and pamphlets, the *pensees* of Aurobindo and The Mother packaged up between covers for shipping to the four quarters.

Up ahead she saw the stained white bunker of Le Cafe Blanc, situated right over the sea rocks, but actually too close, so that the continuous breaking of waves below rendered any conversation beyond a shout impossible at the outdoor tables. But she was nearing the Gandhi statue now, and so even though she had no intention of stopping in at the cafe, she laid her course for it, made it her beacon so that she could continue to navigate down the empty promenade without having to think unduly about where she was going.

Her thoughts gravitated back to the breakfast conversation, and the end point when she had told Josh that her commitments disallowed what he was proposing, a stint of charity work in Calcutta. This was not entirely true. What she had told him about being a publisher, in India to update a travel guide, was true. But it was not true to say she was busy updating. Not any more, at any rate. She had begun the task, more or less routinely, visiting a round of hotels, shops and restaurants upon arrival in Chennai, noting down prices and quality. After a week or so collecting information there, she had taken a bus down to Mahabalipuram, a village of ancient temples by the sea, and worked a few more days before zipping up her bag and moving south to Pondicherry. But it was here, walking the dainty streets of the Ville Blanche, that her resolve had weakened. After years of hard work, and the emotional wringing of more recent times, she experienced the need for a break. A *holiday*. It was years since she had taken anything of the sort. Her body, spirit, her very joints felt worn down. She spent a week in the Palms Guest House, a big and modern place, doing not much more than sitting on her balcony watching the waves break. Then a room miraculously came up at the Sea View, and she grabbed it. She had read, relaxed and rested up – and done no work at all. The days had gone by in sublime uneventfulness, and now the prospect of going back onto the road, the crazy roads of India at that, hauling a backpack for however many weeks, was ever less appealing. She had experienced the odd pang of guilt at her indolence, but knew she could always catch up with her schedule. She knew how much had to be done, and exactly how long it would take. But then more days had slipped by, and more, too many now, and she was aware she should be very much further down the track. But she didn't want to leave Pondicherry, or the Sea View. She didn't feel like budging. For the first time in her life she felt *lazy*. And why shouldn't she be, for once? But the pangs of guilt were getting stronger, and she knew she had to move on. Yet still she hadn't. Couldn't. And so here she was, walking in the potent morning sun, hatless, witless, on course for an ill-conceived cafe she had no intention to enter, and no plans at all beyond that.

She toyed with telephoning Tim, and instantly dismissed the idea. But it recalled the last time they had spoken, her phoning from the airport. The number started ringing just as the final departure announcement came over the public address system in the lounge, and the few remaining passengers started drifting towards the gate. A female voice, drowsy, unfamiliar, young, answered at the other end. Julia asked if Tim was there, and the voice croak-whispered that he was still asleep. At Julia's request that he be woken, that this was important, there was a half-beat followed by a muffle of words spoken behind a hand covering the mouthpiece. The female voice asked who was calling, and Julia gave her name, adding 'he'll know'. Another momentary hesitation, and she heard her name whispered across the sheets of the double bed. She heard the springs squeak as Tim sat up. She could see the squint in his eyes against the morning light, the stubble on his chin. When he spoke his voice was bar-hopped husky.

'Are you at the airport?'

'Just about to board.'

'Well, have a good flight. You got everything?'

'Toothbrush and malaria pills. The lot.'

He laughed a cough that veered towards a morning bout of smoker's cough. He always said he only did it when he worked too hard. She knew otherwise.

'How many did you smoke last night?'

'One or two.'

'Big night?'

'Ish.'

Behind him she heard a blind being opened, then a window. In the airport windows she saw the familiar view: all that white on blue, the aggregate sleek of all those yachts, the Whiteley line of Lavender Bay, the voluptuous bend of the Harbour, the meccano of the Bridge, the shells of the Opera House. Just a few miles from her now, but soon, many thousands. Her eyes went to the queue of passengers being sausage-machined off down the aerobridge.

'You've remembered your copy, haven't you?' Tim was saying.

'Of course. What do you think?' But she still stole a confirming glance down at her carry-on bag, in the unzipped opening of which rested her well-thumbed file copy of the current edition of the India guide.

'And don't let Madras put you off. All the big cities are the pits these days.'

'Tim,' she said, unable to keep a well-worn annoyance from her voice, 'I know Madras. Besides, it's called Chennai now.'

'I remember when we were first there,' he said. 'On the first edition.'

She could hear the girl – what would her name be? Jessica? Nicole? Rebecca? – moving around the room, dressing probably, the muted thud of bare feet on polished boards. An object clattered: a dropped crystal earring glittered in the morning sun before her eyes. It stung, a little.

Almost everyone had gone through the departure gate by now. Julia watched as the last clump of passengers handed their boarding passes to the flight attendant.

'God, I hate flying.'

'Not just flying,' Tim chuckled at the other end. 'Train, bus, foot ... the only thing you ever liked about travel was getting there.'

The flight attendant scanned the lounge for any last passengers. Julia waved to let her know she was coming. The woman gesticulated to hurry.

'I've got to go,' Julia said.

'Already?'

'I'd better.'

'You checked in, didn't you. They'll wait a minute more.'
'Tim, I'll miss the bloody plane.'
She said nothing more, and for a moment neither did he. The line was so clear they might have been feet apart, in adjacent booths looking at each other through a pane of glass, phones foolishly in hand. Between them hung the unvoiced reply: *Then miss it*.
'See you in three months or so,' she said.
'I expect lots of cards, okay? And faxes. Emails.'
The flight attendant waved with annoyed insistence.
'Bye then,' Julia said.
'Yeah,' he almost whispered. 'Bye.'
She held the mouthpiece close, not speaking. She waited for him to hang up. But he was waiting for the same thing.
'You're going to be alright, aren't you? I mean, okay.'
'I'm fine,' she said. 'Don't worry about a thing.'
'Good. That's what I wanted to hear.'
'I know. And now you've heard it. Better?'
She replaced the receiver. A stupid tear came and she stubbed it away with a tissue. She saw the flight attendant had left the gate. As she ran for the plane, she wondered what would happen if they didn't let her on board. Her house was leased out, the cat was in the cattery. All the goodbyes had been said. Her mind raced over the consequences of missing the flight, and all were equally ridiculous, ridiculous as a taxi ride back over to Lavender Bay, to a man she could no longer be with and who no longer could be with her. And if they were to give it another try, it would be like all the other half-tries and the one

really proper try they had attempted over the past couple of years. So there was no going back to Lavender Bay, just as there was no going back to her place in Bondi. There was no going anywhere now but the final destination on her flight ticket, Chennai. In that moment, all the tiny tugs and snares of life drew her inexorably, inexplicably towards it.

But she found herself smiling, for no apparent good reason, as she jogged down the aerobridge and across the steel threshold of the aircraft. She was still smiling when the flight attendant glanced at her boarding pass and directed her to her seat.

'Happy to be getting away?'

'If only you knew.'

II

From his chair in Le Cafe Blanc, he watched her progress in his direction down the promenade. Marco enjoyed taking his breakfast in this useless pile of concrete some idiot must have thought would work well as a seaside cafe. In its age-streaked, sea-eaten boxyness, it looked a bit like something Le Corbusier might have done, a botched sketch rescued from his wastepaper basket. Indians seemed to like his inhuman, prison-like designs: they had even entrusted him with designing Chandigarh, an entire city! Kingston had mentioned one morning he believed an earlier incarnation of the cafe might have been associated with the operations of the wharf, which had been swept away by a cyclone decades before, its remains jutting up from the sea like the snapped-off ribs of a whale. But he himself found it difficult to believe that explanation. The building made such a ludicrous cafe, it had to be purpose-built.

He observed her slow approach, head up in the sun, eyes off

somewhere. She might be meditating, or composing a poem, or thinking about an old lover. But most probably thinking about not much at all.

She passed a circular concrete rubbish bin, the painted sign upon it pleading 'Use Me', and he couldn't help but smile. Yes, the promenade was largely free of litter, but in the black rocks beside it, the sea rocks that held back the tides, in there were rich seams of rubbish. Cigarette packets and plastic chai cups, ice cream sticks and burger wrappers, and oily little bags that once held *baji*. It was all down in there, just inches from the clean sweep of the promenade. How devilishly clever was the Indian mind. They would never drop their litter on the promenade itself: 'No sir, one can-not. That is strictly forbidden.' But in the rocks? Well, they were just as fouled as the rest of India, where every railway line, every street and alley, track and turning, every open space, metre of disused land, every inch that was not presided over by a uniformed security lackey armed with a *lathi*, was covered with a miasma of litter, a *maya* of it, of tangled plastic bags and coils of human excrement, husks of coconuts and rinds of oranges, shreds of paper, forms, business cards and chits, of cow dung and dog dung and pig dung and goat dung, and the cadavers of unrecognisable, long-dead beasts left to rot in the sun and washed by the rain into the stinking rivers and streams. The rubbish in the rocks by the promenade represented yet another victory of the Indian mind. Here reason and hygiene, all the routine strictures of the modern world, were daily routed in a revolt of manure.

Marco's thoughts were interrupted by the waiter, a wordless

young man – it would not have mattered if he had spoken anyway, as he would have found it impossible to make himself heard over the waves on the rocks below – who placed a tray bearing his customary breakfast before him. There were four slices of white toast, decidedly under-toasted, and two small steel saucers containing sickly white butter, and a brand of strawberry jam whose advertising billboards boasted 'No Fruit. All artificial colour.' His standing order for tea – black with no sugar – would naturally be milky white and sweetened to the point where one might expect a spoon to stand in it; and the glass of water dumped on the table with it he had never once touched, it being unfiltered and he a foreigner, yet it arrived every day, sloshing its bacteria across the acned formica. He thanked the waiter, releasing him back to the other staff who dozed in a neat heap by the entrance. Ah, India, he sighed inwardly, sipping the sweet white concoction of his desire.

Knowing how to get what he wanted was one thing. To have adequate table area to spread out two broadsheet newspapers, the *Hindu* and the *New Indian Express*, was another challenge in a cafe, and it demanded his daily patronage of a dump like this which no-one else ever went to, to guarantee adequate space. Each edition of these daily organs carried a catalogue of political and criminal violence, familial, religious and caste murder, a hair-raising saga of mayhem almost unreported in the world outside. You had to be here to know it was going on at all. Yet here it was every day, whole villages hacked to death with machetes over some petty dispute in Bihar, Christian churches torched in Gujarat, Muslims murdered in Mumbai, kidnappings in Tripura, endless chaos in Assam. And of course there were the bombardments up in the mountains of Kashmir, the Pakistani and Indian artillery gunners at their daily diplomacy, always managing to kill and maim a few villagers in the process. So much brutality everywhere, and increasingly these days in the name of Hindu fundamentalism. Imagine that, he marvelled, pacifist hit-squads. Vegetarian mass murderers. Zealots who valued a cow more than a human baby. No, not an elephant, or a hair's-breadth-from-extinction Royal Bengal tiger. A cow. Among millions and millions of cows. Cows everywhere, shitting on streets, chomping on cigarette packets and cardboard boxes, blocking up traffic. *Cows*. And these people, fundamentalists, extremists – it did seem there were too many of them these days to characterise them as fringe fanatics – valued those cows more than Muslim women who fetched the daily water in steel pots on their heads, who tended the cooking fires and who bore children who also happened to be Muslim, and who might happen to end up dead because of that. All in the name of a religion of beautiful sutras and mandalas, icons of gods and goddesses garlanded with blossom and daubed with milk and holy water. Just how had that come to pass?

Half distracted by biting into his doughy toast, a quarter distracted by the woman proceeding his way, Marco's thoughts progressed momentarily to those Hindu gods themselves. He had read there were three hundred million deities in the Hindu pantheon. An impressive figure against just one for Islam and Judaism, and one-or-is-it-three? for Christianity. But who, he wondered, had counted those three hundred million deities?

Had any human being ever counted up to three hundred million *anythings*? But just for a moment assuming there were three hundred million of them, did they each have a name? If so, the human race was richer in names than almost any other cultural artefact. But if no-one had physically *counted* these deities, someone must have come up with a 'ballpark', and a computer done the rest. Who would have done that, and upon what proportional basis had that final number been arrived at? Was there an institute devoted purely to the computation of gods? In India, yes probably.

He returned to the papers. 'Pak Police Blame India For Blast'. *Yet another attempt to blow up the Pakistani PM – by India no doubt*. 'Reduce Defence Expenditure: Sen'. *Some busybody trying to tell the likely lads of the BJP to cut spending on guns and missiles. Would they listen just because he'd won a Nobel Prize? In a pig's eye*. 'Poster Campaign Against Intolerance'. *Some poor unfortunates trying to take on Bal Thackeray's thugs in Mumbai. Sticky end in store*. 'Worshippers Gunned Down In Pak'. *Indian papers love dead Pakistanis, particularly when it's Sunni vs Shi'ite. Even better spectator sport than cricket*. 'N-Test Yield Estimate Correct: AEC Chief'. *More lies about previous lies about size of nuclear test devices*. 'Villagers Shot By Police Over Idols'. *Peasants dug up some old idols. Someone rich must have wanted them. Result: A pile of dead villagers*.

He glanced up. She was getting close. If he wasn't careful she might notice him watching her. Quite lovely. Intelligent, judging by the set of the eyes, and wilful from the chin. She had caught his eye on her first day at the Sea View, and it had not left her. He lifted the *Hindu* in front of his face for the half minute when she passed most closely, then turned in his seat to watch her walk on. Her back was muscular, the spinal discs nicely outlined beneath the skin.

Room 6. *Julia Keefe.* Age – *35 years.* Nationality – *Australian.* Place of birth – *Sydney.* Marital status – *blank.* Passport number – *E1964-something.* Date of issue – *sometime in 1996.* Expiry – *2006 sometime.* Home address – *Bondi Beach, Sydney.* Occupation – *Company Director.* Visa – *Six months.* Reason For Visit – *Tourism.* Coming from: *Chennai.* Going to: *Madurai.* Signature – *expressive, but not over-large or flashy.*

To learn these details he merely had to wait for the Manager to drift from his desk one morning. The Guest Register had laid her bare before his eyes. There was much to intrigue. Why, for instance, had she left marital status blank? Some guests did, considering it their private business. But something about her entry, or lack of one, excited his keener interest. Looking closely he had seen a dot of ink in that space, as if she had put the pen there, considering her response, and then not given one. Was that because she was in two minds about what to say? Had she considered writing 'Married' through a concern male staff might pester her if she wrote 'Single'? Or was there another more intimate reason?

Marco waved his arm for more tea. The waiter looked up half asleep, half-nodded. 'Occupation – Company Director'. What kind of real job did that term mask? 'Company Director' could imply anything from running a nappy wash to selling nerve gas to Iraq. But experienced travellers in India, and she was clearly one, never gave their real jobs, always masked themselves in the generic. There could be no complications that way. He himself always wrote his occupation as 'Agent'. No-one ever asked him what he actually did. Nor did they question the tiny gap he always left between the 'A' and the 'g', by which he registered his true vocation: 'A gent'.

Yet more matters for consideration. Her statement that she was moving on to Madurai. She had initially only intended staying at the Sea View for three days. It was there in the Register, in the Manager's hand. But she had extended, then extended again (much like he himself had done). Her latest extension was for a week. She had to be enjoying herself. Yet whenever he observed her on the shopping streets of the Ville Noire, or in a cafe, or sorting through the postcards, scented candles and trinkets in the Auroville shop, she seemed to be going nowhere slowly. Nor did she appear to have any interest in the doings of the Ashram. She didn't wear the mock-virginal white, and as far as he knew she never went to the early evening meditation at the tomb of Aurobindo and The Mother that the Ashram-ites religiously attended. Certainly she was nothing like so many of the Westerners one saw, buzzing along on a Vespa between the Ashram and Auroville, a sanctimonious look on their faces because they had discovered not just the meaning of their lives and the universe too, but were so evolved that they could ride something as stupidly dangerous as a motor scooter, in India, and without a helmet. Smooth-faced devotees of the goddess Vespa, one of the three hundred million.

So, he contemplated, upon the lovely discs of her spine, what was she doing here, and how much longer did she intend to stay? What was she like and what was she looking for? And did she realise that low-backed dresses possessed the potential to drive a certain kind of man to a certain kind of madness? These were all serious matters, deserving of his deeper consideration. Fortunately enough his tea refill arrived then, divinely milky sweet, and his contemplation was perfect and complete.

She had spotted Mr Manzini in the distance, alone in the shadowy confine of the cafe. She wondered whether she should give any sign. After all, they were neighbours. Someone should simply break the ice. But he looked absorbed in what he was doing, breakfasting over the newspaper, and as she approached he happened to hoist it up in front of him, rendering a greeting difficult anyway. He was obviously very interested in news and current affairs. Or perhaps he had seen her, and wished to avoid contact. But why? There was no reason for that. No, that was a paranoid thought, and she dismissed it. He was obviously caught up in the news, one of those who determinedly maintained a nexus with the world beyond, and all its event.

She took a last peek as she passed by most closely, before, like celestial bodies in their own orbits, the two of them began to be drawn apart by forces more powerful now than those that had caused their approach. She might never see him again, she realised. This could be as close as these two entities got in space. This might be his final day in Pondicherry, the one of his long-delayed departure, a last cup of tea before a midday checkout. By the time she got back to the guesthouse he could be halfway up to Chennai in a hire car, continuing on a slow, grand tour of India. A serious mind in the back seat of an Ambassador, poring over texts on dynasties and deities. Or he might be knocked down and killed by a car in ten minutes time. Or she might be.

So in this moment of possibly greatest proximity, passing by she gained a three-quarter profile. She studied him, the spectre from Room Ten. A face of leanness, abstemiousness, and something of a dignified visage too, she felt, resided beyond the *Hindu*. The cheekbones were elevated, the long, shadowy hollows beneath recalling, who was it, the young Sartre, Jean-Paul? Or was it Belmondo? The lips possessed a Southern European fullness, and the light olive skin had taken on an easy tan she surmised had been gained from incidental rather than purposeful exposure. This was because he looked a thinker more than a doer, in his white shirt with button-down collar, opened only at the neck, and what appeared to be – it was difficult to see properly because of the table – a tailored pair of gentlemen's trousers. He scrutinised his newspaper through round spectacles rimmed with gold so fine they appeared to float on the bridge of his nose, a wisp of reflected light.

Just past him now, she came to the cafe's entrance and, the sun being hot on her bare head, she was tempted to go in. A few minutes in the shade with a lime soda was an appealing notion. But she couldn't, because, ironically enough, the cafe was so empty. Of the dozen or so tables, his was the only one occupied, and in a strange way that made it his cafe. It would feel somehow forward to enter his cafe. After all, he might have caught sight of her coming down the promenade, just as she had of him in his chair. He might be aware she was the person living beside him, in the intimacy of two beds parted by a few yards of floor-tiling. Certainly, he would look up from his paper if she entered the cafe, the change of light alone from the entry of another body into the space would ensure that. Being the sole patrons, they would register each other's faces, admit they 'knew' each other. That registration having taken place, a relationship would have already begun. It might lead to words being called across the room, talk about the weather. He might move closer to make himself better heard — indeed, the cafe's acoustics, or lack thereof, would demand it — and end up sitting at her table, sharing a pot of coffee. And it would all have happened at her instigation.

But, what was the problem with that? The scene as she had pictured it was admirably discreet. She was a fellow guest who had ventured out without her hat. Why wouldn't she want to stop in for the shade and a cool drink? No-one could call that forward. Besides, it might be nice to catch up on the news of the world for once, all those medical advances, and small wars. He might be a terrific conversationalist, shy to make contact but secretly bursting to speak. Travelling, one could spend days, weeks if one wished, saying not much more than 'how much, did you say?' He might be in Pondicherry writing sonnets, or sonatas that would have made Chopin weep. He might be a thinker at the frontier of a vast new mathematical prairie. He could be the most extraordinary lover, deep and tender, sensitive and caring, with whom she might probe the outer limits of delight. He might be the love of her life sitting there, just waiting to lower his newspaper, and the whole thing burst into bloom. And all she had to do was turn left, but now, absolutely *now* and not a moment later, or the turning would be missed, and a return self-conscious and awkward.

But, no, no she would not do it. She would walk by. And so she did, took one step beyond, and then another – away, she felt, from girlish whimsy. Or was it that each step she took away from him, and men like him – from the fantasy of miraculously stumbling across love in a cafe – was really a step back towards Tim? After all, if she and Mr Manzini were bodies spinning in space, then until now Tim had been the big gravitational chunk in the centre of her orbit. And perhaps he still was.

Separating, finally, had been the most painful thing Julia had ever endured. Almost as bad, after the split she found herself cast into the ranks of what the latte supplements of the daily papers called the Merry Widows. These were women in their thirties usually, who, like Julia, had undergone relationship breakdown, or for some reason or other had failed to find enduring love. They were dubbed Widows for the men they had survived (in some cases not even met), and because they wore a lot of black. Cool urban black for some, a flotilla of cocktail dresses for others. But they were not merely Widows, they were Merry too. There were weekends in the country, mountain hikes, yoga retreats, sex in the city. There was merriment in this widowhood. And it was into this group that

Julia had been demographied, after the final torturous tendril untangling from Tim. She despised the term, hated the existence, but still couldn't help but feel it did roughly describe the state she found herself in now, the shore onto which, despite her strongest strokes to the contrary, the surf of life had dumped her.

She and Tim had been together for eleven years. They had founded a business, travelled everywhere. They had spent so much time intensely alone that friends marvelled that two people could be so engrossed in each other and not go at least mildly batty. But being together was easy. They shared preferences in books as in plays, cars as in furniture, in the optimum height of a dining table and distance from a cinema screen, in the hours of sleep and the making of love. All those years they had shared all, wrapped up in each other, and in the publishing business they had brought into existence.

One morning, some months after her thirty-second birthday, as they trekked up a track in Nepal, Julia had mentioned the time was coming when they should discuss whether or not to have a child, and if so, when. In the past this had been something both had thought of more or less in the abstract, a nice idea, for the future. Well now, she said to Tim, as they strode uphill, the future was coming. So did he wish to have a child with her, and if so, when? The almost legalistic wording of her question – which she had been working through in her mind for some time, trying to get it both concise and non-threatening, coming as it did out of the high Himalayan blue – took him aback for a moment.

'I suppose so, yes.'

'So you do want to have a child?'

He took out a chocolate bar, peeled back the cellophane wrapper and, annoyingly, bit in.

'Yes.'

'With me?'

'Yes.'

She sighed, inwardly forgiving him for chewing on that thing at a time like this. But keeping up his sugar level was his current obsession, a new-ish one which, emblematically perhaps for them in these more recent times, she did not share.

'Alright then,' she said, breathing harder as the track steepened, 'do you mind if we stop a moment to discuss it? It's important.'

'I wouldn't mind, except we've got a long way to go today. Can't it wait for a rest stop?'

She felt a tiny prickle in his voice, and felt annoyed, thought about arguing. But that in itself would be self-defeating and childish.

'Look,' she said, 'it's no big deal. I just wanted to air the idea.'

'Darling, the answer is yes on both counts. On all counts. Of course it is. What do you think I'm going to do, run off and leave the woman I love just because the time comes around to have a child?'

She was puffing harder. The other members of the party had started before them while they paid a group of porters, and they were getting further and further ahead. Tim picked up his pace.

'So ... roughly ... when would be right for you?'

'I don't know exactly,' he said. 'The next year or two, I suppose.'

'So, I'd be thirty-four, thirty-five, at the birth.'

Just then he spotted a member of their party perched on a tall rock a couple of hundred metres up the track, and waved. 'Look at Gillian, mad thing. That rock face is almost sheer.'

Nothing more was said for the rest of the trip, nor during the weeks that followed. They were working on a Nepal update, and the days and weeks were devoured by copy deadlines, artwork meetings, map-makers late with their work and typesetters late with theirs, the whole, fraught business of putting together a new edition. When it was dispatched to the printers and there was at last time, her thoughts rebounded to the problem, because that, she realised, it now was. But as the days passed and Tim made no sign of raising it – he was forever closeted in meetings with accountants, with distributors, and with printers (they too were late) – she considered her options. She did not wish to raise it again. That would be demeaning, and could somehow be construed as nagging. She wanted him to raise it himself, unprompted, which would give some indication of him being keen on the idea, rather than merely going along with her. He was after all nearly five years older than her, closing on forty. Surely he must be thinking about a child too, if he really did want one someday. Well someday was approaching, at speed.

But over weeks that stretched into months, he said nothing. In this time he did do an enormous amount of travelling, as did she. They were always being asked to speak in Europe or

America, at conferences, conventions. There were meetings at branch offices in London, in New York, Tokyo, staff to be hired and fired, journalists wanting interviews, writers and artists looking for work. It was endless. Dizzying. It felt a Herculean task to get the pair of them into the same country, much less the same room. Just when they needed to speak seriously about something that would affect their lives forever, the offspring they had already spawned was yowling for attention, demanding they be here, go there, get this and bring that. It was as if they were forever picking up after a tyrant toddler. Weeks would pass in which their only conversations were by long distance mobile-to-mobile, faxes shoved under hotel doors, two-line emails.

As the months passed, however, she began to wonder if Tim wasn't deliberately avoiding the issue. She came to this suspicion, which ripened into conviction, after an opportunity came up for them to take a short holiday. An old friend who ran a resort in the rainforest behind Coffs Harbour, shingle cottages and a blue pool, had suggested they come up for a week. She and Tim had discussed it transatlantically, agreed to rendezvous back in Sydney and drive up. They were both exhausted, beat. A week in a pool in a rainforest sounded just right.

Julia arrived home in Lavender Bay the day before they were to go, and found the house filled with flowers. A bottle of champagne rested in a wicker basket surrounded by nuts and chocolates, covered with a big sheet of cellophane and a blue silk ribbon frilled out by a Neutral Bay giftshop lady. Julia was instantly suspicious. The note confirmed that Tim was very,

very sorry, but he would not be able to make it. Business. Their business. He was in New York still, tying up the deal they had been trying for, that would give them the distribution they needed in the US if they were at last to make a proper go of it there. A quantum leap, his note promised, but it had to be now.

She marvelled, firstly at how Tim had managed to get a Neutral Bay giftshop lady to stop filing her nails long enough to take down such a long message, and moreover get it all down correctly. Then she marvelled at his gall, knowing she was flying all the way back to Sydney for this rendezvous, what it was really about – and coming up with this.

She cleared the house of the flowers. She threw out the basket and the nuts and the ribbon. The chocolate she ate and the champagne she drank. She composed a brief email, saying she would be turning thirty-three in a matter of weeks, and wished to have a child in the following year. She wanted him to be the father, but if he did not want that himself, or could not make up his mind, she would make other arrangements. As she clicked on 'Send' and the message whizzed off into the witchcraft of the Internet, she derived satisfaction from the *other arrangements*. It was understated, coolly divorced from the reality of sex, sperm and egg with a new lover, which lay beneath the veneer of those two words. She switched off the computer, placed the empty bottle in the wastepaper basket, and waited.

Predictably, his response was not to respond. No email awaited when she logged on that evening, nor was there anything the next morning. It was a full twenty-four-hour cycle by then – he must have received her email. Nor was there any phone call. The fax machine sat dormant. Aggravated, she tried to telephone, but the receptionist at his hotel in New York was 'very sorry mam', but he was out. Do you wish to leave him a message? Yes I do. Tell him he's a fucking shit. Okay, thank you mam. Do you have that? Yes I do mam. I'll make sure it goes into his box.

She tried the New York office. There Mel Riley, one of her oldest friends, someone who had been with them right from the start, a Darlinghurst girl who designed street papers and came to work on their very first edition, dear Mel confessed that she hadn't seen or heard from Tim in a couple of days. They knew he was in New York, at meetings, trying to close the distribution deal, but he hadn't been in the office. They had dozens of messages from people desperate to talk to him. She thanked Mel and hung up. Then she dialled his US mobile number, got his message bank, and repeated the message she had left at the hotel.

Putting down the phone, she wondered if she wasn't overreacting. After all, Tim was obviously working under great stress, trying to secure the deal. For us. She could hear Tim emphasising it: *For us*. But even working under that kind of pressure, surely he'd have time for a brief call. He'd had the time to spend on the line with the Neutral Bay giftshop lady, why didn't he have it for a single paragraph email?

He'd been spending more time in New York these past few months. They had an ad hoc agreement that she was covering Europe and Australia, him America and Japan. But he spent almost no time in Tokyo, it was always New York. Of course the negotiations had been going on for some months, and there was a very good reason for him being there, but as she sat in her office chair staring at the blank face of her computer, the sour of the champagne wafting up from the wastepaper basket, she began to envisage a scene.

It was the East Village, a walkup apartment near Avenue A, near, what was it called? – Thompkins Square Park. Of late Tim had been talking a lot about that part of town. How much the City had cleaned it up, how gentrified it had got. How ten years ago all of Alphabet City had been pretty well no-go. So now she pictured the East Village, the cleaned up, gentrifed East Village, and the walkup apartment, and in the walkup apartment a girl of course, the one he'd been seeing these past months, which was why he wasn't in his hotel room at – she glanced at her world clock to check the time in New York – well after one in the morning. Of course he could say he was out to dinner with the would-be distributors, men's business between chaps in suits. But she kept seeing the girl. Her features fleshed in the opacity of the computer screen. She was fresh, bright, educated. A graphic designer with a fancy New York magazine. She knew Tim had a wife somewhere but was 'cool' about it. She had a bedroom right over Thompkins Square Park, and they could hear the streetbeat and yaddayadda while they lay in her bed of an afternoon. Tim had already told her he loved her, but she knew that anyway, with that ease of a woman who is young and pretty, with those good teeth that cost the earth in America, and the good education that costs so much more.

The telephone rang. It was Tim, just arrived back at his room in the hotel, profuse with apology. He had been down in Chinatown, dining with the distributors. A late night. She knew how it was. Yes, she said, she knew.

'Julia, about the baby thing ...'

'You mean, you and I having a child.'

'Yes,' he stood corrected. He inhaled a long, meeting-bushed breath. 'Can we discuss it when I get back? The deal's done. I can come home.'

'What? Right away?'

'Yes.'

'So you mean ... we might be able to go up the coast still, have that break?'

He hesitated, fatally. 'Well, when I say *done*, it's there, but there's still a couple of details to sort out yet. I'll probably be a few days more. A week at the most.'

'Or two.'

'No. Not *or two*.'

'Or three. How long is this going to go on, Tim? How long do you think you can keep this up?'

'What? What do you mean?'

'I know what's been going on.'

'Julia, I'll tell you what's been going on. Today I have secured US-wide distribution for us. For us. We'll be in every major bookshop across the country. It's all we've worked for, and now you're carrying on with some other fucking agenda. I don't get it.'

'No?' she replied calmly. 'Well when you get back here, whenever that may be, I won't be here. Because I know you don't want to have a child with me. So I've been looking around. And I've found someone who does.'

He paused, a long time. 'You've been seeing someone?'

'Yes.'

'How long?'

'A few months.'

'I see.' There was more disappointment than anger in his voice, for now.

'And you? Have you been seeing anyone? New York is a very romantic city.'

'No,' he said quietly. 'I haven't been seeing anyone.'

'No-one at all?'

'No.'

She didn't speak after that. She drew the telephone away from her ear and stared at it, fascinated by the casual destructive power of that dumb chunk of plastic.

'Julia?' he was saying. 'Julia?'

She replaced the telephone in its cradle. Cradle. How apposite that should be where it rested. She picked it up again and left it dangling. Later that day she contacted a real estate agency in Bondi and took a lease on a flat. By the end of the following day she had moved in.

A nasty year ensued. She began seeing someone, and Tim believed this was whom she had been seeing all along. Telling him she had only just begun it, and that at the time of moving out she had really been seeing no-one, only hurt him more and made matters worse. His anger brewed, bitter. He said he doubted she had wanted a child after all, and that she had just been using it as a wedge to get out of a marriage that was obviously making her unhappy. She protested that she really did want a child. Would she be having one with 'the deadbeat'? It hasn't been raised. You don't just jump in with things like that when you've only been seeing someone a short while. Oh, but you're running desperately short of time, aren't you? I thought you'd have raised it for sure by now. After the first fuck even. No, this child thing is just a joke. An excuse. Yes, I did want a child with you, Tim, very badly. But you didn't want it. Didn't I? No. How do you know that? Because you never wanted to even talk about it. You just wouldn't. No, I *couldn't*. There's a difference. *Couldn't*, because I was always travelling and working so hard. For *us*. Oh yes, there it is, the italicised us. Well that's what it was! It was for us! I was in the middle of a crucial deal for us, and had to keep going. That didn't mean you couldn't at least talk to me about things, about how you really felt about us having a child. Julia, there just wasn't *time*. Besides, I needed to talk to you face to face. It's a huge thing. I know that, and that's why we needed to talk about it so desperately, only you wouldn't …

A few weeks later she left the flat in Bondi and moved back into Lavender Bay. A truce had been negotiated. They would take it easy, very easy. They would get through this. Over early, tentative days, a feeling began to grow that although they had been through some treacherous waters, and more probably lay ahead, if they hung on tight they might just still get there. Tim dropped the condom packet into the bathroom tidy. From now on sex would be *au naturel*.

Then Mel Riley was in town for a meeting, and over dinner, just the two of them in a Thai place on Crown Street, after a couple of Singhas and a bottle of red, she admitted to Julia that she hadn't been entirely candid before, and that Tim might have been seeing someone in New York. Who? Some bright young thing? Not exactly – one of the lawyers negotiating for the other party. A professional person that he was dealing with? Yes. But Tim wouldn't do that. That would be ... shitting where he eats? Isn't that the expression? Well, he's a man, isn't he? No, no I don't believe it. Are you sure? No, I'm not sure, Julia. All I'm saying is that he seemed to spend an awful lot of time with Candice. Candice? That was her name? Sounds like a disease. They all do when your husband's screwing them. So, you're certain? No, I'm not. But what I'm certain of is that she has a place down in the Hamptons, and an awful lot of meetings were held down there, and I think that often there were just two parties at those meetings. Okay, yes, yes, I see, I get the picture. Thanks Mel. I mean, I don't like telling you all this. I shouldn't be, but in the end I really just thought you should know. Besides, I'm drunk. I know, so am I.

Tim denied it all, wanted to fire Mel. All was anger, angst and accusation. Mel went back to New York, somehow survived. Tim finally admitted he had slept with the woman, a few times, that it hadn't been important, that he just did it because he was working long hours, living in hotels out of a suitcase, doing all he could. For them. And for the child they would one day have. And although she knew that he was probably telling the truth, and that it wasn't 'important', and that she found herself entirely beyond feelings of jealousy, she was almost inconsolably hurt because nothing could rescue or redeem things now, too much had gone wrong and they were too far gone, so she told him he was a lying cunt and moved out again.

During this very nasty year, the first books went on sale across the US and sold 'quite well', as the US distributors put it. In point of fact they made more money that year than they had in the seven years before it put together. So when she moved out this time she didn't rent a flat in Bondi, she bought a house. More time passed, months, a year, with relations between them best characterised as a wary truce, but one which nonetheless allowed them to keep running the business together. Julia celebrated her thirty-fifth birthday on an air mattress with a daiquiri and a friend in the cool of her garden.

The telephone rang. Tim was back in New York, working on their first guidebook to the entire US. A formidable team had been assembled, and expectations were high it would become the biggest-selling *Hobo's Lullaby* yet.

'I just called to wish you a happy birthday.'

'Thanks.'

'Did you receive my present yet?'

'No.'

'It's coming. I Fedexed it yesterday. I hope you like it. Anyway, that's all I really called for. To wish you a happy birthday.'

'Thank you.'

'And to tell you that I love you. And that I'm very sorry

things have turned out the way they have. And that when I get back to Sydney I want to see you, have dinner with you.'

'Okay. Let's do that.'

'Yeah. Bye then. And happy birthday.'

But they had never quite sat down to that dinner. And here she was now, a Merry Widow abroad, ploughing onwards, putting still more yardage between herself and Le Cafe Blanc and Mr Manzini, who had made such a weak show of hiding behind his newspaper, for whatever reason. She kept on going in the sun, which weighed heavily on her now, and she saw that it was a long way, hundreds of metres, to the nearest place of refuge, the Arjuna Restaurant and Cafe, way up on the right, the entrance marked with a billboard of Mickey and Minnie grinning inanely at each other over the frothy heads of thickshakes. That was to be her course-setting, her new beacon, the scungy Arjuna where the staff would be morning-surly, wouldn't even bring her a menu unless she went out into the kitchen and asked, and would act even more surly when she ordered because all she wanted was a lime soda and a little shade.

She cast a glance back. Seemingly caught out looking her way, he turned his eyes down to his newspaper again. But perhaps he hadn't been looking at her after all, but at something in her direction – a building, a bird, someone passing, or something else high in the quarter of the sky behind her. It was hard to tell out in the sun.

She turned and looked in his direction. What was she looking at? Him? He quickly averted his eyes to the page, which turned out to be a story in the Regional Section about problems in the installation of sewerage pipes in Trichy, and the subsequent loss (to whom?) of some three *crores* of rupees. How much was that in US dollars, he wondered, a *crore* being ten million – and why did the Indians have to have their own silly quantifiers, *lakhs* and *crores*, when everyone else in the world used millions and billions? But he did find interest in the story, as it revealed itself as a small gem, a summation in undug trenches and pilfered plastic piping of the deep subterranean corruption of India, a corruption so rich and ripe you could almost smell it in the newsprint. Ah India, dear Mother India.

He gestured to the waiter who scribbled out the bill, ballpoint cutting into the coarse grey-white paper of his pad, tore the sheet off and dropped it onto the table ready to walk off. But Marco was too quick. He already had a fifty rupee note out, and thrust it down. The waiter shrugged, yawned open-mouthed, walked off and returned with the change. Marco pocketed all twelve rupees of it, got to his feet, folded his newspapers beneath his arm, and walked towards the entrance. It had been an enjoyable morning. A tranquil afternoon beckoned, reading the novel (even worse tribulations in store for the good people of Oran), with just one small task to be performed before evening.

III

Josh was disappointed at how it had gone at breakfast with Julia. There was a reason for this. He had Room Eight, at the rear of the guesthouse. It had the disadvantage of noise, in that gas compressors, refrigeration equipment and generators might come on at any hour of the day or night. But it did possess one advantage, a small internal balcony from which the occupant might observe the other guests going up and down the stairs, to and from their rooms. And the guest whose movements most interested him was the woman in Room Six.

Women usually found Josh attractive. He was twenty-eight years old, smart but not scarily intellectual, a long and large-limbed young man, but not, he considered, a grain-fed American. There was, he trusted, another level to him, a sensitivity which his countrymen often lacked. He liked poetry, genuinely, some of it. He played piano, not very well, but he could play it. Whenever he went home to see his folks on Long

Island – he was studying in New York, living just off the Bowery – his father always asked him to play, a little Mozart which as a child he had mastered, and when the charade was over his father would turn to his mother with a vaguely Yiddish shrug and say 'those lessons, I gave up smoking for him to have those lessons', to which she would reply 'so he saved your life'. They had married older, and Josh had turned up as a surprise addendum. They had been so pleased about it they had almost smothered him with love, his mother in particular. 'You're lucky I didn't turn out gay', he liked to joke with them, to which his father's stock response was 'at least your room would've been clean'.

The streets of his adolescence were leafy middle class, which he escaped as early into his mid-teens as he could, to summer jobs bagging groceries and working as a lifeguard, and bumming round Mexico with his buddies. One summer there had been an early intimation of love, but it turned out to be a fleeting infatuation for the girl, who soon went off with another boy.

Women moving on was to become something of a pattern into his twenties, his med school years. Within a few weeks or months their interest always waned. It didn't bother him so much at the time, why should it? She was always going off to college, travelling in Europe, or else things just got somehow disconnected without much being said. Over time he became aware something was amiss, however, something he couldn't quite put his finger on, an elusive fraying thread. In his darker moods he began to feel it was almost as if when women got the chance to peer more deeply inside him, they were, well, a bit disappointed with what they saw in there. As if it wasn't quite enough to maintain their interest. This was doubly baffling as he prided himself on his sexual performance – *no problems there* – and he was always well-mannered in their company, and conversation flowed without effort. He knew about art and music, could argue politics and debate economics. He was a liberal. He had views. Yet woman after woman drifted away, and although there were ready replacements it became an increasingly disconcerting phenomenon, particularly as he approached his thirtieth year.

When he had first spotted Julia, his feeling was she was just right for his Pondicherry stay. She was attractive, smart-looking, independent. And although he knew she was a little older, there was a growing suspicion in him that a more mature woman might provide some deeper revelation, about himself. That unlike younger women who just moved on when things started to simmer down, a mature woman might put in more effort. She might even be willing to sit down and talk, listen to his baffling problem and hopefully enlighten him on it, if he could bring himself to broach it openly.

Josh had also noticed Lakshmi from his balcony, the young *ayah* in the pink sari, a gorgeously fine-featured Tamil. She always smiled at him, and it felt like a smile reserved for him alone, special. It made him wonder if she ever went beyond a smile, and what it might be like to kiss a girl like that, lips meeting across such a cultural divide. Surely it was impossible even to contemplate. Yet on the street he did sometimes see young Western men, hippies usually, with Indian girlfriends on the back of a motorcycle, clinging with arms locked around their waists. But they all looked like city girls, Delhi girls and Mumbai girls, whereas Lakshmi was a village girl, sent to town to work by her parents, sending money home each month. So he tried not to think too much about Lakshmi. That was plain silly.

What was not silly was Julia, which made the scene at breakfast all the more lamentable. He went over it as he sat with a cigarette on a couch in the foyer. The guesthouse was quiet now. Everyone had gone out for the day. The staff had finished cleaning the rooms, soiled linen and laundry dispatched to the *dhobis*. The Register rested on the desk, no arrivals or departures for a fortnight. Vishnu the security guard was filling in for the Manager, dozing in an armchair beneath a big black and white portrait of The Mother, one of those very late ones, rheumy-eyed, her chin sprouting hairs, smiling with old teeth whose gums had receded on the tide of age.

Julia had thought him smarmy and self-confident. What was the term Australians used? Up himself. He'd pushed the Mother Teresa thing way too hard. Telling her she should go and volunteer herself – it smacked of self-righteousness. He still didn't know why he'd pushed it so hard. He hadn't meant it to come out quite like that, it just had. The galling thing was his supposed self-confidence had deserted him in that moment, and he'd blurted the words out like a nervy teenager, knowing as he did that he was sinking titanically in her estimation, from passionate young man doing good for the sick to pushy Yank who probably hadn't even been to Calcutta.

The thing was, he had. Not for as long as he had implied, but he had. He had given three days of voluntary service with Mother Teresa's order, at the end of which he had apologised and said he couldn't go on because it was just too depressing. There didn't seem any point anyway. The problem was awesomely huge. The garlanded posters of Mother Teresa all over Calcutta (what was it with this country anyway, with these mothers everywhere? They even called it Mother India) carried a caption aphorism of hers, that their work was just a drop in the ocean, but without it the ocean would be less. Well, yes, but less by exactly one drop. In an ocean of leprosy, AIDS, TB, despair. A drop in an ocean that extended off on all sides as far as the eye could see without a speck of dry land to be spied. Maybe working against all that made sense to some people, but not to him. It was too great: it had defeated him.

There were no repercussions when he left, beyond his own inner turmoil. Because if a well-organised relief effort was a drop in an ocean, what about the personal crusade of one young man to save the sick on several continents? Where was his grand plan now? Did he really think there was any point to devoting his life to bandaging the suppurating sores of India and Africa when there were so many more about to burst out? What a useless way to spend your life, running along an endless dike, sticking your finger into leaks while all about you the ocean streamed in. What had he been thinking? And even if others did join him, as he had once fantasised, what could he achieve? Isolated, with just a few followers – nothing. It was useless. He might as well join someone like Medecins Sans Frontieres, except they were so damn French. Besides, that had not been the vision, merely to immerse himself in someone else's scheme. The vision had been of him as something of a latter-day Albert Schweitzer, not just another doctor in charge of a fly-infested hut of babies with swollen bellies in southern Sudan. And so what, if that vision – no, Boy's Own fantasy – had gone, was the plan for when he qualified in a year's time? A residency in Great Neck, then a small practice in Woodbury, all leading to a leafy outlook in Cold Spring Harbor? Jesus Christ, no, please. Whatever, the fantasy was dead. Yet only this morning he had vividly revived it, espoused it all so zealously to Julia, trying to impress her. And it hadn't even worked. She was too smart for that kind of horseshit. If she wasn't he wouldn't have been attracted to her in the first place. She'd seen through him instantly, a talker who'd spent far more time in the Sudder Street bars in Calcutta than in any hospice over the Hooghly in Howrah. She probably pictured him already with the nice wife and the family and the Volvo, the good Jewish boy doing the good Jewish boy thing. She'd been able to see right inside him without any of the usual intimacies. Was she that perspicacious, or was he becoming so obvious as to be totally transparent? Oh, but he had played it so *badly*. The whole situation was a fuck-up. He didn't even know if he could face her again. There she was, his ideal Pondy girl, living just across the hall, served up on a platter, and he'd fucked it terminally on his very first pass.

He coughed. The sound echoed down the lime wash corridor. Why was he smoking anyway? When had that started? He couldn't even remember. Somewhere in India. He thrust the butt deep into the sand tray beside his chair, entombing it, and sat in silence. No sound issued from within the entire guesthouse. It felt as if the building itself were asleep. Then he heard a mouse-like scratching from the kitchen. A girl's voice laughed. Preparations for lunch starting up. He heard the clatter of a pan on a stone benchtop and the girl laughed again: Lakshmi.

Surely, afternoon came. The sun pressed with a firm insistence down upon the city. A breeze gave some relief to the grid of streets of the Ville Blanche by the sea, but back across the canal in the Ville Noire the heat congealed in the stilled air, foamed the waste in drains. The poor slept through it on the pavements, delivery boys on the warm, flat trays of their bicycle carts, the wealthy behind the bougainvillea-covered walls of their villas. Four o'clock saw high cloud gathering, the blue of the sky softly greyed. The sea breeze freshened, blowing right through the city. Beggars stretched and sat up, and merchants rolled up their steel shutters, the clanking announcing the end of siesta and the advent of evening.

Julia woke on her bed, a book propped open on her chest. She realised she had missed lunch, and was hungry. The idea of an afternoon *dosai* was appealing. Her sleep had been heavy, and she felt a little out of sorts as she splashed her face with cold water, dressed, and made her way downstairs. Holding her breath as she passed over the foul canal, she entered the commercial zone on Rue Nehru. Street sellers were laying out their placemats on the pavements, stocking them with toy ray-guns and teddy bears in bright chemical colours, with plastic combs and underwear. She passed a row of beggars, the albino boy selling naphtha balls, and a little further on a puppy no bigger than a human hand, its coat more flea than fur and its forepaw broken, pathetically nosing in coconut husks for a morsel.

She really had to get back on the road. By now she should have been through Madurai, down in Kerala at the very least, ready for the swing back up the coast, the Backwaters north to Kochi, then on to Hampi, where her beat ended. Other researchers were on different tourist tracks, working towards a rendezvous back in Sydney in a few weeks, to compare notes and sit down at the company computer terminals and tap in their data. Photographs had to be sorted, maps updated, sidebar pieces written on the BJP, Sonia Gandhi, Bal Thackeray, the Shiv Sena. And then a few months later the new *Hobo's Lullaby* guide to India would appear in travel sections of bookshops across the world, and Julia would get that little thrill she always got to see the first person at the counter with a copy in their hand.

That was how it was meant to turn out. Only it hadn't, and this time, on this edition, unless she left Pondicherry right now, there would be trouble. And not because one of the kids from the office who had been given a go and sent overseas for the first time had screwed up. Or that one of the experienced researchers had suffered an accident, or gotten sick. These were understandable problems. They were almost allowed for in the schedule. But what was not was the conscious delinquency of someone who, above all others, could be expected to be doing their job: the publisher. No, if the edition was late, and very late at that, it would be because she, Julia Keefe, co-publisher and co-founder, had gone bush. AWOL. Troppo.

She went on past Lord's Suitings and Shirtings, towards Saratha Creations and MummyDaddy's, with its bizarre red-haired mannikin out front in a voluminous orange silk *salwar kameez*. She was about to turn into the Indian Coffee House for her *dosai* when she decided to walk on a little further and buy some fruit at the market first. Fending off the bicycles, rickshaws and motorbikes which came at her everywhichway, she negotiated the cross street, Mahatma Gandhi Road, and was about to enter the market when on the far side of Rue Nehru she saw a shop-sign which had often caught her eye in the distance, Saint Joseph Nighty House. Thinking it might make an amusing snapshot for the guidebook, she nipped across the street, threading a path through freewheeling cyclists, and stopped in front of the sign, which bore the subtitle of Nighties and Churidhars Showroom. The narrow-faced shop had its wares neatly stacked inside, while out front a few items were on display, baggy, unflattering garments in terylene, cotton and silk, their respectively incremental plastic-lettered Pricings above them. She stood looking at those garments, amused at the twee provocativeness of the word nighty, and the reality of those sexless sacks. But seeing them pricked a memory.

It was of another place very much like this, on an equally dusty commercial street, in Mysore. They had eaten dinner, and were about to go back to their hotel. It must have been almost ten years ago, one of their early trips to India. They had passed a nightdress shop, and just for fun Tim had suggested they go in. He chose her the most risque item in the house, still chastely cut but in white silk cool to the skin, and they had rushed back to the hotel to 'try it out'. She recalled making a big entry from the bathroom, how he smiled on seeing it on her, and the love they made. She had kept it for years, even though it bunched up every time she turned in bed. Standing on Rue Nehru, she tried to remember the fate of that nightdress. Purged, no doubt, along with so many other things.

She snapped the photograph, bought papayas and limes at the market, and re-crossed Mahatma Gandhi Road to the Indian Coffee House. It was one of her all-time favourites. She loved the walls, the top two-thirds green, the bottom third orange, the green and orange steel girder columns, the forest of fast-whirring fans overhead, the industrial metal blue of the tabletops and doors. It was an expansive space, with a liberating feeling of height, a great volume of warm air sloshing about inside. Today it was busy as the ever-popular *dosais*, *iddlis* and *uttapams*, restricted to breakfasts and afternoon snacks by the strict chronological regime of Timings, were reinstated to the menu. White-shirted men, foreheads smeared with ash and gold and dotted with red from morning *puja*, sat drinking coffee and breaking their *dosai* crust, filling it with vegetable mix with their fingers, and placing the morsel in their mouths.

Her *dosai* arrived and she started to eat. Then something odd happened. A spot of water dropped into the yellow *masala* mix on her stainless steel plate. It was a tear, she realised. She was crying. Crying about that nighty place, about Mysore with Tim, about the puppy with the broken paw and the albino boy who tried so desperately every day to sell those bloody naphtha balls. Crying about her own indecision here, her inability to move. The tears had come for all these reasons, and a hundred others which reduced to one, to Tim and to her, who used to be one but were no longer, and the stupid, futile way in which it had happened, over a baby she had wanted and now would probably never have anyway, having lost Tim in the process.

More drops fell onto her plate, transparent little islands in the bright yellow sea of *masala*. Tear water, salty pure. Anger followed, boiled up inside her, heated the tears so they squeezed themselves out of her with pain, with fury. Why had she wanted the baby in the first place? What had that been all about? There had been no external pressure, families going on about the pitterpatter of little feet. Where had this mad desire come from? Her own body? Genes? Human programming? Yes, probably. But why? Why couldn't she have over-ridden that urge, that instinct, when it was all too obvious that everyone else was doing a very thorough job of replicating the species. There was no need whatever (beyond her own) to have a baby. So what was this idiotic urge which had wrecked the union she had shared with the man she loved, found she loved ever more dearly now, and had marooned her at this grimy table which had not been wiped down properly since it was manufactured in nineteen hundred and forty-fucking-six. How had she let it happen? What lunacy had gripped her? Why couldn't she have seen herself, as more and more women did, as child-*free* rather than child-*less*? Now she was loveless, directionless. Hopeless. What was the great mystery of this child business, that she had let it ruin her life? What the sociology, the endocrinology, the sub-atomic physics of it? How had she allowed it to happen?

A shadow caused her to look up. A man with a bull-like face and dark-ringed eyes stared down. 'Anything else, madam?'

She looked down, fished up a tissue. 'Just the bill, please.'

She walked back down the esplanade, happy to lose herself in the sunset crowds. Returning to the guesthouse, she discovered an envelope beneath her door. Her name was neatly written on it, and it was sealed. She slit it with her thumbnail and opened the note inside, written in blue fountain pen. It read: *Lunch, 1 pm tomorrow, roof garden at the Aristo?* and was unsigned.

THE
LITTLE
LIE

He sat alone in the Dining Room. He looked at his watch: just past eight. No-one else had stirred in their rooms. In the quiet of morning he could hear the muted motion of the waves on the sea rocks, the wash and scrape of the tide. A sustained and restful rhythm, reassuring.

He had awoken just after seven, and gone up onto the roof overlooking the esplanade. It was a cloudy morning again, almost chilly on his bare arms and legs, the sun struggling up through battleship grey cloud, beams shafting out like searchlights on the sea. People walked briskly down on the promenade, a few jogging in sweatshirts, others meandering in twos, morning chat.

Retiring from the parapet he had seated himself on the roof and done some deep breathing, slowly taking the air in, holding it, letting it out. He had been reading about breathing practices in a book he'd picked off the shelf at Higginbotham's Bookshop. *Pranayama*, it was called, 'one of the eight branches of yoga'. As he exhaled, he attempted to free his mind of all thought, to enter into a meditative state. But the problem was he found himself counting the seconds of inhalation, of holding in the breath, and of exhalation. In other words, thinking about numbers. And thinking about the process had kept him back in the here and now. Unfortunately he had found no reference in the book to this problem, but if there was one it would no doubt merely reassure that with practice it would all become more straightforward.

Upon opening his eyes he initially believed his vision had been somehow clarified by the deep breathing, and wondered if he didn't feel calmer, more 'centred'. He watched the fishermen standing up on their log boats, barcodes on the grey sea, and wondered if he wasn't seeing the scene properly for the first time. But then, with a decided dip in his mood-meter, he conceded that his consciousness was not discernibly changed, and that he didn't feel any more or less calm than usual. Calmness wasn't his problem anyway. He was calm, very calm, verging on pacific much of the time. His problem was more in the 'depth' department. In simple terms, how, if others perceived one to be shallow, to become 'deeper'. He had hoped this sally into the spiritual exercises of the East might light the way into some new depth. But first impressions weren't promising. In fact they were downright disappointing. He reassured himself that it was only a first try, and no doubt he'd get better results up on the roof the following morning. But that was if there was a following morning for him up on the roof, because as he had descended the stairs he was already considering a move, getting back on the road, heading down to Madurai. And as he considered that, he had reflected tangentially that to be chopping and changing his mind so impulsively meant he probably wasn't such a calm person after all. So maybe calm *was* his problem.

In a low swish of fabric on tile someone approached his table, and he looked up to see Lakshmi, order pad and pen in hand. She smiled shyly, placed them at his elbow and waited while he ticked 'Breakfast' and wrote in 'Coffee, milk, one pot' below it. He returned the smile as he handed her back the pad. She wobbled her head and promptly returned to the kitchen.

While he waited for his order, he moseyed into the Sitting Room, and the Library that adjoined it. Each major common space in the guesthouse was furnished with a large aquarium tank – The Mother had apparently believed aquariums made for calming contemplation – and spent a few moments watching an ugly black fish suck its way up the glass wall. He entered the Library, its white shelves dominated by a long row of hardbacks, the collected works of Sri Aurobindo. He certainly had been prolific; there were words in the millions here. There was also a row, only slightly less in scale and number, of the works of The Mother. He struggled to remember the little he'd taken in about the two of them on his guided tour of the Ashram. Aurobindo seemed to have started out as some kind of pro-Independence Indian Nationalist opposing the British. He'd been educated at Cambridge, and written poetry and literary criticism. Naturally the Ashram devotees waxed on about his facility with language, his erudition, his verse.

Sometime around the First World War the Brits had tossed him into jail for his part in the Independence movement, and when he got out he'd jettisoned earthly causes for spiritual ones, and moved to Pondicherry, where he'd met The Mother.

She was a strange one. French-Egyptian, from memory. There were photos of her all over town, from all times of her life. There was one of her as a child looking intense and very sure of herself, not unlike Wednesday Addams. Or was it Tuesday? There was another shot he quite liked, a murky old one of her dancing as a young woman. She was certainly possessed of exotic allure, and the dance looked witchy. He remembered being told she'd dabbled in the occult, in North Africa. Then she'd turned up in India, met Aurobindo, presumably got involved with him (no-one was very forthcoming about what had *happened*) and they'd spent the rest of their lives immersed in yoga and spiritual research. Someone had said – he remembered now it was Britt, in Room Five – that they had attempted to overcome 'dess', and he finally got that she meant 'death'. Well, that was one course of inquiry that hadn't yielded fruit, if their joint mausoleum was anything to go by. Nonetheless they were an intriguing pair. What kind of chutzpah did it take to sign your name 'The Mother'? On impulse he slipped a volume, a thin one, from the shelves before walking back to the table where his breakfast awaited.

He scanned the pages while he spooned his egg. It looked flaky stuff to his eyes, poor dumb humanity toiling up a steep slope towards godhead, with these two enlightened ones ahead, showing the bright path. In the cause of 'depth' he tried to read some, but it all just seemed to reduce to *do good be good*. He shut the book and looked out the window chewing on the last crust of toast. Why did this kind of stuff always end up sounding like *Jonathan Livingstone Seagull*?

Replacing the booklet in the shelves, he heard Lakshmi and another young *ayah* giggling and glancing his way as they swept. Did they find it funny that people actually tried to read these books? But then Guru, the English-speaking steward, approached.

'She is asking for one photo,' he giggled. 'Lakshmi is wishing that one day you will take a photo. She is asking for a photo, in the garden.'

Josh looked towards Lakshmi, who instantly turned away.

'I'd be happy to. Can you tell her that, please?'

Guru looked at the girl and laughed again. 'I believe she already knows this, sir.'

'Mahabarata Not A Myth – Archaeologist', *stating that the ancient tome was really an important source of history. No further mention of this preposterous claim, the body of the article about a conference on marine biology. Curious.* 'Three Gangsters Shot In Mumbai'. *Stake-outs, tip-offs, shoot-outs, the full toughguy lexicon for a trio from the 'Marcheka Gang' gunned down by cops. With Shock Pix.* 'VHP Charge Sonia', *being that a Hindu fundamentalist faction had attacked Congress Party leader Sonia Gandhi for 'behaving like a Christian' for visiting trouble spots in Gujarat where crazed mobs had been burning down churches.* 'Lalloo Out On Bail'

— the nation's favourite fodder-swindling politician from far Bihar rides home to Patna atop a garlanded elephant to applause from adoring multitudes. 'Militants Bid To Blow Up Telecom Office'. *Kashmiri independence fighters (or Pakistani mercenaries) fire a rocket-propelled grenade at a telephone exchange. Miss entire building.*

He read on idly, teacup at his elbow, before setting the newspaper down on the table. The cool of morning, pillows of grey cloud. But breakfast had been disappointing on one count: the waiter had somehow brought his tea as per his standing order, so that it arrived black and unsweetened, not to his taste at all. He'd had half a mind to complain, but knew that could be very complicating, and would probably ruin what had been until then a foolproof scheme. More than the tea though, it was the omen he didn't enjoy.

His eye strayed to an item on the front page he hadn't seen, being drawn first to the Mahabarata nonsense and the gangland splash. Headed 'Thackeray Thanks Sainiks', it related how Bal Thackeray, uncrowned duce of Mumbai, had lauded his Shiv Sena thugs as patriots for digging up a cricket pitch in Delhi where a match was scheduled to be played between India and Pakistan. Now, it said, the Indian cricket authorities were considering moving the game down to Chennai, because of fears the Shiv Sena would disrupt it completely. The question was, what would Thackeray do now? Would he bring his troublemaking to South India too?

That prospect, along with what had happened with his tea, left him feeling somewhat agitated as he paid his bill and headed back down the promenade, towards the Sea View. It was already past eleven, time soon for lunch. Meals came around so rapidly in India, it was surprising more tourists didn't come for precisely that reason. But then, perhaps they did.

Julia edged past shoppers elbowing each other at the bargain trays in those last precious moments before the proprietors shut up for lunch. It was just past one. She was running late because she had dropped in to the Auroville shop up the street to try on one of their hand-knit cotton pullovers. She had also been told the night before, by Britt, over beers in the Penguin Cafe, that the Auroville shop sold some very good ayurvedic body products, including a powder you made into a clay-like paste and applied all over the body like a face-mask.

After a round or two, Britt had shed her Danish reserve and become decidedly playful. When the chat had cruised from Britt's inquiries into the Ashram and its work, onto, almost inevitably, sex, Julia had found herself quizzing the nitty-gritty of lesbian lovemaking, full colour details of which her informant had been only too pleased to give. Sex with a woman was the very best, Britt had sighed into the frothy head of her Kingfisher. And she was not saying this 'in ignorance of the other', as she had not always been exclusively 'with the women'. Men were good for some things, but two women together, well, they could do things no man could.

She asked Julia if she'd ever tried it, and she felt almost cheated when she had to shake her head. And although at no point did Britt suggest she experiment, they walked back with a new sense of closeness, and when they said goodnight, Britt's lips momentarily touched hers. Now, her head fuzzy – usually she drank little in India, treating her stays as a welcome string of culturally acquired AFDs – she wondered what might have happened if they had actually kissed. She had never kissed a woman before, not like that. But with the mood she had been in, her emotional fragility after those hot Nighty House tears, perhaps she might not have made it back to her room. Lesbian sex. She'd only ever thought about it in the vague and abstract. But last night, unannounced, there it had been, a possibility. And now she was a bit muddle-headed, running late, having decided against both the cotton pullover and the body mud, making her way down Rue Nehru towards lunch, curious about who had written the note, still wondering why they hadn't signed it. Who could it be? Josh? Britt? Kingston Chance? Mr Manzini? The Manager even?

Somehow she wasn't quite so surprised when, within two or three doors of the Aristo, she found Josh peering into a shop window, and she called out a 'hello' over the traffic noise.

He appeared to blink in the sun. 'Oh, hi.'

'I got involved in the Auroville shop. Sorry. And now I'm really starving. Shall we go in?'

Still blinking in the sun, he nodded, and she led the way inside and upstairs to the roof garden. They passed through a carved ornamental doorway and by a cage of budgerigars and an algae-tinged fishtank. They were greeted by the maitre d' who ushered them to a table secluded by tubs of flowering bushes. Josh gallantly drew out a chair for Julia, and waited until she sat before nudging it back in. A waiter arrived with menus and asked if they wanted the 'special tea' of the house.

'You mean, *speciality*', Josh said, blinking again. The red hoops of bougainvillea overhead provided only partial covering from the sun.

'No,' the waiter giggled, 'Special Tea.' This turned out to be beer. 'Kingfisher too, sir, none of that Royal Challenge they serve in some places.'

Josh grinned across the table. 'Special Tea?'

'I'm a bit fuzzy today, to tell you the truth.' But then she shrugged. 'Why not? Yes, let's have it. Thanks.'

The waiter disappeared through the crowded tables beyond the flower tubs, and they turned their attention to their menus. Julia was in the process of deciding between chicken *tandoori* and fish *tikka* when out the corner of her eye she saw Mr Manzini walk in and look straight at her. As he looked her way, his spectacles glittered interrogatively, and she thought of all things he might be about to come over and say something to her. But he was interrupted by the maitre d' asking if he would like a table, and she heard him reply, swivelling his head and scanning the diners, that he was looking for someone he had been expecting to meet for lunch. This sounded somehow false to her ear and his room scan concluding in her direction, she again fancied he might be about to cross the floor and speak to her. But after another moment he informed the maitre d' that the person he was seeking would obviously not be meeting him today, turned and left. From her seat she saw him going down the internal staircase, a puzzled expression on his face. Turning her head so that she could see over the parapet wall and down into the street, she saw him emerge onto Rue Nehru a few moments later, negotiate the rush of traffic to the far side, and stride off down the pavement past the beggars outside the Indian Coffee House, back towards the Ville Blanche.

The bafflement of his behaviour almost made her suspect that he had written the invitation instead of Josh. But that was an absurd idea. She did not even know the man, not even his first name, and he had never given any indication of desiring to meet her. Rather than inviting her to lunch, his past behaviour had been to avoid all contact, even eye contact. Besides, there was Josh. If he hadn't written the invitation, what was he doing waiting outside the hotel, and what was he doing sitting here now? No, it didn't make sense. Mr Manzini was just strange, or for some reason didn't like her, or both.

'You know, I've got to confess something,' Josh said, startling her from her thoughts.

'Yes, what?'

'I'm having a real hard time here. I can't pick between the chicken *tandoori* and the fish *tikka*.'

The waiter hefted an earthenware coffee pot containing their Special Tea, and set it on the table with two coffee mugs. They gave him their order – opting for both the *tandoori* and the *tikka* – and he left them with a parting wink. With drinks poured, Josh paused a moment to take stock. It seemed sublimely fair fortune to find himself in this position. But how had it happened? Had she been intending to meet someone else downstairs, and was this a misunderstanding of some form? Or was her manner of suggesting they eat lunch just kind of weird? And if she had been intending to meet someone else, where were they? Surely they would be here by now.

Their orders came promptly, a generous succulence of chicken *tandoori*, and tastebud-tingly morsels of fish *tikka* arranged in a circular pattern on the plate, served with slices of cucumber and ripe red cherry tomato. They had also ordered a vegetable *pulao*, and *naan* bread, the latter arriving perfectly crisped but unburnt. They ate studiously, as if they hadn't eaten properly for days, and this was probably much the case for both, restaurant meals taken alone tending to be frugal affairs.

'You know,' he said, 'I've really got to apologise for yesterday at breakfast. I mean, like, wanting to push something on you.'

'Oh, you didn't do that.'

'No. I did. And I was way, way out of line, preaching at you like that, like some zealot.'

'No,' she said, 'you *should* have been like that. It was a fine thing you did in Calcutta. Giving your time to such important work. All that disease ... poverty ... to me it's just so overwhelming. Didn't you ever feel like that yourself?'

'Of course I did.'

'But that didn't stop you, did it,' Julia persisted.

And although he had been on the verge of telling her what had really happened, he was also happy enough now to fudge it. Because, he realised, he could avoid telling her a direct lie. To omit, mislead, he could handle that – but not to tell an outright lie. As a boy he had been caught out too many times, and had learned the lesson that omission was safer.

'It didn't stop you because you really wanted to help those people,' she continued. 'You had a mission. Felt part of something bigger than yourself. And that's why I can ultimately understand you being evangelical about it. Because it *is* something we should all be doing. I mean, imagine if everyone came to India and gave a month of their lives to helping people. That would be something. That wouldn't just be like a drop in a bucket. That'd make a difference.'

'Definitely,' he said. 'More beer?'

'Oh, I don't know if I should. I don't usually drink during the day. What do you think?'

'I think why the hell not?'

He grinned, found that she was grinning back. He summoned the waiter and more Special Tea was on the way. He felt her lean in closer across the table. There was something propitious in that lean.

'So, you're from New York,' she said. 'And you're, what, twenty-seven?'

'Twenty-eight. You?'

'Thirty-five.'

'I would have put you at no more than thirty.'

'Thank you, but I'm thirty-five.' She smiled: 'See, you invited an older woman to lunch.'

The waiter arrived with a fresh pot, froth flowering from its spout, deposited it at Josh's elbow, and left.

'Only, you didn't sign it.'

'Sorry?' Josh said.

'The invitation to lunch. You didn't sign it.'

He played for time, pouring for her.

'Why didn't you?' she asked.

He finished pouring the beer. Her question hung in the air between them, demanding a reply. Should he admit now he didn't write any invitation? That he didn't know what she was talking about? And where was the person who had written it, and why weren't they here now?

'Well, I ...'

'Yes?'

He hoped she might run on to something else, give him time to think. Or a waiter appear and spill something over her. Or rain just tumble out of the sky. But nothing happened. He was left with the question hanging over him. About this invitation, which now seemed so important to her. And if he admitted he didn't write it, he sensed, that might spoil everything. The serendipity of the afternoon could be squandered. The beer and the sun felt suddenly very strong. What to do? Lie? But surely he would get found out. Or would he? The real person hadn't even shown up. And what, really, did he have to lose?

'No,' he said. 'I didn't.'

True enough, up to a point. He hadn't signed any invitation. No-one had, apparently. So although technically it was a lie, it was a small one. In the Goebbels-scale scheme of modern things, minuscule.

She frisked him with her smile. 'Why not?'

'Because I wanted it to be a mystery.'

Just as it was to him.

'A mystery ... yes, I suppose that makes sense,' she said. 'Not that I really minded you not signing it. I suspected it was you, anyway. And even though people usually think it's, you know, not utterly courageous of someone to leave a note unsigned like that, as I said, I thought it was brave enough of you to ask me at all, especially after I'd been a bit short with you.'

'Only because I was an asshole.'

'No you weren't.'

'Yes I was.'

'No, you weren't.' And to underline the point she reached across, and touched his wrist. 'I mean it. You were just feeling enthusastic about something. About something good. And there's something else too. You didn't let things rest there, in that difficult position for us both. You did something about it. Wrote that note to say, "Hey, come on, let's go to lunch, let's be friends, let's not allow some silly misunderstanding to ruin everything".'

She had left her hand on the table near him, and for a mad moment he thought about taking it to his lips and kissing the tips of her fingers. Some women liked things like that, impulsive acts, bold gestures. But maybe Julia wasn't one of those women. Or did she just scare him a little?

'I was feeling a bit strange when I got back to my room last night and found your note,' she was saying. 'Personal things, you know. And I found it and I thought, great, this guy is good. He's not afraid. I was impressed. So impressed that I went out and had a few drinks with Britt. Not because I was feeling down any more, but because I felt good. So thank you.'

As they walked back in the late afternoon, the old gold of the sun blending harmonically with their newly shared sense of wellbeing, Julia marvelled at how things could turn about so quickly. She liked Josh. It felt like they might spend some time together, explore Pondy together. He had already asked if she would like to visit Auroville with him the following day. And so the only cloud on the horizon now, the usual leaden ones having been pushed away for the time being, was Mr Manzini, and his continued odd behaviour. But fortunately that remained the only off-key note in a day which had turned out far better than the one before it, and the one before that, better than any day for a seeming age.

Josh felt good too. It had all been smoothed out. Fate had intervened while he'd been looking into the window of that cookware place on Rue Nehru – ironically enough, trying to avoid her as she came up the street – and everything had changed. The prospects looked bright. He was not completely sure of his next move, but that would come. Only one little cloud on his horizon – a baffling one though – which was how to handle it if and when it came to light that he had not written that invitation. After all, he'd had to go well beyond possible misunderstanding and purposeful omission, into the telling of an actual lie. A little one, but a lie. It was worrying, a problem, but a minor one, he felt. After all, if fortune was running his way as it had been at lunch, surely a little white lie could be taken care of. And so he walked with a confident stride down the street, so much so that she had to catch him up. He was going too fast for her.

Passing Room Ten towards bed that night, Julia saw the light on inside and was tempted to knock and confront the man in there, demand to know why he had been behaving so oddly towards her. But, she asked herself outside his door, had he really? Wasn't it true that he had just been ignoring her? And that, however hurtful it might be, was his prerogative. No-one could make him speak to her if he didn't want to. It was up to him. Just as it was up to her whether she wished to speak to him. And did she? In some ways he was more of an enigma, the subject of intrigue, than someone she might or might not wish to meet. Most probably it was the mystery that made her think about him at all. And if she wanted to dispel it, solve it as it were, all she had to do was knock on his door. He was in there. His door padlock was off, and his light on. She heard him cough. He was reading, writing in his journal, or sitting out on the balcony, unaware of the turmoil his actions had prompted in her. Would he like her to knock on his door? Would he want her not to? Did he care an iota either way? The answer to each of these questions was an irksome *perhaps*. The wisest thing, given all the circumstances, was to continue on to her own door. And that is what, after a few moments more of indecision, she presently did.

11

Josh sat in the Dining Room. It was early again, but he was not entirely alone this time. The Indian couple from Room Four had for once ventured out to eat, and sat over the yellow remnants of *masala pooris*. They looked so elderly and fragile up close, a tap on the shoulder about what time did to flesh, how it undermined and sucked it dry, how it curved and twisted bone, turned it to chalk. There was also the Canadian woman from upstairs, Mildred. She sat in a corner reading a fat volume of Aurobindo. He was almost tempted to ask her about it, what she was seeking in it and what she was getting, but he resisted. He had overheard some of her chats about the master and his works, and they were always earnest and never brief.

He had been up on the roof again, done his deep breathing, trying to clear his mind of thought. But what was it Woody Allen said? Something like, whenever he tried to meditate his laundry list came up. Josh hadn't got a laundry list, nothing so useful. Just a lot of half-formed thoughts running out onto his mental stage, dancing silly pirouettes and running off giggling. Unwelcome thoughts, amateur players. But you couldn't keep them off the stage.

One of these unwelcome thoughts had caused him to wake sweating in the middle of the night. It was a memory from schooldays, the time he told another child that he wasn't Jewish. Bloom wasn't only a Jewish name, he had said. His family had migrated from ... Manchester ... plucking it, of all places, from a school project on the Industrial Revolution. The other boy, who suspected anything he ever said anyway, had asked some pointed questions about Manchester, and Josh had been unable to answer with much conviction, because he was having trouble remembering anything about that project beyond cotton. But he was able to counter that they had been living in America for several generations, and that was why he knew little about his 'ancestral homeland'. In fact, the family had been in America for three generations. His grandfather had arrived from Poland clutching the cardboard suitcase of the huddled masses, and sold hats, gloves and spools of thread on First Avenue. Now his father owned the factory in Newark, and the old trademark, Bloom's Gloves. Bloom was a lot easier on American ears than their plosive-intensive Polish name, so they had taken it on. That had been his father's explanation anyway, though as he grew up, Josh came to the view his father had been trying to distance himself from the Jewish tag too, perhaps believing, as young Josh had, that somewhere there might just be gentile Blooms.

His father had followed the name change with behavioural

ones. He worked all Saturday, and didn't even walk by the synagogue. He made a point of serving Chinese food when guests came to dinner. But still he was Jewish. It was there in the rhythms of his speech, the gestures of his face and hands. His father's denial of the obvious made it all the worse for Josh when his own denial came to light. His father's fury, rarely sighted, was frightening, and young Josh, an eleven-year-old boy of the American suburbs, could not work out whether it was the denial of race and culture which had so disturbed his father, or the telling of the lie itself. It was certainly that, the word *lie*, which his father kept shouting as he strapped his bare behind with his belt.

After that Josh had never been able to tell an outright lie without significant unease. And it was another lie, yesterday's, the one which circumstance had seduced him into, that had caused him such anguish when he awoke sweating at ten to three with the dull break and shingle-scrape of the waves in his open bedroom window, and sat straight up in bed. *What had he done?* Beer and bonhommie worn off, the peril of his situation was manifest. He had lied. Openly. Clearly. *Detectably*.

Of course, social lying was something everyone did from time to time. It was a part of life. People who sat screening on their sofas while their answer machines picked up calls, they were lying in a way. Their taped messages told callers they weren't there, but they were. And friends who feigned other appointments, headaches and family crises to get out of social engagements they didn't feel like going to, they were lying too. Even the 'fine, thanks' when you felt like shit, that was a lie. They were all lies. People lived their lives spinning webs of little 'Seinfeld' lies. Everyone did it, everyone knew it. It was accepted because it made life easier.

There was the occasion, however, when a social lie got found out. You might have told someone you couldn't meet because you'd be out of town that weekend, and then you run into their best friend – or them – trying on a jacket in a store. *Caught.* And although no-one really cared too much about it because everyone knew that everyone did it, the real misdemeanour was getting caught. Because then everyone is confronted with the reality of the Lying Game. Everyone is embarrassed. You, the person you were meant to do the thing with, and their friend who caught you out. It's useless emotional work for everyone. But among friends, okay, maybe not such a big deal. What's a little lie between friends? They just thought you were a schmuck for getting caught. And the schmuck-tag only stuck for so long. People forgot about it soon enough. That was how it happened on 'Seinfeld', when George lied to Jerry and Jerry lied to Elaine and Elaine lied to George. (Kramer never lied.) And that was pretty much how it was in real life too. You just started a new episode.

But lying to people you'd only just met, while at the same time accepting praise for things you hadn't done – why did she have to make such a big deal about the invitation and about his heroic fucking humanitarianism in Calcutta, was she drunk? (yes, probably) – that was dangerous. If the person who'd actually written the invitation turned up as he (Josh presumed a he) no doubt would, he was well and truly in *stuckville*.

Because confronted with it, he had no room to manoeuvre. He couldn't pretend he didn't understand, or change the subject as you might try to do with very, very, little lies. No, the stark choice was this: to try to bluff his way through, say he had written the note and that the other person was lying (why would they do that, it didn't even make sense!); or, gulp, *admit it*. *Admit* to Julia that he had allowed her, all through the cruise of that afternoon, to continue under the misapprehension that he had invited her, and capped with a straight-out lie that he had. A patent untruth. An unequivocal lie.

So, accepting now that he could not bluff his way through if it came down to it – and he sensed that it would come down to it, that it was his karma – the only option was to admit he had lied. What an appallingly Pinnochio-nosed, Clintonesque situation he had blithely skated into. Such thin ice, with a moral quagmire beneath. And so all he could do now, if it did come down to it, was to throw his tainted character upon her mercy, accept the guilt, tell her he had done it out of confusion when she approached him on that busy street, out of indecision, out of human weakness, and out of a misplaced desire to set things right, make up for the previous day out of his pathetic desire (at the very bottom circle of the Hell of the lie) just to spend some time with her, a woman he liked.

Actually, this was sounding better. Maybe that was the pathway out of the mire. Flattery. It might just work. But then, gloom returning as he had lain there waiting for sleep, hoping it would come soon or the day would be even harder to handle, he saw that each way was equally problematic, vexed, so vexed that it would probably ruin things with her, so that she would never trust him again, certainly not with her confidence, just as certainly not with her body.

This was the depressing landscape he contemplated in the Dining Room, as the staff began to move around, hands unreeling his rattan placemat, others setting down the regulation four slices of toast, the butter and the lurid pink strawberry jam, while any hunger was leaching from him like life from the dying.

'The brainchild of The Mother!' Julia was shouting into his ear, reading from a guidebook as they bounced along. 'The physical embodiment of their ideas of the nobility of work ... a response to the alienation of worker from the product of their labour, in an almost Marxian sense ...!'

Julia shouted on as the autorickshaw jerked and jolted, swayed perilously on the road north to Auroville. A few short kilometres though the journey might be, it was a sharp reminder of the real India that spread beyond the tiny Pondicherry enclave. Now they were back in Tamil Nadu state, well and truly back in India, with its teeming traffic, buses excreting stupendous quantities of black carcinogenic smoke straight in your face having almost killed you in the process of overtaking, driven by crazed men ready to meet their maker. He recalled once naively asking a hotel desk clerk if there were many bus accidents in India, and the clerk didn't even look up from his ledger, murmuring 'numerous, sir'. So every time he took a bus he found himself asking if he was ready to meet his own maker, whoever that might be. Mind you, did it really matter? In fifty years' time people wondering that would at least have an answer. General Electric. Or is she a Sony?

It didn't help that Julia was shouting in his ear. She was doing it with the best of intentions of course, to ensure that they arrived at their destination properly briefed. But all Josh wanted to do was concentrate on the road, telepathically soothe the pathological urges of their mad-speeding, klaxon-squawking driver by the transference of calming thoughts into his pea-brain of pine forests, desert islands and mountain streams. Incredibly, Julia appeared as unconcerned about the road as the driver, reading on about Auroville from her guidebook, its starting up in a rush of idealism in the sixties, 'a new community where all races and nationalities would mingle and there was no private property and transactions were conducted by barter ...' reciting its square kilometrage, its population count in Indians and foreigners ... about the villages of Auroville with names like *Certitude, Verite*, and *Discipline*, some growing vegetables, others making leather goods, paper, even designing software ... and how they had nearly finished building the great centrepiece, the Matrimandir, and that if the original plan ever got finished the civic centre of the whole place would be a complex of futuristic white buildings swirling like a galaxy around the 'eye' of the Matrimandir ...

She read off these grand details as they lurched down the road past shabby shops and stalls, meagre houses and vacant lots.

The words bubbled forth so readily that when she paused he couldn't help but chuckle that she almost sounded like an Auroville enthusiast herself.

'No, just a fascinated onlooker. But who knows, with all they've done in thirty years, maybe they will just realise some big dreams here.'

And maybe not, Josh thought. He'd heard whispers in town about this place. That the foreigners stuck together in their national ghettoes: French, Dutch, German, Italian. That the whole thing was turning into an exclusive retirement village for superannuated European hippies. But he was nonetheless pleased at her enthusiasm, not so much for the facts and figures that marked it, but because she seemed genuinely to want him to share her interest.

The autorickshaw swerved hard, almost dislodging him from their bench seat in the back as they turned into Auroville and left the coastal highway behind. As they followed a bumpy, once-sealed road uphill past the first vegetable gardens and orchards, Julia was saying that no matter what one thought of Aurobindo and The Mother, one couldn't help but accept that the Society had transformed what had been dried-out orange earth into thriving villages producing fruit, vegetables and grains, and intensively reafforested too so that the place was like a well-shaded Garden of Eden.

Josh nodded, but it still looked like a scrubby mess to him. There were trees, yes, but all unkempt in that Indian way. And how did anyone navigate the place? The driver kept taking pot-holed dirt tracks off pot-holed dirt tracks. If this was the roads system of some quasi-socialist utopia, they'd better get a sub-committee onto it and quick.

They lunched at a place called New Creation Corner. Julia enthused over her slice of carrot pie, but Josh found his omelette oily and spent the meal swatting flies. They moved on to the Visitors Centre, and after queuing in a stuffy room with a coachload of tourists, managed to procure tickets for that afternoon's organised visit to the Matrimandir Chamber, the primary objective of daytrippers to Auroville.

Waiting for visiting time to come around, they whiled the afternoon away in the Visitors Centre cafe, talking about art in New York and beaches in Sydney, hiking the Adirondacks and the feel of the Outback — and her confession that she too had been terrified out on the highway, but had dealt with it by reading him all that 'guff' about Auroville. It was comfortable talk, the pair of them idling over coffees, the understated bliss of conversation conducted without pressure, finding its own way. He charted the growth of intimacy in how closely they sat and how quiet their voices, in the occasional physical contact when speaking, the fleeting touch on the wrist for emphasis. It pointed pleasantly on. She was open in that manner of Australians he had met before, at ease as she revealed aspects of her personal life, even the mess of things she had made with her husband, and how bad she felt about it. Josh could tell she still loved him, and so he coaxed the conversation away, back out into the mainstream of relationships in general, to the degree of difficulty of love, the tumble, pike and twist of it in the dumb rush of life. He had experienced that himself too, he said, enticing her back towards the personal, the singular, but that singular now being him. But he had hardly broached it when she glanced down at her watch and with a touch on his wrist informed him it was time they got out to the Matrimandir, unless they wanted to be shuffling along at the end of a mile-long queue.

The driver dropped them in a red-earthed square where they joined hundreds of others waiting. The pilgrims sat on concrete benches beneath an enormous banyan tree, making small talk as the last of the afternoon heat asserted itself, the women fanned and the men dozed and the clock hands dawdled towards four. The atmosphere was subdued beneath that gnarled spread of branch. Voices were muted except for the occasional child's cry or half-stifled adult cough. Everything pointed to them being in proximity to a holy place, and preparing themselves to enter its holy of holies: all switching, consciously or otherwise, into church-best behaviour.

Josh and Julia had a bench to themselves. He was chuckling through a travel vignette about a Delhi taxi driver who had tried to overcharge him, and Julia was sitting back listening, one arm settled easily on the other, when she noticed Mr Manzini perched at the far end of a bench occupied by an Indian family, reading intently. Narrowing her eyes to a squint, she saw his book was *The Plague*, by Camus. Cheery reading. But it spoke again of a serious mind, and he was so engrossed he did not look up when two children brushed by him playing. Nor did he when their mother reprimanded them. Julia watched him as Josh went on, while still nodding and smiling appropriately at each beat and twist in his tale. Mr Manzini's eyes possessed a ferocious intensity in their gold-framed glasses, every part of his being trained down through the lenses onto the page, every seeming corpuscle of him directed into it. He looked trim, comfortable in a white T-shirt and khaki shorts that showed off tanned, fit legs and healthy feet in their Birkenstocks. A white cotton squashable sunhat sat on the bench beside him: that said he had to be unusual indeed, a European who respected the sun.

Josh finished his story and sat awaiting her approval, and enough of her had been listening to get the gist, and give him the approbation he wanted. Just as she finished speaking, the uniformed attendants gave a sign, and people were on their feet making for the gate, almost running some of them, and the attendants started forming them into a snaking line that looped back on itself again and again, waiting for the gate to be opened and entry to the holy ground that lay beyond.

Julia regarded Mr Manzini as he rose, eyes still fixed on the page, and began toward the gate, moving with ease through the crowd yet never once lifting his gaze. The closeness of his attention caused her to wonder whether he had seen her first and was avoiding her, or whether it was, as had been her initial impression, that he was immersed in the book and had no idea she (or anyone else) was there.

She felt Josh's hand close about hers and draw her up to where he stood. Helping her to her feet, gentlemanly enough, yet with the connection established he did not let go, and drew her through the crowds to the end of the queue. But it happened to suit her to be hand-to-hand with him then, because with subtle pressure and tugs of her own she was able to mediate their course and speed, so that they reached the queue only a few places behind Mr Manzini. Closer, she marvelled even more at his concentration, reading in public, standing in a crowd.

The plague had to be at its worst now. Perhaps he feared for the doctor, or the doctor's wife away in the hills, or had an intuition about Tarrou, the dilettante who had turned up in Oran just before the plague. She remembered what reading about the peak of the plague had been like for her, how she had not been able to close the book herself. She stole a quick glance. He was two-thirds of the way through. Perhaps he was reading about the death of the child, that long, shrill cry. Compelling, horribly so. She had almost been physically ill. When had she read it? Years ago. They had been in Varanasi, staying at Scinidia Ghat, next to the Burning Ghat. She remembered their talks about the dead and the rites that surrounded them, how the bodies were carried on bamboo stretchers by chanting men down to the banks of the Ganges for cremation, and how the pair of them watched the wood pyres late into the night, flames burning the dark sky orange, luridly rouging the ghats and the buildings that rose so precipitously above the waters. It had not seemed macabre or even strange to watch it, the open incineration of the dead, the public consumption of flesh and bone by flame. Rather it had been beautiful in its resignation. In the end, the human body, along with all our passions, needs and desires, burned down to nothing, or very nearly nothing. The gold was sifted from the teeth and rings, and the ashes sprinkled on the Ganges. She remembered Tim had remarked what an odd choice for Varanasi reading matter *The Plague* was. She had asked him if he'd read it himself, and he'd said no, he wasn't sure he'd like it, and that had turned strangely into what almost became their first real argument, but not quite. Instead it had transmuted into lovemaking: there would be plenty of time for arguments later.

Josh was jibing about the officiousness of the attendants as the queue began to move off, and, with a commandment that they now observe total silence because of people meditating in the realm they were about to enter, they were admitted through the gate to a pathway running through a mandala of well-tended gardens. People kept chattering to begin with, but after a minute or two they fell quiet, and the only sound was the scrunch of sandals on gravel.

She saw that Mr Manzini had put the book away now, and walked briskly. His long legs progressed him through the dawdling knots of Indian families. With a squeeze of Josh's hand Julia urged him forward, and he readily responded so that they overtook the families too, and left them in their wake.

Turning a corner they gained their first view of the Matrimandir, a massive sphere now only a couple of hundred metres distant. 'Looks like a giant golf ball,' Josh breathed into her ear. She nodded agreement, wondering how many thousands of people must have said exactly those words at exactly that spot. Because it was true, it did look like a ball for a deity-sized golfer, being pure white and covered with portholes which corresponded to the dimpled surface of a golf ball.

Ahead Julia saw attendants directing people to remove their shoes and line them up in rows. Mr Manzini was already taking off his sandals. Not wanting to lose him, she manually urged Josh into the shoe-divesting area where she flicked off her slip-on sandals and waited with some impatience while he unlaced his Timberland hikers. Then she drew him rapidly through the barefoot crowd to the carpeted up-ramp that was the final, airstrip-like approach into the Matrimandir. She bustled him past attendants and signs demanding *Silence* until she overtook the last family parting them from Mr Manzini. As they walked in silence up the flight of steps into the interior, they comprised a trio: Mr Manzini, apparently unaware of their presence; Julia, puffing a little from the pursuit; and Josh, who having taken little notice of other guests at the Sea View beyond Julia, had no idea who the man in front of them was.

Workers remained busy on the structure, and once inside they climbed scaffolding steps past a landing stage where two ultimate attendants, serene-faced devotee women, made ultimate, finger-to-lip injunctions to silence. Then they found themselves on a futuristic moulded concrete walkway that swerved through a half-turn up to the concrete chamber high above. As they climbed past support struts and more scaffolding, Julia felt Josh's lips on her ear, touching this time, kissing a whispered smile: 'The silence is nothing to do with meditation – they're just afraid the whole thing'll come tumbling down.'

At the top they were ushered into a connecting hallway, like a miniature aerobridge. Julia saw people up the queue being summoned forward so that they could stand, three at a time, at a barrier and peer within the chamber. Mr Manzini remained unaware of their presence as they moved closer and closer in the line to the viewing barrier. Then, with a mathematical precision that was entirely fortuitous, they were gestured forward as a threesome so that they arrived together at the barrier. As they peered within, Julia felt Mr Manzini notice her peripherally, with surprise (or was it a small recoil of distaste?), but there was far too brief a time allocated to them now for anything beyond that. There were mere momemts to be had here, so she trained her attention on the scene within.

The chamber was wedding cake white, the interior, to her eye, shaped like a lotus flower several metres high. The air they breathed was cooled and filtered, the floor padded with white cushions, bottom comfort for the meditating devotees. A circle of slender columns, themselves white, stretched upwards. Following them, she saw a beam of natural light where it entered the room at its highest point, and shone down onto the focal point of the chamber, a globe of opaque green glass, a metre or so in diameter, which rested in a gilt cradle adorned with the lotus symbol of Aurobindo in the centre of the floor.

Julia had just registered her snapshot perception when their seconds at the barrier expired and they were motioned to move on and allow the next trio in. And so they did, descending the down-ramp, observing the long queue of people on the up-ramp, all impelled to silence. To a final annoying silence command back outside in the sun, Mr Manzini was heard to reply: 'Yes, yes ... I'm going.' To which the attendant said

'Sshhhh!' and the man replied in a bored voice, 'Yes, yes ...'

As they exited the great white orb and walked barefoot back to their shoes, the three almost abreast, Julia spoke up, addressing herself to both men.

'So, what did you think?'

'Fucking outrageous,' Josh breathed. 'All that money spent to build some meditation chamber, when there are all those lepers on the streets desperate for medical attention. You know they're going to cover the whole thing with gold, don't you?'

'What?' Julia almost gasped. 'Not real gold though, surely.'

'I think a gold wrapping would be quite fitting,' Mr Manzini interposed. 'A giant, gold-wrapped Ferrero Rocher. After all, people can't get enough of chocolate. They eat it religiously.'

Julia smiled. 'You're staying at the guesthouse, aren't you? In Room Ten?'

'And you are in Room Six. And the young man in Room Eight,' Mr Manzini replied.

Julia extended her hand for him to shake. 'I'm Julia.'

He took it and shook it. 'Marco.'

'Josh,' the American said, putting out his own hand.

They retrieved their shoes and started putting them on looking back at the Matrimandir, from which a column of people entered and left simultaneously, as if being processed inside.

'And what did you think of it?' she asked Marco.

'Oh, remarkable. Remarkable that the human mind has evolved far enough to imagine and build a place like that, one purely for the practice of meditation. If only it were for pure meditation, and to further the development of the human mind, I would applaud it.'

'But?' Josh interposed.

'But it's merely a shrine to The Mother. The old Frenchwoman. Got her followers to build a monument to herself. She is there you know, inside that big glass ball, in the Holy of Holies, exulting.' He looked up coolly, straight at Julia. 'Just the usual human way of doing things, of course. Cult of the personality, iconography, homage to relics. Denial of reality. Weakness. Do you know there's a letter box at the Ashram where the faithful can post letters to The Mother? And she died in 1973.' He fastened the buckles of his sandals, stood up and stretched. 'So that is what we see there, in that Holy of Holies. Human weakness, human vanity. And that is how I found it. Vain, and revolting.' A beat of silence ensued. 'And you?' he asked Julia. 'What did you think?'

'I found it quite beautiful.'

'Really?' Marco said.

'Yes, I did.'

Marco's response was to half raise an eyebrow, and allow himself half a smile.

Josh reassumed Julia's hand, and they began the walk back toward the banyan tree and the car park. Even though the imperative to silence was effectively lifted, and people chatted all around them, few further words were spoken between the three, each immersed now in their own thoughts.

Upon their return to Pondicherry in the early evening, Julia became aware of a heightened sense of expectation from Josh, expressed in a growing physical familiarity. When he suggested they dine together, he appeared to assume she would agree. Did he think she had signed over some proprietorial deed to him? But then, they had found the guesthouse unusually quiet: almost everyone was out. There seemed no prospect of dining with Britt, or with Mildred, with whom she had shared a meal once or twice. The elderly Indian couple had closed their door and would not reopen it until morning, and needless to say Kingston was nowhere to be seen. Nor had she lodged a Dinner Order Form with the Manager that morning, so she would have to eat out anyway, and if it was not with Josh it would be alone, as it would be for him too. So it was convenient for them to dine together. But she hoped her acceptance of his proposal would not give him the wrong idea. To hope was the best she could do at this time, however, as there was no easy way she could have a conversation with him of that degree of trickiness without possible misunderstanding. So she made a show of considering before she replied, quite formally, as though his suggestion had come unexpectedly, from a stranger, that yes, that would be nice.

She was torn between dressing up or down. To dress up might be seen as some kind of invitation, but to dress down was equally problematic, interpretable as easy familiarity, perhaps inviting his own easy familiarity. In the end she opted for jeans and a simple, loose-fitting top and sandals. Her hand hesitated at the lipstick, then applied it. Already unfamiliar to the eye, the rich viscous red was almost shocking when she saw it in the mirror. But it was evening, and she was going out to dine, and there was no problem, surely, with a little lipstick. At home she wouldn't have thought twice about it. And Josh wouldn't jump to any silly conclusions, just from that. He was sophisticated enough, surely.

Quitting her room, she considered inviting Marco too. But what would Josh make of Marco turning up with her, when he had been expecting to eat with her alone? As she passed Marco's room she saw his lights were out anyway, and the padlock on his door. Had he come back and gone out since they parted in Auroville? Or perhaps he was still out there, dining, or staying the night. After all, she still had no idea about who he really was, who he might know (and who he might be with).

She went by his door and down the stairs, at the bottom of which she saw Josh waiting. He himself had dressed up, as if for a date. He looked uncomfortable in pleated chinos and a 'wacky' fifties-style shirt, all jazzy blue guitars and green checks. He smiled what she interpreted as a forced smile, and stepped forward with his hand extended, ostensibly to steady her as she reached the bottom of the stairs, but also, she knew, to reassert himself. She took his hand and shook it with a 'good evening', and let it go. Released, it hung in space before him, as if not quite knowing where to go now, before retracting mechanically to his side. But if he was discomfited he did not otherwise show it.

'The fragrance you're wearing, what is it?'

'I'm not wearing any.'

'No?'

'I don't wear perfume.'

He studied her for a half moment, almost seemed to see her differently.

'But you smell so nice, what is it?'

'Soap, I'd say. Tea-tree.'

'What's that?'

'It's a kind of soap they make in Australia, from the tea-tree. Highly antibacterial.'

'But you do wear lipstick.'

'Sometimes, yes.'

'What shade is that?'

'Why?' she laughed. 'Do you want some?'

'No,' he said, relieved at least at the apparent lightening in her mood.

'It's red. I'm afraid I don't really know beyond that.' She took it out of her pocket and looked at it. 'Actually, it's called *Vacances*.'

'Well, I like it.' Then he grinned: 'On you, that is.'

They ate at the Penguin. It was her choice, but the hyperactive air-conditioning felt as if it would give him a kidney chill, and there was a general mild sense of malaise besides. Things had seemed to be going so well, but now they'd reached what felt like a holding pattern, in which he got the impression he might forever circle the runway but never get tower clearance to touch down. Conversation rambled, a mix of books, movies, India. In many ways it was an addendum to the chat over coffee in Auroville. But where that had been comfortable and easy-going, this was somehow forced. He felt dull, off form. What was wrong? It was all turning to jelly. And where out at Auroville she had sat inwards so that their voices could be softened, now she had her chair pushed well away from the table, so far that he sometimes missed her words over the air-conditioner. And he couldn't reach out for her hand now, even had it felt like the right moment to do that — which it obviously wasn't — because he couldn't physically reach that far. She was literally drifting out of reach. Things were starting to end without even properly beginning.

What had changed, and when? He tried to pinpoint the moment. It wasn't so difficult. It was at the Matrimandir, from when they had met up with that guy, Marco. It was that speech he had given. The clever-sounding English accent with the tiny hint of something else beneath. The big speech about The Mother inside the big glass ball. She had totally gone for it, even if she'd expressed a contrary view about the place herself. He knew that Marco's speech had just been a performance piece, a bit of oratory which would always impress women, particularly smart ones like Julia. To his ear it had been delivered before, that speech. Couldn't she tell that? Apparently not. But from that moment he had felt her receding tidally from him. Was it a temporary thing, the sheen of the newly met? Or was it something worse? For one terrible moment he wondered if Marco hadn't written that damn invitation. Perhaps some intelligence had already passed between them, while she was upstairs back at the guesthouse, changing for dinner. Had a few words been spoken then, which would explain why she was so cool with him when she came downstairs? Did she – sitting opposite him in a pale blue blouse which outlined her breasts maddeningly and made him want her even more – already know of his untruth, his lousy fraudulence?

This at least was an explanation, an ugly one, but an explanation, for her cooling. But surely if she'd found that out she wouldn't be here eating with him. She'd have refused to see him again. Or would've she? There was a certain *je ne sais quoi* about a man who would risk a lie to be with a woman. Maybe that appealed. Maybe she knew everything (*everything* – as if one stupid little lie was a hanging offence) but didn't care. Maybe it had made her *more* interested. But why then was she being so cool now? Was it a game, playing hard to get? Or was she really going cold on him, like the others, but this time before there had even been any heat? What a horrible prospect: a 'pattern' that was becoming a 'condition'. Something that could only end up with him sitting (or lying?) in some psychiatrist's rooms paying Christ only knew how much to have some equally fucked-up person tell him he was fucked up. *Dr Katz*. And him? *He was turning into Dr Katz's son!* That total loser who couldn't even take a plane trip alone without having to call his dad every five minutes, from the plane, from payphones, cellphones, to tell him he was 'fine'. What was his name? *Ben*. Ben the loser. Ben the total fucking bore. And even as he was thinking this, mentally mouthing the words *Ben* and *bore*, he saw Julia yawn, undeniably, whipping her hand to her mouth and apologising that it had been a long day and the sun strong out at Auroville. And before the word *bore* had even died on his mental lips, she was making moves, fussing, manoeuvring her chair squeakily on the tiled floor, getting up with more protestations of fatigue, saying she had to go back. In one awful moment, dinner was over.

As he walked her up the stairs, she did feel tired, very much so. Amazing how filled the last two days had been. She had a sense of things starting to move. Was she entering a new phase, in which the chaos of the last two or three years would resolve into some kind of order? She recalled climbing the steps at Lavender Bay with Tim beside her, after a night in many respects like this one. They might have dined out at an Indian restaurant in Crows Nest, or across the Bridge in Little India, Cleveland Street. Tim would be talking, making a joke. From downstairs the hush of the stereo, late night jazz on Radio National, while they undressed and stretched out on the bed looking at the Harbour and its lights, their 'million dollar view' (it hadn't cost them that, thank god) and maybe make love before they let sleep take them. Such certainty, comfort, for all those years, now gone, evaporated as if she had never lived through such an era, as if it had never once been hers, a time of peace.

She looked at Josh on the stair beside her. He had not touched her all night, as she had not touched him. That was how she had wanted it tonight, although she wasn't quite sure why. Certainly she did not want any more adolescent hand-holding. That time had passed. She hoped Josh understood these unstated things, and that nothing occurred now to make things difficult. Because tonight's feeling might pass too, and tomorrow she might feel different, more open to him again. But for now she just wanted to be in her bed, alone.

Reaching the landing, with the doors to the five upstairs rooms running off it, she noticed light leaking from Room Ten. Marco was in residence. She felt an impulse to knock right then, but it wasn't appropriate, returning from dinner with Josh — questionable manners towards both men — and she continued to her door escorted by him. They came to a halt and she felt in her pocket and located the key to her padlock. Josh was standing close and partially obscured the hall light, and she found it difficult to find the lock with the tip of the key in his shadow. Finally she did, and the padlock sprang open, and she turned to bid him goodnight.

She could not easily read what was in his face in that moment.

Something like sadness, tinged with a nuance of annoyance. But mostly it was confusion, in the weight of the brow of the forward-tilted head, in the brown of the eyes yearningly intent upon her. She felt his hand on her arm, his other hand on her hip. Then he was drawing her up to him, as easily as if she weighed nothing, enfolding her in a tight embrace that verged on crushing the air out of her. His mouth was on hers, spicy and slippery from oily food. Half surprised, she let the kiss go on a second or two. Then his tongue thrust in through the beachhead, and that she did not allow at all, stepping back decisively to break the contact.

'Josh, Josh ...' she was saying, but the mouth was coming at her again, he obviously deciding he might as well try her resistance with male persistence-cum-coercion, but this time she turned her head so that his lips attached themselves sucker-like to her cheek. They tried, almost slobberingly, to crawl their way around the curve of her face, blindly seeking the warmth of her mouth like some deep sea crustacean, but she had firmed, and in placing the flats of both palms against his chest gently but insistently held him back. Now the only way for him to continue would be by force.

His response was a lowering of his head, so that he stood before her defeated, almost melodramatically, and she felt for him straight away, but not anything like enough for him to be allowed to continue. So, he realised, even the lowered and defeated head would not work. It was over and he knew it. Everything had been lost in the space of seconds.

'Sorry ... I just thought ...'

'It's okay,' she said. 'It's fine.'

'I mean, I thought …'

'I think we should just go to our rooms now, okay?'

He looked at her, one more time, puppydog-wise.

'We're both just tired, I think,' she said. 'Goodnight Josh. And thank you for a wonderful day.'

She went into her room, glancing back through the crack with fleeting reassurance before closing it with finality, sliding the bolt home and leaving him where he stood.

Around fifteen minutes later, as he sat on the edge of his bed feeling all the more like Ben Katz, not just a copy now but the human original for the cartoon character, he heard a door open onto the landing outside. A padlock went on, and footsteps followed across the tiles. He heard the tap of a knuckle on a door, and, moments later, the internal bolt of a door sliding back. Then a murmur of voices, a greeting, followed by the sound of the door being re-bolted.

Opening his own door, Josh looked across the shadowy landing at the doors of the other rooms. He saw that Marco's was now padlocked, remembered that it had not been when they passed a few minutes before. Listening carefully, he could hear sounds from Julia's room. Marco had to be in there. He was tempted, sorely, to sneak over and listen. In the heightened sense of the moment it felt as if in some way his life depended on it, upon hearing what was being said and done in that room. But he couldn't do that. What was he, a Shakespearean villain eavesdropping on the heroine? Yet her door was only feet away, and the sounds from inside indicated they were some way back from it, far enough to give him the chance of escape should they decide to end their conversation abruptly. That was unlikely anyway: they had only just begun it. Marco would probably be in there for some minutes at the least. All night? No, she wouldn't, she couldn't.

He stood framed in his open doorway, staring at the door of Room Six, a crack of white fluorescent light from within falling in a white strip down the middle of the landing. Barefoot, he took a silent step, then another. The padlocks were on Rooms Seven and Nine, and so there was a risk those guests would come back up the stairs soon, returning from dinner. Then he had an idea, and nipped back into his room and grabbed a book, his *Solo Soles*. People were forever knocking on each other's doors with questions about travel, guidebook in hand. It gave him licence to be out on the landing.

Tensed, almost trembling – how had this crazy situation come about? – he approached Room Six, standing back in shadow, then inching forward, careful not to fall into the light coming from the crack between the double doors. Closer – he was very close now, right beside her door, trying not to make a sound – he worried about the heaviness of his breathing as he crouched to listen.

When he picked up their voices, he was relieved to find they were some distance away, on the far side of the room. He had been shown Room Six when he first arrived. He remembered it was long, with two single beds and a couch at the far end. That was where they must be now, sitting side by side. He didn't like that image, and tried to dismiss it by straining to hear what was being said. Annoyingly, their voices remained indistinct, and the sound came and went in waves like the sea, with the same muted monotony. Then came a lacuna. Had the chat dried up – or were they kissing? Next he heard a laugh, loud and close. They were right beside the door! He panicked, and in the moment of his turning fumbled the guidebook, which fell to the floor with a loud slap. No time to pick it up, he scurried, silently as he could, and had just managed to get through his door and shut it when he heard her door open and someone step outside. He stood tensed against his door, breathing heavily, listening. There was more laughter, male and female, a melody of it. The door closed, and Marco started walking back to his room. But then he heard him stop. What was he doing? With a stifled gasp Josh realised he must have seen the fallen guidebook outside Julia's door, was picking it up and looking at it. Josh sighed with gratitude that he was not one of those people who wrote their names in books, and there was no other distinguishing mark. No-one could prove it was his, nor how and why it happened to be discovered outside Julia's door. He was still okay, he thought. Safe. He breathed more easily still when he heard Marco continue across the landing and unlock his door. It opened, closed, the bolt was bolted.

Josh relaxed. The immediate danger had passed. Within a minute or two he was wondering what had happened in that room. It had been a very brief conversation. What could have been said? Brushing his teeth, his eyes white awake in the mirror, he thought again about the laugh that had ended their talk, their harmonic laugh together.

He stretched on his back and waited for sleep. It would not come easily tonight. It wasn't much past ten, and the hall lights would not be turned off until Vishnu The Ever-Vigilant locked the front gates at 10.30. But sleep surprised him, descending swiftly out of the white swirls of his mosquito net, and he slipped away with a pair of laughing voices distantly echoing in his head.

In Room Six, Julia drifted towards sleep too. We cover so much territory in a single day, she was thinking. Like sailing blue uncharted waters to terra incognita in seventeen waking hours. Or that is how it should be, if we are truly alive.

THE
MUD
PARTY

It was past nine when he awoke. Nearly twelve hours of sleep. Why had he slept so long? He rose gingerly from the bed, feeling stiff as if from hard labour the day before, and saw a note beneath his door. It was from Julia. She trusted he had had a sound night's sleep. She herself was going out for much of the day and wouldn't be around. She wished him a pleasant day. And there was a PS, asking if he had lost a guide-book. One had been found on the landing, a current *Solo Soles*, the same edition she had seen him with. If it was his, it had been left at the front desk and he could claim it there.

The thing he wondered, looking down at the note, was how she had got the book from Marco, and so quickly. There must have been more contact between them.

Having spent some several minutes re-arranging the ruler, pocket calculator, pair of matching ballpoint pens in their velour-lined case, pencil and rubber, and around five seconds glancing at the official form before her seeking conversion of foreign currency, the clerk in the smart purple sari with the stick-on hi-fashion *tika* spot on her forehead sighed with the collective fatigue of all the human race, and slipped the brass token, worn by generations of fingers to a smooth-faced disc, across the desk.

'You will take it to the cashier now,' she instructed Julia with a fidget of her spectacles. 'Your number will be called presently.'

The penny-sized disc which Julia carried past several counters to the cashier's booth bore the name of the bank, the branch and various other official imprints, along with cuneiforms of Tamil script, no doubt repeating the same information, and was further stamped with the number 621. She located a bench in front of the wire cage booth, and sat down beside a white-robed woman furiously fanning herself with a booklet, which Julia saw had been printed by the Ashram, titled *Death*.

'Any big new insights?'

The woman looked up at her with plain annoyance. 'What?'

Julia instantly regretted having spoken, even in half-jest. 'The booklet. Does it have any ... fresh insights into death?'

'How should I know?' the woman shrugged in heavily French-accented English. 'I am only using it as a fan.'

Why had she bothered? She turned her eyes forward, and let them run over the expanse of the bank, at the rows and rows of desks where clerks laboured in the close air over their forms and ledgers. A bank without computers. It was hard to comprehend how a modern institution could function without them, or even why it was, considering every second billposter in Chennai was for computers and software. Yet computers or no, experience had taught her that provided one did things entirely by the book and requested no service beyond the ordinary, Indian banks were very efficient. Her one-hundred-dollar US traveller's cheque was at this moment being moved about this ledger labyrinth, collecting signatures and stamps at every stop. Within minutes it would arrive at the cashier's booth, each detail attended to and authenticated, and her number would be called, and she would slide the brass disc across the counter. The cashier's fingers would fly through the forty or so one-hundred-rupee notes, and they would be presented to her for checking, and the amount would be correct to the last rupee.

And that was exactly how it happened. When she put the money away and returned to her chair to collect her hat, the Frenchwoman was still there fanning, and for some reason, which Julia could never understand in herself, she felt constrained to say goodbye, which was acknowledged with a half-raised eyebrow and a look away.

Over their lunch table at the Aristo, they agreed that Josh was a very strange young man to have pretended to have written the invitation, and gone along with things as he had. Yet, Marco said, 'that he did it one may discover in due course to be the most interesting thing about him'. When he asked Julia how she intended to deal with Josh, she had to confess she wasn't sure. She was even undecided about whether to confront him with it. After all, he would be travelling on soon, and she might never see him again. Where was the logic in confrontation?

'But he might not move on for a while. And he is rather keen on you, isn't he?'

'He seemed to be last night. It was all I could do to hold him off.'

'In which case he may need a clear signal from you to desist. The embarrassment of you knowing he lied would certainly be that. If you wished to deal with it that way, that is.'

How strange. Yesterday Josh had been a breath of fresh air, and being with him enjoyable. She had been relieved. Happy. Now he was a problem to be dealt with.

'It is entirely up to you, of course,' Marco added. 'You know him better than I do.'

'Yes. And I hardly know him at all.'

'An American, isn't he?'

'That's right. A medical student, or young doctor, I can't remember which. With aspirations to working in poor countries. He did some volunteer work for Mother Teresa's order in Calcutta recently.' She stopped. 'That's what he said, anyway.'

'Yes, unfortunate that, isn't it?'

'What is?'

'How one proven falsehood tends to bring everything else someone has ever said into doubt. But the ability to tell a single lie, the ruthlessness of it, taints every other word.'

'Ruthlessness ...'

'Lying is a ruthless act. An easy and callous betrayal of the confidence of others.'

'Even little lies?'

'Of course.'

'But don't you ever tell white lies? Such as, I don't know, to get out of some inconvenient social arrangement?'

'I don't have social arrangements, inconvenient or otherwise.'

He chuckled at his own open disingenuousness, and she smiled back: 'Your lunch invitation to me, that was an arrangement.'

'No, that was a *de*-rangement. Mitigated only by us being here today.'

She recalled the scene for him, the puzzlement on his face at seeing her, the sharpness of his turn away from the maitre d', the irritation in his step as he went off down the street.

'I have to admit I was a bit put out. I kept on thinking, I've invited this woman to lunch. And I've made it a tiny bit intriguing – or so I thought, poor fool me – by not signing the note. And then I arrive to find you seated here with the young man from Room Eight, studying menus at a table for two! I simply couldn't believe my luck. And it took me a long, slow walk along the promenade to realise there would be an explanation for it, some silly misunderstanding. Fortunately all was made clear last night, and here we are at the lunch I invited you to in the first place.'

He turned in his seat, touched the passing drinks waiter on the arm and asked him to bring out their wine.

'Wine?' Julia said. 'In India?'

'It's not so unheard of down here in the south. They grow grapes outside Pondy. Good red earth and good French wine-makers interfering. The French owned the wineries until a few decades ago of course, when Pondy was still a colony. I've tried some of the local wines and they're not at all bad. But today we're having one of my good honest Valpolicellas.'

'You have a cellar?'

'Of a sort. Room Ten is quite large, more like an apartment really, and I have a small cache in my dressing room.'

The waiter returned with a bottle, uncorked it and poured. The red of the wine tumbling into Julia's glass was a delight in daylight: she had missed it. They clinked glasses and sipped. It was good, better than she remembered any Italian wine being. When she mentioned this he replied, with a gentle intimation of humour, that not all Italian wines were the watered down stuff they served up in the boulevard bistros of Venice and Florence.

'Good wine is home,' he said, 'and bad wine is tourism.'

She considered confessing her profession was precisely that, decided to hold it back for the time being, took another sip and let her eye rove the vista of Pondicherry stretching beyond Marco's shoulder, the street below with its shuttered shopfronts, the jumbled concrete roofs on the far side, square, rectangular, irregular, punctuated with TV aerials and satellite dishes, and washing billowing out on lines, flickering in the wind, a morse of shirts and smalls.

'Tell me,' she said, watching a crow peck in a saucepan on a far-off window ledge, 'those things you were saying after we'd been in the Matrimandir ...'

'Yes?'

'Are you usually that cynical?'

'Of course.'

'Why?'

'Because it is the only position which does not require endless retreats and the digging of fresh philosophical and ethical trenches.' He lifted his glass by the base between thumb and forefinger, closed one eye and peered into the wine as if a show judge, or someone spying out a hair. 'Besides which, I can't help myself. To me, afterlives, karma, cosmic consciousness, the whole kit and caboodle of Eastern thought, is rot. All that mumbo-jumbo should be reduced to one easily comprehensible thing: compassion. Because compassion is a fair goal for humanity. It's worthwhile, it's achievable, within our grasp. But it is, sadly, still, a hopeless goal.' He sipped from his glass and set it down. 'There, you see, not a bad wine at all.'

'Why do you say that?'

'Because it's not.'

'No, I mean, why do you say compassion is a hopeless goal?'

He grimaced and lifted his hands while turning out his palms, the movement like a cod facsimile of Italian gesturalism, fully at odds with the portrait of the well-reasoned Englishman (who now rolled out more tailored yards of argument).

'Well, take, for instance, I don't know, something simple. The doing of a good deed. It's the basis of our Western Judeo-Christian system of ethics. We would all swear by that, doing something to help another, with no advantage to ourselves, wouldn't we? Yet to me it's hypocritical.'

'Why?'

'Because good deeds don't exist. There are only self-interested deeds, deeds that make you feel better. If they didn't, you wouldn't do them.'

'But can't the deed be of benefit to both?'

'Yes it can. But experience shows us that if it doesn't make the doer feel good, it doesn't get done. So no matter how it benefits the recipient, it's really for the doer.'

'So, you yourself wouldn't ever do a good deed? Help others?'

'Of course I would. I do. But I *admit* that it is for me. That I benefit too, by feeling better about myself, thinking that I'm not such a black-hearted creature after all. So it's not a good deed. It's a *mutually beneficial* deed. Of benefit to both, as you put it yourself.'

'But what about love? Surely love is given freely, without thought of personal return. Isn't loving in itself a good deed?'

'Precisely the opposite. Love is ultimately a selfish emotion, gratification and aggrandisement of the self. Which is why it never lasts, because our egos constantly need inflation from new sources. We can't extract enough ego strokes from the declarations of a lover forever. We tire of it, just as children tire of their toys and want new ones. And it's all so will-o'-the-wisp, fanciful and chanciful anyway. If you read about someone saying how shattered they were by the death of their loved one, you can be sure that if the terrible accident hadn't occurred, the very next week they would've been thinking, "Perhaps I don't really love Richard any more. I don't know if I still feel the same way. Perhaps we should call it quits." But when something like that happens, someone is killed in an accident, it's as if the event itself takes a snapshot of the lovely couple. One of those "Richard and Sally in happier days" ones the papers are full of, only now they are in those happier days forever because the relationship is frozen in time, and they will never have to deal with the removalists and the divorce courts that would almost inevitably have come later on, in the normal full term of things. Them being "in love forever" is a fringe benefit of Richard's death. The essential problem is that human beings aren't built to deal with *ever*. We're just watery bags, skins stuffed like sausages with big ideas, like *ever*, which we can't even conceptualise, much less act upon. No, we love until we're bored and then we move on. It's altogether subjective, capricious and selfish, like everything else we do.'

He had spoken poised on his elbow, glass set down to one side, its placement precise as a prop set by a stage manager for a performance of a play. He rubbed his hands together, as if feeling a sudden chill now that he had stopped talking, and she thought how strange, but this man is *simmering*. He's on a slow boil about something, something important to him, and all this clever talk is really to mask that simmering self.

'And is that what you're doing here in Pondicherry?' she asked. 'Moving on?'

He took up his glass again, drained it and re-poured for them both. 'No, I'm not doing anything here.'

'What, nothing at all?'

'Virtually nothing, beyond reading the papers. I like the newspapers here. They're colourful and quite well written. There's always so much to read. Scandals, tribal conflicts, trouble at the borders. They're not like the papers in Britain or America, which are quite stuffy and conservative.'

'Just a minute. You mean to say you're really doing nothing here but reading the papers?'

'That's right. And the odd book.'

'How long have you been here?'

'Some months. A year perhaps, I'm not really sure. I enjoy Pondy. And especially the Sea View. If only I could find an hotel with such atmosphere in Europe, I'd be there.'

'But with your views ... I mean, don't the Sri Aurobindo people annoy you?'

'In the extreme. But most of the time I'm able to ignore them, which is the best way to deal with people like that.'

'But ... what were you doing out at the Madrimandir then, when you feel that way?'

'Idling.' He flicked a speck of non-existent dust from his shirt sleeve, ran a hand over the smooth of shaven cheek. 'And you, are you travelling?'

'Yes.'

'You appear to be rather stationary for a traveller.'

'I enjoy Pondy too,' she said.

'Hmmmm. And how do you travel, when you are at it?'

'Train. Bus, car. I'm here updating a travel guidebook. So I try to do it the way our readers would. By a mixture of means.' A tiny movement attracted her attention, an ant hauling away a boulder of sugar. 'I don't much like travelling on the roads though. They're too chaotic.'

'They are to our eyes, yes.' He saw her glass was empty again.

'More wine?'

'That would be my third, and we haven't got our food yet.'

'Please, don't count. It's anathema to civilised drinking. How can you ever derive the full and proper effects from wine if you count? It interferes with the modus operandi of nature's gift to humanity.'

She surrendered her glass. 'You make it sound a blasphemy.'

'Not to drink wine properly is.'

She watched the wine whirl its way up her glass. *'To our eyes. Are you saying the roads here are only *subjectively* chaotic? That they're orderly to some people?'

'Oh, India is very ordered. To the Indians, of course it is. Every iota of existence is allocated and accounted for here, like a Bombay pavement. The low-caste woman whose baby squats on the street with those big black eyes while her mother washes her from a bucket, that baby already knows who has the right to be on every inch of the broken pavement, just as the local shopkeepers have the rights to their shops, the well-off to their houses. That baby has already imprinted all that in her mind. It's perfect. The gods are content to crowd the heavens, the people to crowd the earth. No-one is ever lonely. All are surrounded all their days with the reassuring sounds of prayer and politics, commerce and gossip, of animal husbandry and human reproduction.'

He was still on a slow boil, she thought, still steaming beneath his lid with what he really wanted to say but which for some reason he dared not, and thus substituted all manner of wordage which he could invest with the suppressed passion. And what was that passion? Closet romanticism? Thwarted idealism?

'So then, you enjoy living in India,' she half asked, half said.

'Not at all. It's much too hot and dirty. But thankfully I'm not living in India, I'm living in Pondicherry, and Pondicherry is not India. Pondicherry is India made acceptable for Westerners. And I wouldn't dream of living anywhere else in this country. It is all dung, dust and plastic bags out there. A republic of flies.'

'But no matter what you say, you're still inside India. So if you feel that way, what are you doing here really? And don't say "nothing", or reading the newspapers, because I won't believe you.'

'No?' He raised an eyebrow.

'No.'

The waiters began bringing out their food, the full palate of dishes Marco had ordered: the kelp-green *palak paneer*, chatty yellow *tikka* morsels, the cushion of steaming rice, the lip-red pickled lime.

'Ah, but that would require the full story.'

'And I wouldn't want to hear that?'

'I don't know. But I warn you, it's a tale of some length. And would require at the very least a long post-prandial stroll down the promenade.'

'That sounds ideal. Shall we eat?'

And so they did, and beyond that took *masala* tea, which they sipped as the afternoon took its first tiny dip towards evening, like an airliner in that exact moment of shifting from cruise to descent. At last Marco gestured to the waiter, and he came over scribbling figures.

Julia reached for her bag, but Marco's hand on hers stopped

her. 'Please. Allow me this small sexist act.' He slipped two one-hundred rupee notes into the leather wallet which held their bill, but Julia replaced them with two of her own.

'But ...' he attempted to protest, 'you're my guest.'

'Put the money away, please,' she said, 'along with the sexism. You invited me the first time, but today I invited you.'

Gradually, as if nothing like this had ever happened to him, he retrieved his notes. Grateful for the tip included in the payment, the waiter inclined his head to Marco, but he directed him on to Julia, and the man repeated the action for her, raising his joined hands to his forehead and uttering the word *namaste*, to which she responded in kind.

As they walked through the hooped bougainvillea and down the stairs, Julia mused on the word. '*Namaste* ... Hindi greeting. People don't use it much in the south.'

'Perhaps he's from the north.'

'I honour the divine in you.'

'Do you really?'

She smiled. 'No, that's what *namaste* means.'

'I know.'

Marco's mother came from the West Country, where her parents were doctors with a country cottage and medical rooms in Chippenham. Angela had attended a college for young ladies in Northampton Street in Bath, her moment of greatest remembered excitement being witnessing a stick of Nazi bombs excavating the gardens of Royal Crescent. She showed an early artistic bent, as her father termed it, and begged to go to art school rather than university. Believing she would soon realise that the poverty of the artist was even more arduous than the hours of medicine, they packed her off to London with its ration cards and smog, its gloomy postwar countenance. But Angela soon found herself disappointed with college. Designing Tube advertisements for medicaments and hoardings for haberdashers was not what she aspired to: she wanted to be an artist, a real artist. And she yearned to travel. She had a fascination with the East, Near and Far, for all things Arabian, Oriental, Indian. And while her fellows learned to draw cigarette packets and underwired brassieres, Angela was swept up in the romantic literature of the East, of young Englishwomen who took a steamer to Algiers or turned up in Damascus with little more than a hatbox and a silk scarf. There was always a young Arab man reclining in the shadows of these daydreams, dashing, gallantly amorous. She of course told her parents nothing of the fancy, only that she now wished to study the art of the Near East, and they took her at her word that she was travelling escorted, with several other young ladies. How could it be otherwise?

Her route was easily plotted: Southern Europe, the Levant, Arabia, and her ultimate goal, India. This last, gossamer-veiled destination had come from a book of her father's, which she had discovered on a neglected shelf of his library as a young teenager, and had kept as her own ever since. It was titled *Views of India*, and had been published by the Times of India. There was a handwritten inscription to her father, in a lady's hand which

Angela knew was not her mother's: 'For my darling. Xmas, Madras, 1921.' That mysterious inscription exerted an intoxicating attraction over the girl, melding the exotic of India with the allure of her father's former life as a colonial doctor in India, and the forbidden love he must have tasted there. Because Angela knew that by 1921 he was already engaged to her mother, and that they were to be married as soon as his term expired and he returned to London. There was even the faintest smell of something still in that page, a perfume or a spice, a potion perhaps, and Angela spent many hours with her nose to the inscription, seeking to divine its secret.

The book was a pictorial tour of the marvels of colonial India, its reproductions of colour photographs interleaved with onion paper. There was 'Calcutta, The Pagoda, Eden Gardens', a spired pyramid with a rowboat lazily adrift in the adjoining pond. There was 'Bombay, The Municipal Offices and Victoria Terminus', a brace of brickwork Victorian civic structures, magnificent in scale, with a green trolley tram in the foreground, running down on a quiet street where well-dressed Indians strolled shaded by parasols. 'Ootacamund, The Lake, Race Course and Bazaar', showed a green racecourse and blue lake, as glimpsed from a pine-studded hillside. And there was 'Lucknow, The Residency', a lone forlorn cannon in the foreground, the battle-scars of the Mutiny on the walls and turrets of the ruin, the Union Jack limp on the flagpole, all of which bespoke poignantly of the decline of Empire. The last image was Angela's favourite, 'Pondicherry, The French Quarter', an avenue of walled, whitewashed mansions by the sea, under a powder pink and grey early evening sky. Angela marvelled at it, being both Indian and French, doubly exotic. She imagined gendarmes on the street corners, cognac drunk in boulevard cafes, affairs of the heart. The picture showed a poster on a wall announcing a recital of the works of Chopin. A carriage had pulled up nearby, and a young lady in a dark dress was alighting, leaving a hatted man alone. There was something so perfectly wistful about it, evoking a sense of loss, departed love. And it was this last photograph which inspired Angela to make India the ultimate goal of her journey to the East.

So, aged just twenty, this petite and delicate Englishwoman with soft blue eyes and a too-fair complexion set off on the boat-train to Paris, and purposefully struck south. A week later she met Carlo in a hotel foyer in Nice, where he was negotiating a deal with a French hotel group. Marco's father was a tall man, one of those who in later life gained an habitual stoop from speaking to so many less than tall others. But in those days he was straight-backed, charming and good-looking. He had several foreign languages, English foremost among them, and over the round of cocktail parties, dances and dinners for two that followed their first meeting, he swiftly wooed Angela. It transpired that the Veneto region of Italy was as far east as the would-be traveller got. They were married within weeks, honeymooned in America, and returned to live in Carlo's family villa in the Dolomite foothills. One might have wondered whether Angela did not feel that she had cheated herself out of her journey, but she later told Carlo she had found she possessed little real enthusiasm for travel. The French train down to Nice had been quite enough: the back of a camel unthinkable. Nonetheless, she still spoke often to him of her desire to travel to the East, and, most particularly, to see India. But as the years passed and British India subsided into history, so too did her desire. The India of Mr Nehru was no longer the India of *Views of India*. The romance was over. One day she realised, with a tiny pang, that she had no idea where the book was. Lost to the years; or, at the very least, to the impenetrable jungle of her closets.

Carlo's family originated from Treviso – 'Three Faces'. It gained its name from an historical footnote. When Attila the Hun descended the Alps into the Veneto, this pretty market town was one of the first he encountered. Besieged, the city fathers pleaded with him to spare their town, and to encourage him so had three of their prettiest maiden daughters delivered naked before him on a velvet-lined platter. This triple delicacy proved to the conqueror's taste, and he spared the town. Sadly, the maidens were not spared him.

Much of the town's wealth was founded in the Dolomite stone trade, and like many others the Manzini family had been in it for generations. Carlo inherited the virtually bankrupt company upon the death of his father Lorenzo, just after World War Two. War-ravaged Italy presented few prospects for the marble and granite trade. Before the hostilities, the company staple had been lintels, flagstones and tombstones, but Carlo foresaw a very different kind of future: bathrooms. It wasn't easy starting out. Postwar Europe was hardly clamouring for marble tubs. But over the next two decades, Carlo resolutely refashioned the business, so that when the wave of postwar prosperity finally began to roll, he was ready.

Not much income came from Europe to start with, though Carlo did manage a deal or two with hotels, such as the one he was negotiating when he met Angela in Nice. Inevitably, the first real prospects came from America. Carlo had had the foresight to visit the West Coast on their honeymoon, and after a subsequent trip he set up a branch office there. Ten years later it was generating the kind of money his Manzini forebears could only have dreamt of. Carlo knew that making the business succeed meant keeping the market broad, and it was *Manzini* which first brought black granite floors and white marble bathrooms into middle class homes in San Francisco and Los Angeles. But he also realised the kinds of windfall sums that could accrue from the top end, and for the rich and the famous he designed heavenly showers with solid gold faucets and filigree shower roses that almost sang arias, sarcophagus-scale marble bathtubs, jacuzzis with all the trimmings in turquoise and opal, handbasins with the patron's name and astrological sign inlaid with lapis lazuli and curlicues of precious metal. Such flair proved irresistible, and those years became a bonanza.

Marco was born in the first year of his parents' marriage and grew up a child of the fifties, which despite the looming shadow of atomic doom was irradiated with an optimism that humanity had put the worst years of the twentieth century behind it and everyone could safely re-mortar their masonry and start making money. A cock-eyed optimism, but it was infectious. As the years advanced so did prosperity, like the battalions of the previous decade, establishing beach-heads and fanning out into the countryside. By decade's end the good times were starting to return to Europe, and with them came *Manzini*.

Even as a young boy, Marco realised his father's success offered him opportunities others would never have. His mother insisted on an English education, and his father was not opposed. There was a suspicion in Carlo's mind that the English might do one or two things better than Italians, such as minding their own business and educating children. Just as there could be no doubt that Italians made better cars, coffee and love than any Englishman. So he agreed Marco should learn about words and numbers in England, just as he would surely learn about life in Italy. His only stipulation was that the school be Roman Catholic. Angela went one better, making it Jesuit. And so young Marco, the only child — something went awry after him — of Italian businessman Carlo Manzini and his artistic English wife Angela Lamprey, was delivered into the black enfolding robes of the Papal defenders, to be immersed in books and learning through those long boarding-school winters, emerging each spring to shake out his wings and fly home to Italy for the summer with its own curriculum of Vespas, cafes and girls.

At university Marco read English literature and Marxist economics, and dabbled in Eastern philosophy. When he graduated his father invited him into the family business as American branch manager, a generous offer which Marco politely declined. He wanted to travel before beginning his career. His father was somewhat annoyed, believing it was time for him to face the realities of life, but his mother pleaded his case, saying she too had wished to travel before starting on her career, and had her own parents not wisely assented she would have missed out on the most wonderful gift her life had offered – he himself, Carlo. Moreover, she had been consulting a fortune-teller of late – Angela's fascination with things Eastern had nudged her towards the arcane – and a Tarot consultation (the Marseille deck, which the gypsy fortune-teller assured her retained the Secrets of The Ages the others had long forgotten, and was in fact the book her people had carried with them all the way from their ancient homeland, India) had forewarned her that Marco's destiny would pattern itself in crucial ways upon her own. This being the case, Angela said, he had to be allowed to follow his fortune. Carlo, ever shrewd, knew when he had a hope of winning and when he didn't, and acquiesced.

Marco journeyed firstly through Africa, then on to Asia, to China, Japan, the Americas, the Pacific, and, briefly, to Australia. It was taken at a leisurely pace. How, he wrote to his mother, could one gain anything from travel beyond a few exotic sights and smells unless one lived in a place at least some weeks or months? This philophy of travel, combined with the physical scale of the world, meant his journey took some years, which grew into a decade, then beyond it.

Although he accepted a small remittance from his father during this extended peregrination, he supplemented it with odd jobs. He washed dishes, waited at tables and tended gardens. As the years passed, he found an interest in computers, and undertook a course of study. He graduated to consulting: a good word, he wrote home to his mother, covering a multitude of equally useless time and money-wasting activities, but it allowed him to continue his journeys. He had by now an aversion to staying anywhere too long – an ironic but perhaps inevitable reversal of his younger man's philosophy of travel – and the idea of 'settling' anywhere filled him with unease. With consulting as his ticket he was able to work a beat through Hong Kong, Singapore, Bangkok, Manila, Jakarta, living at a standard commensurate with his maturing years.

When, towards the end of this period, he contracted malaria, in Singapore, he was nursed by a Singaporean he had met through his work, and whom he later married. But that all too quickly began to fade, just as, he wrote home, the consulting work got 'denser and denser, drier and drier, emptier and emptier'. Sometimes, awakening in the night, he found he was no longer sure of who he was and what he was doing, where he was going beyond the urge to pack his bag and move on. He felt increasingly adrift, directionless; running, he conceded, but from what? Responsibility, existence itself?

Occasionally he would fly back to Italy, to his mother's kisses and father's admonitions that drifting around Asia was all very well for the young, but one was not young forever. By the time his father said this to him for the last time, and most stridently, Marco was two months off his fortieth birthday, and beginning to think his father might just be right. But something happened then that changed things forever.

Shopping in Treviso, slipping between traffic, Angela stopped to comfort a woman whose bag had been snatched by a boy on a scooter, and was herself struck by a passing car. The police pursued and arrested the driver, a young man drunk because his girlfriend's father had demanded she not see him any more and sent her into exile with relatives down in Rome. Angela was dead on arrival at hospital.

A huddle of overcoats assembled in the snow around the dark wound of the grave. Not a muscle of Carlo's face moved as the casket was set into the earth. Over the weeks that followed, he sat in his armchair staring down at the half-lit winter streets. Marco knew his father loved his mother, but his awareness of it had been diminished by his decade and a half abroad, and by belonging to a generation for whom love had a use-by date and always went sour in the end. Though grieving himself, he watched his father with awe that anyone could love so unreservedly. As he observed his father in his silent chair, a chill hand settled onto Marco's shoulder that made him wonder whether this might not be what love was all about, or meant to be. The white ash of grief that crept from his father's pores testified that love was worthy, had dignity, that somehow it progressed the human being, even in the moment of final despair. It brought something else home to him too: the admission that he himself had never been in love, allowed himself to love. Why not? It troubled him.

But Marco had misjudged his father in one respect at least: the older man himself felt no dignity in the pain he endured. Images of a life fully shared haunted him. Worst of all, he could not escape the memory of his last day with his wife, when over the Sunday lunch table laden with food and wine, noisy with relations, he had marvelled at Angela's loveliness, her abiding childlike sweetness, at how love had endured.

Finally venturing out to the confessional, Carlo confided his concerns about an omniscient and omnipotent God who would permit Angela to die in the manner she had. His confessor, the brothel-creeping cardinal, a friend from childhood, was attentive to these concerns. He was patient and understanding. But, by slow degrees, this became a cautioning that he should stop his questioning of the All-Powerful One. After all, Angela was happily in heaven. At the very least he could rejoice in that. Carlo found himself being told to deal with the loss, to grow through it, that God's plan was not revealed, that he must draw strength from the tragedy. In other words, the cardinal told him to shut up and have faith.

But daily at the wheel of his modest Fiat entering the gates of his factory, and sitting down before the charts and accounts, Carlo recovered a diminishing personal return from the empire he had created. His work, life, existence itself only made sense if there was something, *someone*, at its centre. Until now Angela had been enshrined in that place, and behind her, the Virgin in a grotto, and behind Her, mistily, God. But with Angela gone, and taken so brutally, the centre could not hold.

Marco watched his father's lifelong dedication wither, literally before his eyes. Marco himself had abandoned the faith many years before. Even as a schoolboy, altar boy, a perfect mute on retreats, he was all the while questioning his religious faith, and continued to question to the point where, like a love too zealously examined, belief faded away.

During those long wintry retreats, eyes fixed upon the crucifix, the boy had asked the blond and mournful Jesus why the Church did not sell up its possessions, its properties and its treasures, to feed and comfort the wretched of the earth. It was a simple question, a child's question, but also one he realised his superiors did not enjoy being asked (and prudently kept it to himself).

In early puberty it was the issue of contraception that further disturbed him. He questioned whether the Vatican had made that prohibition because of its interpretation of God's will, or a notion of the sanctity of human life. But where, the young Marco asked, was the sanctity of a life lived out in the bondage of crowded poverty, the grip of disease?

Marco's eventual rejection of the Church and its doctrine propelled him on irrevocably, and although for some time afterwards he classed himself as agnostic, as his Jesuit boarding-school years came to a close he arrived at what became his lifelong stance: that there are no gods, no demons nor angels, no designer behind leaf nor star, nothing to it all but a great deal of carbon, a wealth of sunlight, aeons of time, and chance.

Then had come university, a grooming towards the family empire. Questions wrestled with in adolescence became irrelevancies in a life of study, walks on the Heath, Charing Cross Road bookshops and West End plays, and a girl in an attic room, windows rattling with rain, waking before first light to read some crucial textbook chapter, peering out to see if any dawn was leaking yet past the chimneypots, then snuggling back into the warmth of her for another half hour. And after the years of study had come those of travel, until his mother's death, and his father's own loss of faith.

Carlo's breach with his creed was no soul liberation, nor an intellectual freeing from shackles, as it had been for Marco. Carlo felt as though his faith was being extracted like a wisdom tooth without anaesthesia. The spiritual agony had become corporeal. And it seemed for some months that he would mortally succumb to the double blow, the loss of Angela, and of God. So Marco was startled when, a few weeks after his father's return to work, as they sat in the office with staff shuffling files around them, Carlo looked up and announced he would soon be departing, on a journey to India.

India. It wasn't so much a country as a dreamscape from which people returned with a wisp of cloud seeping out from their widened eyes, stomachs tightened, wallets picked clean by beggars and saints. It was no place for a grieving old man. Despite his years in Asia, Marco himself had never even visited India. The crush of population, the disease and poverty, the chaos all disturbed him too much. Even though he felt habituated to them in other parts of Asia, Indian poverty, Indian disease, Indian chaos appeared of a different order altogether. His only direct experience of India was from refuelling stops in Bombay, and what he saw in the airport terminal was quite enough to confirm that he did not wish to see more.

Marco tried to persuade his father against the decision, but Carlo's mind was set. He had interrupted Angela's journey there: now he would complete it, he said. And so he did, departing in the spring, on a jet merging into morning haze. After that communication was sparse, confined to a brief, crackly call, a few lines scrawled on a card stamped with the image of a cow or Gandhi, faintly spiced with India. Then nothing. Meanwhile Marco found himself running a company he'd never had any intention of even joining. When his cousins coveted his position while complaining that he was doing nothing to rescue his poor unbalanced father, Marco only said he respected his father's wishes, which in fact he did. Then the final postcard arrived: 'I shall not be returning.'

Several years had passed when one morning a fax arrived informing Marco of his father's death. It had occurred at a place called Auroville, outside Pondicherry in southern India. He had committed suicide.

That preyed on Marco's mind. He had always thought of suicide as an act of cowardice or defeat, a last selfish act by someone who didn't care about the pain they left behind. But Carlo Manzini had been a moral force, a beacon. He had been robust, good-hearted, fully a man. But family and friends had not seen him during his Pondicherry years, a shambling figure, meditating alone within the walled gardens of the Ashram, or turning a leatherworking tool by candlelight in his tiny cell out at Auroville, grey beard grown down to his chest. The sallow skin clung to cheek and jawbones, and as the years lengthened he became ever more stooped in the stance of the melancholic.

The truth was that the loss of his faith had not been mitigated by his excursion into Eastern mysticism, his prolonged spiritual self-excoriation. Rather, the more he stripped away from himself, the more he 'freed' himself from earthly attachments and became 'ego-less', the less he felt he truly *was*. In the end he felt himself little more than a scrap of tissue paper being shredded in the breeze off the Bay of Bengal. By his seventy-fifth birthday he was a mute recluse.

He celebrated the date with his long-planned suicide. The *ayah* who discovered the corpse found a withered old man face down in a half-filled rusty bathtub, an empty bottle of sleeping pills on the floor. He had left no note. Yet, Marco thought, taking one's life alone in a grubby bathroom on the far side of the world, that was a note in itself. Reading the faxed police report, typed laboriously in English, he pictured his father as he drifted in that tub, in the never-never of semi-consciousness. He sensed there was no last minute Act of Contrition from his father for the mortal sin of taking his own life. Rather, Carlo had marched across the frontier into the void with a resolve to die and be done with it. His father's suicide, he sensed, had been that of a man desperate to believe, but who could no more. Putting down the police report, Marco realised that his father now knew – or did not know – whether it had been prudent to push his convictions all the way, and wondered if he could ever possess the courage for such trial of belief himself.

When he arrived in India, and sorted through his father's things, in a pile of old papers Marco came across a few words scrawled on the back of a grimy envelope, in his father's hand: *Existence is a sweet sentence. Followed by a full stop.* His very last word on the matter perhaps, and the only thing approximating a note that he had left. There had been few other things of any apparent importance at all, except for a battered old book of photographs from the colonial period, rendered droll by the years, titled *Views of India*. Then Marco remembered his mother's story about a book of photographs of her father's which she had treasured a girl, and realised, remarkably, that this was that book. His father had kept it to the end.

Taken together, the deaths of his parents left Marco to ponder how ultimately each person's destiny was not their sum of dogmas clasped, dreams chased and opportunities grasped, but so much more about the inchoate passions and clawing ambitions of the others one interacted with, whether they be the struggling shopkeeper who sells you a wormed apple because he feels he has no choice but to, or the drunken lover behind the wheel of the car that runs you down because he had no other escape from the despair of lost love than the oblivion of alcohol. Or the father whose heart breaks in a rusty tub, and out spills all his disbelief. It was as senseless as that.

Evening had come. They had strolled back and forth along the promenade, and sat watching the crowds taking their sunset *passeggiata*. Courting couples passed by or sat on the sea wall, close but not touching, speaking in low tones in a sustained and searching premarital intercourse of the mind.

'Your father is buried here?'

'Out in Auroville,' Marco said. 'I knew he wouldn't want to go back to Italy.'

She saw two pale faces against the darkening esplanade, coming their way. It was Mildred and Kingston, walking slowly side by wide.

'And so, now for you?' she asked.

'I don't know really. All his life my father wanted me to take over the business. Until right at the end, when he didn't care. He left it to me in his will. But what am I going to do, sell taps? My cousins are happy to fight over it. It's of no interest to me. I draw a little money, just enough to live here. And there's the house and apartment too, should I ever wish to return to Italy, which is unlikely.'

'Why? Because you like it here?'

'No. Because there is nowhere else I can be now.'

They sat in the encroaching darkness, the rush of the waves and the wind off the sea filling in the silence. She peered down the promenade, wondering what had happened to Kingston and Mildred. She spotted them at a stall opposite the Gandhi statue. He was buying her fairy floss. The incongruity of the sight made her point it out to Marco. A smile parted his lips, and he watched them a moment before turning back to Julia.

'And so now I have told you my story, what about yours?'

'There's not really much to tell. I grew up in Sydney. We were reasonably well off. I went to a girls school where they made us wear silly straw boaters. I moved out of home when I was eighteen and went to university. And then I met Tim, my husband, though we're not really together any more, and we headed off overseas. And we founded the guidebook publishing house together. And you sort of know the rest.'

'How embarrassing,' he said. 'You tell me the story of your life in a few neat sentences. While I take up hours of your time with mine.'

'That's because yours is interesting.'

'And yours isn't? I doubt that. I'm sure there are many fascinating depths to be plumbed.' He removed his spectacles to clean the sea-hazy lenses, squinting into the glass. 'You know, when I first saw you I thought you were an Ashram devotee.'

'Why?'

'Put it down to your serene expression. Only yours isn't contrived.'

'Thank you. May I record that as a compliment?'

'You may.'

'You really don't have any time at all for them do you, the Ashram people?' she said.

'Do you?'

'I don't mind them.' She watched Mildred's hapless attempts to negotiate a pink beehive of floss. 'I'm surprised you can stay at the Sea View if you feel that way. After all, it's run by them.'

'As I always say, it has atmosphere.' He turned to her. 'And some of the guests are interesting. And you, why do you stay there?'

'Oh, because it's perfect. And I've got an open mind on the Ashram.'

'On Aurobindo and The Mother too? Then your mind must be a very model of openness. Wide as the Grand Canyon.'

'I take that as another compliment.'

He responded with a small ironic bow of his head, and they watched as Kingston and Mildred meandered through the market, stopping at a shooting gallery where they took turns aiming at a pasteboard wall of semi-inflated coloured balloons. The fairy floss had been discarded.

'No matter what you might think about them, their ideas, the Ashram, Auroville – all of it ... I think they've helped make Pondy a unique place,' Julia said. 'It wouldn't be the same without them.' She turned and looked at his profile, against the glossy dark of the sea. 'I think you liking the Sea View probably has something to do with you growing up Catholic.'

'You mean, I miss the incense.'

'Incense, chanting, saints. Something like that.'

He laughed softly, the sound somehow in tune with the sea. 'So then, here you are staying in Pondicherry, obviously not doing what you're meant to be doing for this publishing company you and your husband have set up, and you are ...'

'Yes? What?'

'Taking revenge.'

She looked up startled. 'What?'

'It's a normal enough human reaction in your kind of circumstance.'

'Not to me, it isn't,' she said with studied calm, trying to control an anger welling in her stomach. 'I don't operate that way.'

'Everyone does.'

'Well I don't!'

She was clearly upset by what he had said, and he feared he had gone too far. He had only meant the comment to be provocative, more in fun than anything else, a riposte to her jibe about Catholicism, and in teasing her alluding to the degree of intimacy between them, the newly attained plateau of it.

'I'm sorry. I didn't mean you to take it like that.'

'It's alright,' she said. 'I over-reacted. I'm sorry.'

She got to her feet.

'Julia …'

'It's alright. It's fine.'

'Are you sure?'

'Yes.'

She waited for him to get up, and they began walking back towards the guesthouse. They passed the Gandhi statue, and before too long went by Kingston and Mildred, sheltered behind a stunted tree, kissing gastronomically.

II

A power cut punctuated the walk back, and they continued on in tepid darkness, the esplanade crowds thinning. Approaching the Sea View, they saw candles lit in the garden and the open vestibule. The hotel generator had not been turned on. Standard practice: the Manager usually waited up to half an hour before doing so, in case the blackout was short-lived.

They stepped out of the freshening breeze into the entry hall where the Manager sat alone at his desk. He was half turned away, reading, his brooding profile illuminated by candles placed in water-filled metal bowls, the flickering light of which played across the ceiling like the interior of a crypt. His face was habitually impassive, and he appeared not to notice as they passed on into the Dining Room and from there to the stairs, and went up. The place was silent, seemingly devoid of staff or guests beyond themselves and the Manager.

On reaching the landing, Julia perceived something odd, and

brought it to Marco's attention. The door to Room Eight was open. She stepped forward to peer in. No candle burned inside, but in the spill of starlight through the window she could see that the room was empty. It lacked the accoutrements of travel, and the bed had been made up.

'He must have checked out today,' Marco said, joining her in the doorway.

Julia kept looking around the room, as if for a clue.

'He probably couldn't take being found out,' Marco said. 'About the lie.'

'Possibly, yes,' she agreed. 'Poor boy.'

They heard bare feet on the steps coming slowly up, and were joined by the Manager. The indications were he wished to speak with them. This was much of a surprise, as he rarely communicated verbally with guests, that task routinely delegated to Guru. The Manager was an unobtrusive man for a leader, Julia noted as he drew up to them, his sole defining characteristic being his idiosyncratic mixing of Lacoste polo shirts with the long 'male skirt' *lunghi*, both bleached a searing white. But at this moment, in the gloom of the blacked out guesthouse, it was the whiteness of his teeth which stood out, approaching as he did with a set, and, to Julia's eyes, forced smile.

'Did you know Mr Bloom?' he enquired.

His funereal tone, in combination with pointed use of the past tense, made Julia start. 'Yes. Why, is he alright?'

'He is gone,' the Manager said. 'There was an incident.'

'Incident?' Marco put in. 'What kind of incident?'

The Manager eyed them both, as if considering whether to

impart a confidence. 'With one of the female staff members,' he continued. 'An *ayah*.'

The incident as described by the Manager had begun entirely innocently, as he put it, when the young *ayah*, the teenager Lakshmi, asked Mr Bloom to take her photograph. This was a common occurrence, he said. The *ayahs* would tee it up with a guest, usually for a religious holiday or festival when they would be in their best saris, and adorn themselves with jewellery and *tika* spots. They would pose among the frangipani blooms in the courtyard, and the guest would have the film developed before they left Pondicherry and give the *ayah* a set of prints, often with a duplicate set for her family, as a friendly gesture.

Mr Bloom, the Manager said, had taken a number of photographs of Lakshmi. There had been a good deal of laughter. He had heard it himself from his office, a lighthearted occasion. Not long afterwards, Mr Bloom had returned to his room, and the girl to her duties. All had seemed well. But half an hour later the guesthouse quiet had been shattered by an uproar from upstairs, and everyone rushed up to see. It was soon revealed that while Lakshmi was cleaning his room, Mr Bloom had made improper advances, witnessed by another *ayah*, Durga, who had seen the girl struggling with him, and both females had begun to scream. With the arrival of other staff, Lakshmi had been safely released from the man. Upon being fully apprised of the facts, the Manager said he had given Mr Bloom fifteen minutes to pack his things, and should he be there when that term expired the police would be summoned.

Mr Bloom, the Manager noted with obvious satisfaction, 'did not need telling twice', and had thrown his things together and departed in a taxi. Asked if he believed him still to be in Pondicherry, the Manager replied that he believed not, as the taxi driver, knowing something had happened involving his passenger, had returned to the guesthouse for the full story. He said he had dropped the American off at the bus station, adding that the agitated young man had said his intention was to 'get the hell out as soon as possible', nominating Madurai as his probable destination.

'And Lakshmi,' Julia asked, 'is she alright?'

The Manager's head wobbled affirmatively. 'I have sent her back to her village.'

'But she will come back?'

'In good time, I hope so madam.'

The three of them peered in at the room so recently occupied. Now it housed a linger of disinfectant.

'Did Mr Bloom provide any account of his actions?' Marco asked. 'Protest his innocence, or try to put forward any mitigating circumstances?'

The Manager eyed him with an undertaker's gravity, his face almost invisible on the darkened landing. 'No sir,' he replied, 'he did not.'

Josh watched the traffic streaming towards him in the darkness, all of it coming at the same velocity as this rusted-out cadaver of what, back at the dawn of time, might have been recognisable as a government bus. The tragic old leviathan overtook and was constantly overtaken, bleating its horn in demand or protest, the driver barely ever easing off. Other buses, equally overloaded, and massive crudely-built trucks bore down constantly, and Josh spent much of the time with his eyes clamped shut, unable to watch. This conflicted with his usual practice of telepathically soothing the driver, but tonight's seemed beyond help, a loon with a licence and sixty or seventy unfortunates jammed within his tin-plate confines, fated to trust their souls to him tonight.

The bus had arrived late in Pondy, and so a journey of a few hours scheduled to be taken during daylight hours would now have to be taken all through the night, and he would arrive in Madurai God only knew when. How would he find a hotel at four in the morning? He might have to spend the rest of the night sleeping on the bus station floor. If it had one. If they made it there at all.

During the five hours of the journey so far, he had been trying unsuccessfully to work his way backwards in the bus, but the mass of people, the density of human flesh both seated and standing, had rendered that impossible. Usually passengers and bus drivers were happy for foreigners to ride at the back of the bus: that was where the bumps were worst. Not a few travellers had bashed their heads on the metal roof as a bus sped over a pothole. But this bus was too packed to allow for any change of position. And there was his bag too, his backpack, which he had to admit took up the space of two average Indians. So it wasn't just a matter of trying to squeeze himself back in the bus, it was like trying to take two other people with him. The solid wall of humanity faced him with blank unconcern, and he knew it was hopeless.

Josh's keenness to get further back into the bus related in part to a traveller's tale told by a German he had met in a hotel back in Mahabalipuram. His informant had been on a speeding bus in Mexico which had been involved in a head-on collision with another bus in the middle of the night. The German had been standing at the back of the bus, and watched in slow motion horror as the rows of seats in front of him peeled up from the floor like flower petals in a wind, crushing row upon row of passengers between them, leaving heads fractured, limbs twisted and organs pierced. The German himself had been extremely lucky. From his standing position he had been thrown by the impact against a pile of baggage, and escaped injury beyond shock and bruises. One victim who had been sitting near the front said the driver appeared to lose concentration because he was having an argument with a passenger about football. And so now, trying not to imagine the immensity of the force of a head-on collision and what it must feel like to spend hours critically injured, trapped between the teeth of the twisted steel frames of seats, Josh stood with eyes shut, while at the same time trying not to remember the scene that had taken place at the guesthouse that day.

Serving his breakfast, Lakshmi had said this was the day she wished him to take her photograph. It was a religious festival, and she wanted to be photographed in her best clothes for her family back in the village. So when he had finished his breakfast, he went up and fetched his camera and met her in the courtyard. Lakshmi was excited, constantly laughing and running off to re-emerge in a variant of her outfit – a different scarf, new earrings, a change of pantaloons. It went on like that for twenty or so minutes, until he ran out of film. She didn't believe it at first, until she heard the film automatically winding back inside the camera. Then she cheekily demanded 'two copies, give me two copies!' before running inside with a parting laugh.

Josh went back in and climbed the stairs towards his room. He was, it had to be said, weary of Pondicherry now. It was time to move on. He didn't want to face Julia again, not after the humiliating rebuff of the night before. He saw the padlock on her door as he unlocked his: she had already gone out. As her note had said, she was busy today. With Marco, no doubt. The two of them joking about him.

He had begun packing when there was a gentle tapping on his door. Lakshmi stood there smiling, back now in her signature hot pink sari.

'Clean room?'

'Yes. Please.'

She brought in her buckets and brooms while he went on with his packing, rounding up bathroom things. How many toothbrushes had he lost in India? He could navigate himself all the way back to Delhi by them.

As he re-entered from the bathroom, Lakshmi stood up and faced him. She was smiling, shyly, but she appeared to be doing something else with her eyes, the same flirty, funny movements he had seen in South Indian dance performances. In that moment she looked like a heroine from a Hindi movie, he thought, because those girls were always fun and spirited, unlike the Indian girls you got to meet, who usually looked sour and depressed, or incredibly studious. It was as if they were in denial of their fun and sexy sides, in denial of it everywhere but in the fantasyland of the Bollywood big screen.

'Check out today?' she asked.

'Yes.'

Her expression didn't change at the news. The same flighty smile played on her lips, inviting him perhaps. Or was it mocking him? Or maybe she was just asking for a tip. She laughed delightedly, her laugh full of music, a laugh freer than he had heard from any Indian woman, and in two steps he was with her, looking down into those eyes that didn't stop smiling. He reached out, taking her in his arms with infinite care. He needed to. Her body next to his felt amazingly thin and bony, a thinness you couldn't tell just from looking. And *she wasn't resisting*. The realisation flashed through his mind like a headline over Times Square. He exulted, having so boldly bridged the unbridgeable divide. But even as he was doing so, exulting, she was turning herself in his grasp. Gently, not sharply, but turning away from him. He couldn't kiss her now. Maybe she was telling him just that, that it wasn't safe then and there, but she still left his arms cuddled around her waist. Only he couldn't see the expression on her face any more, so he couldn't be one hundred per cent sure of how she was reacting, beyond that she felt at ease in his arms.

His left hand found itself inside the loose fold of her sari, made contact with bare skin. His fingers started running over her, in circles around her tiny belly. The skin felt wondrously smooth, and his fingers glided over it, gaining in confidence with each moment. Still there was no sign of struggle, no sound of protest, and emboldened even further he slipped his hand under her top, cupping her breast and taking her nipple gently between forefinger and thumb.

But in the very instant of that touch, Josh realised two things. One was that she had left the door part way open when she came in. The other was that another *ayah*, an older one he had never noticed before, was standing out on the landing, mop in hand, watching. He would never know whether Lakshmi screamed because he was making advances to her, or that the advances had now reached her breast, or that, like him, she realised in that moment that they had been seen. Whatever the case, the sound that erupted from her lips was a teenage girl's shriek of distress, a scream for help. He heard it resound down the halls of the guesthouse and bring everyone running upstairs, just as it summoned the older *ayah* into the room, staring at him with eyes horror-wide, as if he had been on the point of raping and murdering Lakshmi.

Instinctively he released her, and she turned on him, face contorted with pain, with terror, with anger, with all these in part and with something else too, a hatred for him, loathing, disgust. He feared she would leap at him scratching with her nails, but the other woman had her now, drew her away, cradled her, and already the room was filling with people, the downstairs staff summoned by her cries, more people than he had ever suspected worked in the place, and they were all talking among themselves, listening to the accusations she spat out between sobs, and the wide-eyed pointing and shrieks of the older woman.

After the Manager arrived it had been a simple matter of being ignominiously kicked out of the guesthouse, a place he could never return to now. It struck him as he went down the stairs for the last time, backpack over his shoulder, watched by a line-up of silent faces from above, and out through the courtyard to the taxi they had summoned for him, that so much in life turns on the random fortune of a single moment, and that in a different circumstance he and Lakshmi might have beaten the taboos. Because, he sensed, wrongly or rightly, she had been willing. But it was not to be, just as it had not been with Julia, which was sad because he genuinely liked her and wouldn't even get a chance to say goodbye, and now that he was leaving Pondicherry he wished that he could stay longer. But that's just how it goes, he had thought, as he took his seat in the taxi, observed with curious bemusement by the driver in his rear-view mirror. That's just how it turns out sometimes, he thought now, as he stood trapped halfway forward and unable to get any more than halfway back, stuck in the grievous injury zone. The moment goes against you, everything turns to shit, and all you can hope for is the next town.

The Manager took his leave and returned to his post downstairs, leaving them alone on the landing. With Josh's room now vacant, and Kingston and Mildred out still, the upper floor's complement was accounted for. It was quiet, no sounds came from downstairs. It felt late, even though it was not.

'I'm at a loss to know what to say,' Julia said.

'Yes,' he agreed. 'Quite extraordinary.'

Marco was not, however, quite so much at a loss or astounded as he indicated. The young American had obviously tried his luck with that young *ayah* he'd been eyeing all along like a sweet tooth a parfait. How far it had gone, the degree of transgression, the intricate interplay of suggestion, accession, coercion (if there had been any) or the use of actual force (unlikely, he thought) was a dark zone into which little light would ever reach. The offence was likely to remain a mystery, the outrage of which would no doubt grow with each re-telling. But the facts themselves could not be elucidated because there were, probably, no facts, only a person (or was it two?) who had fumbled towards something that had gone wrong. But only those two parties knew the absolute truth of it, and one of them was in the asylum of her village, and the other expelled and fled to ports beyond.

Thus, he thought, as he followed Julia towards her door, was the stuff of legends made. From perceptions of things that had happened between other people, heightened in telling and re-telling, agonised and aggrandised by time. There was a complicating factor, in that the American was a paying guest, the girl a low caste domestic. It was a power relationship weighted entirely in favour of the man, and it was a position of power which Bloom had, wittingly or unwittingly, abused.

Interestingly though, when the pendulum swung the other way, as it had here, all that power was suddenly weighted against him. Now instead of him being a paying customer and her a virtual slave, Bloom was a sexually depraved foreign oppressor and Lakshmi the wronged flower of Indian womanhood.

Could he discuss it with Julia in terms like these? Not really. As they stood outside her door exchanging parting pleasantries, he concluded he could share none of these thoughts because Julia was a woman and he a man, and there was a muddy channel of correctness to be negotiated between them. One misinterpreted word could create all kinds of unforeseen complexities. He resolved to play a dead bat.

'It's just so strange about Josh,' Julia was saying.

'Yes,' he agreed.

She sighed, and felt for her key. 'I enjoyed today.'

'So did I.'

He had been debating what to do at this point. His intuition said a kiss, even on the cheek, was out, especially in light of what had most recently been placed upon the agenda. In the end he put out his hand for her to shake. 'Goodnight.'

She took his hand, but then went up onto her toes and placed a kiss, warm if brief, onto his cheek. Then she unlocked the door and went in. She lingered there a half-moment, smiling goodnight, before closing it.

He felt very alone on the landing, swung around and walked quickly to his room. He went straight onto his balcony and stood at the railing, looking out at the waves. The wind was fresh in his face, ran light massaging fingers over his skull. It had blown away the clouds that had hung out to sea earlier in the evening, and the sky was starkly starred. The courtyard palms rattled in the rush of air. He exhaled slowly, emptied his lungs, then breathed in deeply, diaphragmatically, the air filling his lower back, abdomen, chest. He held in that fresh clean air, then exhaled gently, not forcing, letting the air escape from him. Repeating the procedure twice, he began to feel the effects, the lightheadedness that oxygen brought, partially relieving him of the weight of the body he stood in. Then he thought about Julia. How much, he decided, he liked her, for her intelligence and wit, but also for her obvious torment. Her openness of mind, too, he liked: he could only wish it for himself. She was a rather noble creature, he decided, but then wondered if it wasn't the oxygen talking. Perhaps all he was saying to himself was that he was well disposed towards her. But then, that was very clear.

Returning indoors, he settled onto the baize-green couch which the guesthouse management had provided with this room, in a setting with a pair of matching armchairs. They were arranged at the far end of this grand space, which might once have served as a suite of offices, or reception hall. He poured a glass of brandy from a decanter on the sideboard and picked up the morning's edition of the *Hindu* from the coffee table. He leafed through it, but for some reason found himself too tired to read. He sipped the brandy. It was decent stuff, from an importer in Chennai, the same one who maintained his wine cellar. The man was also good at getting champagne, two bottles of which he kept stored in the refrigerator in the kitchen downstairs. He took another sip, fingertips toying with the paper, and idly scanned the headlines.

Thackeray was in the news again. Now he was making noises about coming down to Chennai to try to disrupt the cricket test against Pakistan. Marco sighed and shook his head, drank down his drink, rose, stretched, yawned. He went out onto the balcony for a final breath of air before bed.

Out there, he heard faint but familiar sounds. Through the opened door off the adjoining balcony, he heard the kissers of the promenade wrestling body and soul, their whimpers a gentle accompaniment to the rush of the wind and sigh of the sea. So Mildred's journey was not in vain. She had discovered something here after all, love, which was what she had desired all along but had clouded it all up with hocus pocus. And Kingston? He might now begin to dismantle his great wall of books. Let the breeze blow through.

Almost asleep, he wondered if Julia was sleeping, or reading, or just lying in bed thinking. Could she possibly come to his door tonight and knock? No, that would not be Julia. Nor could he knock on hers.

As she lay in bed she tried not to think about Josh much, in fact not at all. Nor think about the unsettling thing Marco had said to her, about revenge. And she did not even try to digest the saga of his life. Instead she tried to clear her mind, rinse it clean, blank it for sleep. But her mind resisted. She tossed in her bed, within the white shroud of her net. She knew if her mind had its own way she would spend all night going over things, so she willed her thoughts to fly off in either direction, her mind to clear. Oddly enough, next thing the Lycee Francais came into her mind. On, where was it, Rue Dumas or Rue Suffren? She saw the *tricolore* on its pole in front of the neat school building, and the lines of equally neat *étudiants* outside it. The *tricolore* recalled the Consulat-General, and the elderly guard who sat outside it and always greeted her with a 'bonjour madame', his cheery bonhomie straight out of a Yoplait commercial.

Her mind's eye reading of those two French words progressed her further, to something that had happened the day before when she had been crossing the park in the main square, and a very old woman had begged her for 'something'. She was tiny and bony, her clothes grubby and limp, and she was lying on the stubble of yellowed municipal grass beside a sleeping man, equally old and tiny, her husband, Julia had concluded; and as she passed them the woman's toothless mouth had shouted out '*Donnez-moi quelque chose, madame! Donnez-moi quelque chose!*'; and she had given the woman two one-rupee coins, and as she walked away thought it possible both were well into their eighth decade and living in that park, and that their only clothes were those tatters on their backs, and those two rupees, one each, the only money they possessed in the world. She glanced back at them, the woman staring down happily at the coins in her palm, the sleeping man with the dark skin stretched tightly over his skull and receded from his empty mouth, looking like the corpse he would surely soon be.

She had walked on through the square, dotted with the prone shapes of the poor who seemed to sleep the misfortune of their lives away. What was the name of that square? It eluded her now. But she should know it, because knowing places and names was her business. And thinking that brought back what Marco had said, so that she finally admitted it, resignedly, to her consciousness, dragged it inside her walls, along with the Trojan Horse of that forgotten place name.

Revenge. Marco had asked the question, and she had dismissed it out of hand. High-handedly, as if it were utterly beneath her. Why? Probably because the desire for revenge was one of the low emotions, like jealousy or rage, things one did not like to detect in oneself, something vestigial, from the old brain, from back in evolution, a scaly tail. But had she really left it behind? How subtle is something like revenge? Could one be taking revenge without realising it? Was she taking revenge on Tim now with her inactivity, and had Marco put his finger on it first time? Was she effectively on a sulky strike, not doing the work Tim and so many other people were depending on her to do, and would she be doing that unless it was at least in part motivated by revenge? But revenge for what? Any realisic consideration of their split-up had to lay the blame primarily at her feet. She had initiated the troubles, and carried the whole thing through to its conclusion. She had lied to him. She had moved out. Twice. From the man she loved. What was she, masochistic? Or just impulsive? Or proud? Was it that what had started as an earnest desire for a child had ended up in a power play in which her self-esteem had demanded she make all the running and play all the big cards? Put that way, it was her who had destroyed the whole thing. It wasn't really quite as one-sided as that, and she knew that in the morning she would apportion more of the blame to Tim, but for now it was deep night in India and she was alone in bed, aching that familiar ache, and for now she was willing to shoulder the blame, the lot of it, her lot, just as she was willing to countenance that over the past few weeks she had been behaving petulantly, motivated by an unexpressed, unrealised even, desire for revenge, a passive *fuck you* to Tim, to the world.

She took a deep breath, trying to remain calm. How far was she behind schedule? She wasn't even sure. And she was due back in Sydney in just six more weeks. And if she wasn't, the whole edition would be held up for weeks, months. People would lose work, income, because of her. The entire credibility of *The Hobo's Lullaby* guides might be damaged because of her behaviour.

There was only one thing to do. In the morning she would go to the railway station and book a ticket. She would only have time for the major places now, so she would do less on the Kerala beaches. They were easy anyway. Considering it closely, she decided it might be wiser to start in the opposite direction, go back to Chennai and take a train to Bangalore, and from there up to Hampi. With its wealth of Hindu ruins, Hampi was popular with *Hobo's Lullaby* readers. After that she would go down to Mysore, and ports south. Ooty, Kochi, Allepuzah, Quilon, and finally the Kerala beaches of Varkala and Kovalum, and whatever this year's new beach was. Then by train from

Trivandrum back to Chennai, and her flight out. It was daunting to think how far she had to travel, and how much data she had to collect (and what about the places she would miss now, like Madurai? – she would have to pick that up by email as best she could with the Tourist Commission) but if she started as soon as possible, it could still just be done.

It was decided. She would get up early in the morning, book her ticket out for the following morning and spend her last day in Pondy collecting all the information she still needed. That would be another stretch in itself, but with effort she could get the essentials. She would also have to say goodbye to Marco, which was a pity as she was just getting to know him and liked him. She would have liked very much to get to know him better, but she knew now was not the time for that. She had no time at all, in fact. She had to go.

These matters resolved, Julia rolled onto her side, expecting merciful sleep would now be bestowed upon her. But it was not, because there was yet more unfinished business. Josh. And so, defeated, she returned to the flat of her back and looked up, eyes wide, and faced that one too. Not that there was so much to be faced. His transgression was symptomatic of his behaviour all along. Obviously he was a young man with problems and needed to work them out, *viz.* the pathetic business with the invitation, his lie. Part of a pattern of behaviour? Probably. And Lakshmi, the incident? Julia intuited it was something relatively minor, awkward groping. Of course it had got him into hot water in India. It would outside India too. Where was the line? There was no easy one. Plenty of disgusting, manipulative men, and enough women keeping up with the Paula Joneses. Add to that old-fashioned sexual repression and media titillation, and you got moral quicksand. Josh? He was a silly boy. Probably not much more than that. She felt more sorry than anything for him, although she felt far sorrier for Lakshmi having to go through it, whatever he had done or tried to do, and the sad end effect of her going (or being sent) back to her village like some kind of fallen woman. That was the worst thing about it, and of course Josh wasn't here to see it, the possible loss of precious income, a whole future perhaps, because of his foolishness. Well she wasn't going to cause the same sorts of problems herself, with her own folly.

Sleep still did not come easily, even after that. Her pulse was rapid, she was more jumpy than sleepy. Her mind went back over the day like a balloonist over a savannah. She found herself wondering, of all things, whether a full stop could be said to follow a sentence, or whether it was part of it, the end-part; and finally conceded this was not the time for such debate, but rather for sleep.

By slow degrees her body calmed, and by the time the *muezzin*'s distant call to prayer drifted into her window before dawn, she dreamt.

III

She awoke around nine, later than she might have wished: there was a lot to do today. Leaving her room fifteen minutes later, she discovered the note she had not seen beneath her door. It said: *Lunch, 1 pm today, roof garden at the Aristo?* She penned a quick reply: *Sorry, lunch not possible today. Dinner perhaps* and slipped it under Marco's padlocked door on her way out. Walking downstairs she wondered what he was doing this morning, and remembered he would be at Le Cafe Blanc, with his papers.

The streets were full of people. 'Harvest festival', a boy volunteered. She had no time to seek out any higher authority, thanked him and continued on her way. The railway station, which served as a terminus for the branch line that ran up to the main Chennai–Madurai line, was crowded with holidaymakers, all waving tickets, trying to change them for this reason and that, or just wanting tickets back home in a couple of days time when the festivities ended. After being pushed and shoved for fifteen minutes she reached the counter and managed to procure a ticket to Chennai the following morning.

Returning to the guesthouse for breakfast and a shower, she discovered another note beneath her door, proposing: *Sunset cocktails on the roof, Sea View, 6 pm?*, to which, running out again half an hour later, she responded *Yes, thank you. But isn't it time we introduced ourselves? I'm Julia*.

A full morning followed. She took rickshaws across town, garnering prices from hotels and guesthouses, looking over the rooms and facilities of the Palms, the Villa and the Krishna, and as many others as she could jam in. She checked menus and prices from the Aristo to the Rendezvous, compared quality in the shops. She took an early lunch at the Indian Coffee House, just beating the cut-off time for morning *dosais*, jotting down notes as she ate. After lunch she was sightseeing, at the Ashram, the Pondicherry Museum, the Toy Museum and the Alliance Francaise. By late afternoon, marvelling almost at her own efficiency, she was able to slacken off, feeling that she had made at least a half decent job of it. The information for Pondicherry was pretty well there. As for Auroville – well, she had her visit to the Matrimandir, and that lunch at New Creation Corner. From that, and the guff in the current edition, she could put something together.

She walked back through the streets of the Ville Blanche towards the seafront knowing now which was Rue Dumas and which Rue du Bazaar Saint-Laurent, and to which deity the temple off Rue de la Marine was dedicated, and that the proper name of the esplanade was Avenue Goubert. She also knew –

obvious when you thought about it – that the seafront Ville Blanche had gained its name from the white French colonists who had lived there, while the Ville Noire beyond the canal was where the Indian population had lived. And although the Indians had long ago crossed the canal and recolonised, the old French names abided.

Her work done, she was free to leave Pondicherry. Inevitably, that realisation, particularly on a calm and sunny afternoon, meant the streets acquired an entrancing beauty. Her walk back to the hotel became a slow stroll up Rue Suffren, with its candy pink and green houses, its lime and ochre yellow walls cascading jasmine. Billowing banks of bougainvillea flashed scarlet tips across the blue of the sky, alive with flitting finches.

She stopped and noted down names for a sidebar piece she could include, 'The Villas of Rue Suffren': Villa Carlos with its floral nameplate and Virgin Mary shrine inside a walled courtyard; D'Armaraza-Mahall, a white monolithic facade with coat of arms crowning its entrance gates; Villa Rathina with its wrought-iron gateway of leaping carnival horses; and Villa Rose, with eponymous rosy walls.

She took her time, working for detail she thought readers would appreciate, realising as she laboured with her pen that she was probably doing so in the thrall of Revenge's cousin, Remorse. And so the afternoon slipped away, her last in Pondicherry. A glance at her watch confirmed it. In twenty minutes it would be six o'clock. That reminded her of the arrangement with Marco, and putting her notebook and pen away she hurried back to the Sea View where beneath her door she found the latest in their flurry of sub-portal communication, confirming: *Up On The Roof at 6. Marco Manzini.*

Julia drew on the black cotton dress. *Dhobi* beaten and frayed, it was hardly a cocktail frock, but it was the best she had. With a parting glance in the mirror to check her lipstick, she climbed the whitewashed stairs and crossed the flat, sun-warmed roof, past snaking TV aerial cables and scattered broken crockery – the archaeology of some long-forgotten tiff? – and the turret of the semi-derelict building next door, squealing with bats.

Marco greeted her from the parapet wall at the front of the building. She joined him peering down at the esplanade where children rollicked along while their parents strode heads down in conversation. Bicycle *rickshawallahs* jangled bells and food hawkers wailed. There was a holiday feel in the air again, the tropical night so breezy up here it made her want to extend her arms and let it blow right through her.

Marco pointed out the seated-gnome shape of a saffron-robed figure on a tuft of seafront grass, staring into the black surf.

'He's from the American state of Iowa,' Marco said. 'Do you know it?'

'Only vaguely, from the map.'

'It's a vague kind of place, apparently. A lost horizon of wheat. He was an agricultural scientist, so I've heard. The story goes that he was happily married – forgive the oxymoron – until his wife got mixed up in a religious cult of some stripe and ran off. Took the children with her and vanished. After a few months skulking around the house waiting for word from her, he drove out to the airport, left his car in the car park and got on a plane. He didn't even think of where it was going, he just flew. Connected flight to flight and kept on going till his money ran out. That's the mythology anyway. Turned up in Pondy a year ago and he's been living here in the Sea View ever since. And the next thing he's garbed like a monk sitting cross-legged down on that patch of grass every night, staring out to sea. He's the one in Room Three downstairs, that you hardly ever see.'

'I've never even seen him at all,' Julia said. She looked down at the small rounded heap of a man who used to be a scientist with a life he thought he knew, and ended up a spectre in the lime wash halls of a guesthouse in India. When he was soothing his babies, or telling a farmer how they might bump up their yields, or making love with his wife half-drunk on the sofa on a Friday night in front of the TV, could he ever have foreseen such a fate? Surely it was a different person down there, wrapped in orange cotton. Only, it wasn't.

'We have so many people, fates, endings inside all of us, it's frightening,' Julia murmured. 'If we can be anyone in the right circumstances – or the wrong ones – then where's the centre, the truth to us, the essential part that can't change?'

'I believe you're looking for the soul.'

'Perhaps,' she said. 'I don't know.'

He reached into a pool of shadow and produced a bottle of champagne, and a pair of glasses. A mildly clichéd tableau, she thought. Them and the night and the wine. A *New Yorker* cartoon from the fifties, or was it a *Playboy*? But the invitation had been for cocktails. And of course she liked champagne, as she liked Marco too. Understanding could come so easily, given the right working conditions.

Marco levered the cork while Julia's attention remained upon the stilled man on the esplanade. 'Lives an utterly monastic existence,' Marco said. 'I took a peek through his door one day. Empty cell.' The cork acquiesced with a muffled pop, and he poured.

'Do you know his name?' she asked.

'It's Dwight.'

'Certainly an all-American name.'

'Yes. But apparently he hates America now and says he never wants to go back.'

'He couldn't. Not with the parking fine he'd have.'

Marco smiled at the quip, and raised his glass to hers. 'But then India's like that for a lot of people.'

'Like what?'

'Last refuge. A place to come to when all else fails. And Pondy is the case *par excellence*. Like one great big pleasant psych ward.'

'Is that why you're here?'

'Oh yes. And as last refuges go, it's quite ideal.'

She clinked and sipped. The champagne was crisp chilled and very good. 'Well I'm certainly going to miss it.'

'You're leaving?'

'Tomorrow.'

'I'm sorry to hear that.'

'I'm sorry too. Because I was enjoying myself here. And I was enjoying getting to know you.'

'But you're moving on.'

'I have to. The work I'm doing ... the guidebook research ... I have to get back to it. Too many people are depending on me. And, well, actually, what you said to me, about taking revenge on my husband ...'

'But ...' he admitted a minor exasperation into his voice, 'I didn't mean it to be taken so ... seriously.'

'I know that. But you were right. Because I *was* doing that. I've been taking revenge. Childishly. And I'm not going to any more.'

The full lustre of night had settled upon them now, no moon yet and the stars obscured by cloud. It still surprised her how quickly night came here, a stage curtain dropped on the day. Only shapes, outlines could be discerned below, intermingling photon eddies in a dark particle stream. Dwight had been swallowed whole by the black of the sea, a saffroned Jonah.

Marco saw her glass was half-empty, and topped it up. 'Galileo said wine is light, held together by moisture.'

She held up her glass in the spill of streetlight, watching the pale gold bubbles rise. When she sipped, it tasted even better than before.

'So where to?' he asked.

'Back to Chennai, first of all. Then a Cook's tour of South India in double quick time.'

She could feel the first effects of the wine, track it through the tracery of her capillaries, dropping off its delicious little packages of release, quanta of ease.

'You know, I envy you,' he said. 'This might surprise you –

but perhaps it won't either, I don't know – but I envy you going *there*.' He gestured towards the crowds down on the promenade.

'But I thought you didn't like India.'

'I don't. I hate it. But that doesn't mean I wouldn't want to go there. Who wouldn't want to journey into this country? It's so dirty and disgusting, mediaeval. But dazzling too. Undeniable.'

There was a curiously supplicant sense about him as he spoke, of him reaching out further than he was accustomed, almost to the point of overbalance.

'I would love to see what you will, experience all those things. And alone, like you, so that I might savour true disorientation, in such an orientated world. But, you see, I fear I lack what you have. And so I do not.'

'I don't have anything special.'

'Well, you have modesty, even if it's false,' he laughed. 'No, you have, I don't know, the urge for wonderment, the need to know things immediately and truly, to experience them more deeply. You have curiosity, and you have courage. You seek. And what else is there for us to do? How tragic when for one reason or another, we don't. Ever, in some cases.' He paused. 'I did, once. Or thought I did at least.'

'But not now?'

He shook his head. 'I live in a single room. Perhaps that's big enough for me now.'

'Why?'

'I don't really know,' he said, appending it with a tiny, abrupt smile.

She reached and touched his cheek. 'You'll surprise yourself yet, I think.'

'I can only admire your faith.' He took her hand in his. 'I had been thinking of asking you to my room tonight. But of course, with you going tomorrow ...'

'You thought the moment had passed?'

'Something like that.'

Of all things, she was thinking about Dwight of Iowa as she rummaged in the wardrobe in her room. She wondered if he was still out there, cross-legged on the grass on those dark and windy rocks. More to the point, she wondered why his wife had left him, and the nature of the sect she had run off to. It was like running off with the circus, only taking the kids too. She wondered where the woman was now, what she believed in and what the children would grow up believing, whether the sect leader had started articulating the end of the world yet, and stocking up on rat poison. Poor woman. Poor kids. Poor Dwight. He probably thought it was all religious madness when she first told him about it, and now look at him.

She located what she was looking for, a packet of condoms. She trusted he would have his own – an attractive enough man living alone in a hotel through which a succession of solo females passed – but she liked to be sure they were fresh. She broke the seal on the packet and took one out. Would that be enough? Should she take two, three even? Marco had to be some way into his forties. Two would probably be ample.

The door to Room Ten was ajar. The candlelit space inside was so vast it made her feel slightly giddy. She looked up to where shadows played on the stout-beamed ceiling, the whitewash purple-bruised with sea damp. It had to be twenty feet high, or more. A lounge settee, armchairs and table stood grouped at one end, two single beds veiled with mosquito nets at the other. A pair of regulation black and white framed portraits of Aurobindo and The Mother surveyed the scene from the wall.

She called out a hello as she stepped across the tiled floor to the balcony, where she expected to find him. But he wasn't there. 'Marco? Where are you?'

'In here!'

'In where?'

'The bathroom!'

She went back inside and walked to the far end, where she heard the splash-tinkle of a shower not far off. She passed through the dressing room which intervened between the main chamber and the bathroom, saw the racks of wine stacked, and ahead saw another candle burning before a chipped bathroom mirror.

Stepping into the golden glow of the bathroom, she was amazed and somewhat taken aback by what she saw. Marco stood naked before her, and down his bared chest, stomach and thighs a runny mud ran and mixed with the flow of the shower into a pool at his feet. The face was heavily caked with mud, the eyes and teeth contrasting an almost unnatural white. The lips and mouth looked obscenely pink. His hand held an opened bottle of champagne.

'Come on,' he grinned. 'I'll put some on you. It's wonderful stuff. You'll like it.'

'But what is it?'

'Don't be shy.'

'I'm not. But what is it?'

He poured her a glass of champagne, careful not to taint it with drops of muddy brown liquid. 'You mean you don't know about The Mother's Touch? Minerals and herbs mainly. They use these kinds of mixtures all over South India. They say they're much better than soap because they don't strip the skin of oil. And The Mother's Touch is the best. Made out in Auroville.'

'You say all these nasty things about The Mother,' Julia chuckled, 'but still you like her touch.'

'Would you like to try it? Your skin will feel wonderful afterwards.'

'Actually, someone told me about this stuff the other day. Or something like it. I tried to get some at the Auroville shop.'

'So, do you want to you try it?'

'Alright.'

'Then,' he said, 'you'll have to take your clothes off.'

'To shower – will I really?'

She drew her dress off, and joined him beneath the flow of water. He took her hand, opened the palm, and shook the tan-coloured powder from a sachet. He showed her how to make a paste with it, funnelling in drops of water until it reached the right mud-clay consistency, and together they applied it to her skin.

'It smells like the earth,' she said.

'That's because it is mainly, I suppose.'

They covered her completely, legs, arms, breasts, torso, face. When they were finished she couldn't help observing it was like they'd been transformed into a pair of ash-covered *sadhus*.

'And now it's drying, we wash it off. I like this part. Like washing away the travails of the world.'

'I almost thought you were going to say *sins* for a moment,' she laughed, as they embraced beneath the shower, the pale brown mud running from their bodies.

She rose early, left him sleeping, and penned a note which she left propped between two limes on the bedside table. She settled her account with sleepy-eyed Guru at the reception desk, and hailed a rickshaw for the station.

How she loved India, she was thinking, as the cycle squeaked down the empty shuttered streets of yawning dogs and infants on their backs on the pavement, dreaming in tangled blankets in the arms of their dreaming mothers. How beautiful these deserted streets, this new blue day. She felt it so intensely that for a moment she sensed herself rising above it all, looking down on the scene, as was said to happen when you were near death. But she didn't feel near death. On the contrary, after so long a time of virtual non-being, on this morning she felt herself near life.

The note she left on the beside table read:

Dear Marco,
One must be shrewd as well as foolish, frivolous as well as wise. I can't remember where I read that. (A quote from The Mother on a cafe placemat?) But it sounds vaguely right. I'm sure Dwight of Iowa would agree anyway. Thank you for a very pleasant evening. I trust our paths will cross again.
Julia
PS: Namaste

THE HOBO'S LULLABY

Every journey begins with a single step. Axiomatically. But, she wondered, which step? Was it the one across the iron threshold of the jet at Sydney Airport? Was it the step away from the kitchen when the approaching taxi blew its horn, or the stumble from bed when the alarm went off? Or was it turning away from a bunch of tipsy well-wishers at a restaurant the night before, or running from a basin of hand-washing to answer the telephone dripping suds, to a request from Tim that she update the South Indian section of the guide because (he pleaded) no-one else was available, nor (he flattered) could do it so well. No, she decided, rather than a single step, a journey started with a lot of them, a sequence of steps, a kind of dance that meshed seamlessly with the other dance routines of life: the mating *pas de deux*, the rock & roll of sex, the family square dance, the techno aerobics of work, the dying swan. All of one's life, she continued – warming to this theme now – comprised interlinked steps, danced journeys linking the far destinations of infancy, maturity, age and senescence. And beyond those lay the ultimate ports of embarkation and disembarkation, awakening from a dream to find oneself alone at the railing of a ship, looking down into the oily waters of some nameless foreign port while the dock ghosts into dawn mist and a brass band brays godspeed this ship of fools.

Julia watched in the window of the train crossing the plains of Karnataka state. She was en route to Bangalore, nine rail hours west of Chennai. She was lying on a top bunk of the compartment, lulled by the bumping rhythm, head cushioned by her backpack. She shared the compartment with a trio of shirt pocket-penned men of the Bangalore technocracy, and a plump, dozing woman, rich-looking in an emerald green sari shot with gold, her braided black hair pomaded with coconut oil. There was something sour, perhaps, in her face, even in sleep. Usually by now Julia would have been drawn into conversation with her fellow travellers about her country of origin, family, marital status, cricket, politics, religion, the meaning of it all. But today her companions sat squarely behind their computer magazines, clicking their ballpoints, while the woman slept on.

Julia recalled the first time she had travelled on an Indian train. It was in the north. Delhi, Agra, Rajasthan, then down to Bombay. Tourist Route Number One, Tim had dubbed it. He loved the Indian trains. He was one of those people who could spend thirty hours on a train yet prize each moment, always pointing to new vistas, paddy fields with yoked oxen drawing a plough, peasants with their heads covered with high-piled hay going home in a line like ducks, framed by a glorious sunset. Or simply mile upon mile of green rice, running away to the horizon, tricking the eye, like one of those geometric patterns child psychologists use, into believing the world has no end, not even in the purple range in the distance.

She and Tim were new lovers then, very much so. They made love, talked and made love into the night in hardboard box rooms in wayside rests in a hundred towns whose names ended in *puram* and *ipur* and *abad*. It had been intoxicating just to lie together beside an open window through which drifted gentle laughter and the waft of *bidis*, the aromatic smoke of a distant fired paddy.

In the window now she saw the same vistas: the farmers, the ducks, the oxen, the same kingdom of mud and straw. Not a detail appeared to have changed (beyond the occasional satellite dish). It was all so peaceful to the eye, a utopia of sorts, if one did not strain to look too closely. But the memory of first seeing it all with Tim tainted it now, tainted her mood, which after the elation of her departure from Pondicherry had been gradually ebbing back into more familiar territory. She saw the accumulation of sadness in the eyes reflected in the railway glass. If we bought our lives from a shop, she mused, we would be forever trying to take them back.

Arriving back in Chennai, she had decided not to email Tim from one of the streetside cyber booths. She wanted slower words with him. Instead she posted him a card, a foxed 1940s black and white photograph of the Pondicherry esplanade, with the Sea View in the foreground. She wrote that she was well, work was proceeding, and that she would be back when planned. She hoped all was going equally well for him, adding that it would be good to see him on her return. Her hand hesitated then. Surely she could say more than that. But the hand did not move. In the end it merely signed her name and added a kiss, stamped it and slid it over the counter for franking.

She was thinking about Marco too, as the train bumped towards Bangalore. How had he felt about their night together? Disappointed it could only be a 'one night stand'? She was. Yet it also felt good to be leaving it at that. Obviously, she was not ready for the possibility of him. There was Tim, still Tim, somehow always Tim. Because if she and Tim really wanted it, they could have it again. The opportunity was still there, dangling before them, waiting to be grasped. Neither had become seriously involved with anyone else. There remained a real chance that in the not too distant future they could be lying in bed, their bed in Lavender Bay, laughing quietly together. And a baby could be in the adjoining room, and they would get up to check on it, and spend ten minutes just looking down into its sleeping face, marvelling at its tiny fingers. It all remained possible. Yet for now here she was, going away from him, even further away, because that was part of it too. It felt somehow pre-ordained, as if she were caught up in the workings of a larger mechanism. Again she thought of the two of them lying in bed back in Lavender Bay, and her mentioning that she had felt all these things on the train to Bangalore, and they would both smile at the picture she painted. But for the time they had been destined to further separation – and they would in the end smile at that too.

If that time did come, would she tell Tim about Marco? There would be a few lovers for them both to relate, if they felt inclined. But Marco? How could she explain to Tim why she did what she did last night? That knowing she was leaving in the morning and would probably never see him again, she had slept with him nonetheless. Tim would ask, as anyone might, if there was something about him that might have caused her decision – great wit, charismatic charm, an irresistible physicality – but she would have to reply that it was none of these, nor even a combination of them, but something else entirely. She couldn't even say precisely why she had done it, except that there was something she had needed from that man, something to do with the anguish he failed to conceal beneath his cynical visage, and the love that she had squandered, and that these in combination with champagne and a rooftop in a tropical breeze had been more than enough to make her desire to spend the night with him. And what had happened in bed with him, if she could tell Tim detail like this, if he actually wanted to hear it (she certainly didn't want to hear the details of his other lovers) had been akin not so much to a meeting of souls as a sharing of burdens, a span of gentleness, understanding, across those few hours they had shared. How would Tim take that? She tried to conjure his face in the green windowglass, but couldn't beyond an outline. So strange that, how one could find it hard, after even a short time apart, to envision the face of a long-loved one.

Her eyes moved from the window, casually down across her fellows. Two of the men had now laid aside their computer magazines, and noddingly dozed where they sat, along with the plump woman. Only one of the men remained awake. He looked up from the page and caught her eye, and the intensity of his gaze intimated something that disquieted her. It said that with everyone else asleep, they were alone. His eyes retained hers, then began roving over her, her neck and breasts, before deliberately coming back up to her eyes, his hard black centres daring her to keep looking. That was a difficult choice: it could be taken as provocative to keep looking, but a sign of weakness to look away. So she stared back at him, until a lewd little smile crept like a lizard from the corner of his mouth. Her reply was a hard shake of the head. She kept staring at him until the lizard crept back under the rock it had emerged from, and she looked away through the window and did not look back, feigning interest in what she saw outside.

The train was passing gangs of stone crushers, working in the sun by the tracks. She had seen these gangs many times in different parts of India. They broke up grey slabs from the quarry and turned them into gravel by hand. This is a country, she thought, watching them work, feeling the man return his attention by degrees to his magazine, that manufactures computers, cars and satellites. It has atomic power and nuclear weapons. Yet it makes gravel by hand.

It was a microcosm of caste and karma, the work of the stone crushers. The luckiest got to strike the biggest rocks with the biggest implement. And they got to stand while they did it.

These were mostly men. The next degree down, women mostly, squatted hammering rocks the size of a mango. Then a workforce, exclusively female, progressively reduced egg-sized stones to gravel, building a mound for collection. They worked every day in the sun and rain, for a few dollars a week, yet looking up from their hammering, they laughed and waved at her, at the *memsahib* in her well-made Western clothes. How could they, she wondered? How could they smile at all? But they did, one toothless crone proudly holding up a black, fist-sized stone she had broken with her mallet, cheekily threatening to throw it, then guffawing and waving madly until the *memsahib* and her train had passed on.

As much to avoid the man, she encouraged her thoughts to wander further, a longer excursion. *India*. It wasn't like, say, Japan, or Thailand, with a Western veneer appliqued over a culture which denied even the merest inquiry. On the contrary, India felt wide open. People were eager to talk about their history and religion, their lives and beliefs, and in her own language. A wealth of information was accessible, from heavyweight academic treatises on the Aryans, Dravidians and Moghuls to the comic-book versions of the *Mahabarata* and *Ramayana* on the news-stands. One was deluged with information, with histories, ideologies, ethical codes and philosophies, a welter of gods, goddesses and more gods. India seethed with deities in their esctatic, psychedelic multitudes, sweated them up in sweltering days through open drains, and rained them down in monsoon torrents, so that sometimes it all felt too much, as if you were caught in the open without an umbrella while gods hailed against your temples. Comprehending India was exhausting, sisyphean. The deeper one scraped a hole in the sand, the more sand ran back in. Mostly she delighted in the very impossibility of understanding. Other times, tired of trying, she vowed to give up, stop wondering, stop thinking about it, just be here and enjoy it. But at that very moment, the scales would fall from her eyes about an aspect, however trivial, of Indian life, a caste behaviour or historical note, and spin her back into the spiral of all those half-knowns, unknowns and unknowables. In the end, she concluded, she knew just one thing about India – that there was no-one, anywhere, no leather-elbow-patched academic in Calcutta or mystic on a Himalayan peak, who knew it all, who could take in the entire mosaic of India in a single look. And that was probably why she so loved it.

She looked up, and her eyes inevitably strayed back to the man, as one's eyes do when they want to check that something they don't want to be there isn't. Only they found that it was. He was staring at her, his tongue stuck out at her, impudent, pink as a phallus. She shook her head as at something sad which she felt powerless to change.

'Put it away,' a female voice chided, and the tongue darted back in. The plump woman in the shot-silk sari had awakened. The man flushed deeply, and hid behind his magazine before getting up and leaving the carriage. Julia flushed too, internally, embarrassed at her earlier snap judgement of the woman, and thanked her.

'They are rascals,' the woman said. 'Some of them are, most

of them are.' She prodded the other two men awake and told them what their companion had been up to, adding that if he returned to the carriage she would call the conductor and make a report.

As was his habit, upon waking he did nothing but lie in bed and watch the listless curtain in the breeze. The guesthouse halls were silent, and he surmised from that, and from the sharp rectangle of sun across his exposed feet, that morning was well advanced, if not already given way to afternoon.

Sitting up, he detected few reminders, even pale clues, of the events of the night before. It had always been cause for mild surprise that, the total evaporation from a room of a night of lovemaking. It had all departed, gone out the door with Julia. Yet the reminders were there, if one looked more closely: the empty champagne bottle and glasses, the condom wrapper. And of course the note she had left, on his bedside table.

He picked it up and re-read it. *One must be shrewd as well as foolish, frivolous as well as wise.* Her decision to move on, continue with the work she had come to India to do, presumably. But that had already been decided before their night together. Was this, in some understated way, an expression of regret? Yes, he supposed. And although she had directly said as much to him on the rooftop, before their little *tete-a-tete*, he found himself touched. Perhaps it was that she had gone so far as to commit that regret to writing, or that she had chosen to frame it so quaintly epigramatically in mock 'Mother-speak', which she knew he would find amusing. *I can't remember where I read that. (A quote from The Mother on a cafe placemat?)* This she had followed with the confiding remark: *But it sounds vaguely right. I'm sure Dwight of Iowa would agree anyway.* An agreeable touch, a reminder of intimacies shared. Then the well-brought-up young woman: *Thank you for a very pleasant evening.* And the concluding sentence, *I trust our paths will cross again.* Interpretable as a formality, but for the word *trust*. She *trusted* their paths would cross again. So much of a different nuance to 'I hope our paths cross again', or 'I think our paths may cross again'. No, this was trust. And trust is something not given or received lightly. Among the most precious of human intimacies. And here she was, extending it to him. Or was he reading too much into that word, *trust*? After all, it might only be a turn of phrase, an idiomatic usage, an idiosyncrasy. It might signify nothing much at all. But no, he intuited, as he sat propped up on his elbow, the sun warm on his feet, the old white curtain billowing mainsail-like with the noontime breeze off the sea, she had *chosen* that word. That conscious choice had to signify something, that she really did trust their paths would cross again. Then, lastly, there was her signature, *Julia*, expressive, again, but in no way overdone. There was no X for a kiss, which was slightly strange considering how many kisses they had shared during the hours leading up to the writing of the note – the thought quietly disconcerted when it expressed itself in those terms – but perhaps she was not someone who ended with Xs for kisses. And then there was the *PS: Namaste,* which was a kiss of sorts, recalling as it did their lunch, and their sharing of that word. *I honour the divine in you*. Did she? And did he honour the divine in her? Because if they did then they were already in love. Love of the kind one stranger should ideally have for any other stranger, at the very least. Perhaps love of another kind too. He put the note down and worried the stubble on his chin. All in all, at the best it was a promise of sorts, and at the least it was an artefact of remembrance, from a night already subsided beneath the sands.

Dressing, he went downstairs, and surprised himself by sitting at one of the tables in the Dining Room and ordering breakfast. Guru chortled over this and that, and took his order with no hint of any surprise of his own. As it happened, he had managed to arrive just before the end of Breakfast Time, as stipulated in the Timings posted on the wall, and two or three other guests dawdled over their eggshells and tea-leaves. Mildred sat in the corner, intent over a volume of Aurobindo, but Marco noted that her eyes lifted every now and then, in the direction of Kingston, who sat at the largest table in the centre of the room across his *New Indian Express*, and whose eyes also happened to stray every now and then in her direction. The frailty, the sweet frailty. And when would she finally toss that prodigious tome aside, rush across and kiss him on the mouth, and he cast down his newspaper and kiss her with equal abandon? Another disconcerting thought, because it posed the question of when would he throw down his own newspaper? Right now, he answered, readily. I would throw it down right now if Julia were to come into the room. I would leap up from my chair and kiss her. And again he thought, my god, perhaps I love her.

It was this thought, and others akin to it, that he took with him on his strolling of the Pondicherry streets that day, during which he considered, of all things, taking to the road himself and trying to catch up with her. She only had a day's start, and despite the fact that India was a definitively big place, there was a fair chance he would find her along the way, in some traveller's hotel or tourist cafe. But, returning to the Sea View in the tawny light, accepting his key with a half-nodded greeting from the Manager behind his counter, and making his way through the Sitting Room where the old Indian couple read as if they always had occupied that particular pair of chairs, he resolved not to go after her, not so much because he did not want to, but because to do so would subtly risk everything that might ultimately happen between them. Either of them as pursuer or pursued was not how this could be.

Sitting in the Dining Room for tea before mounting the stairs, he wondered whether he wasn't being foolish about this anyway. They had known each other for mere days, spent one night together. It all might mean nothing, as these things usually did, *trust* or no *trust*. And perhaps it would be better if it did, considering his track record. Or was there still youth enough left in him to hope?

Immersed in this, he raised his cup to sip, when he experienced, almost with shock, the realisation that there were strangers in the room. A spry, elderly woman in jeans sat on the far side by the window, looking out at the garden. And at the next table, a young man, blond dreadlocks tied up in a red bandanna, digested his *Solo Soles*. They were the new residents, of Rooms Six and Eight. And that was how you knew you would die one day, that someone could take your room and live in it as though you never had been.

The bus lolloped down the red dirt road skirting the temple ruins, banana groves and a boulder range, and halted just outside the village of Hampi. Julia hefted her pack and walked in the desert-dry heat up and over the rocky hill which parted the bus stand from the village proper. As she approached she saw the high *gopuram* of the Hampi Temple rearing up like a gargoyled pyramid from the burnt orange plain, which was scattered with the vast spread of ruins of the Kingdom of Vijayanagar.

The Hampi bazaar was a dirt strip of cheap hotels, cafes and souvenir stands for tourists and pilgrims from all over India. Passing beyond it, she entered a shady thoroughfare paved with a jigsaw of flagstones, a lane of bald-faced houses whitewashed for the most part, but the odd one peppermint green, pale blue, siena. A sleeping dog attended each stoop, beside a chalk-drawn lotus that would be worn away by the feet of the day. Crows watched from roof terraces and monkeys chewed on filched sticks of sugarcane and tossed the ends down. Women observed her passing from their meshed windows, giggles behind shy hands. Children played cricket with a stick of firewood for a bat. Two or three tiny ones ran up crying out for 'one pen, one pen!'

Hampi was all sub-single star, and her room that night was a cell with barred windows and an anorexic mattress on a concrete floor. A dandruff of limewash dusted down from the walls. The other guests were French and German, hippies who were not hippies the second or third time around, but prototype hippies from the sixties who'd never made it back to their office jobs in Munich and Lyons, and now excelled at doing nothing.

Her sleep was deep and dreamless, a well-tired traveller's sleep, and when she awoke she was unsure at first where she was. A strange and lovely music floated in on the early morning air. She realised it must be coming from the temple, rousing the pilgrims who had slept the night in its courtyards and sending them shivering into the chill so the temple could be swept out and *puja* begun. She lay on her back listening to the music. It was jingly as mid-seventies pop, yet also classical, Vedic, genetic. She listened contentedly, an old cotton blanket pulled around her, as dawn sketched the cell bars of her window.

She took the track through the red boulder ridges out to the ruins of the Vittali Temple. It passed through a peculiar landscape, something like New Mexico to her eyes, or the Bedrock of the Flintstones. Boulders the size of apartment blocks were shunted together into winding ridges and red pyramidal hills. Aromatic herbs flourished by the wayside, as did *sadhus*, beggars, chai stands and *ganja* hawkers. Herds of piebald goats strutted through the rushes by the river, marshalled by goatherds with their whistles and whoops.

The Vittali Temple manifested itself at the top of a rise above the river. Julia entered the serene enclosure through a massive stone gate, and submitted to the guidance of a young local, who demonstrated the various tonal properties of the pillars of the Music Temple. The stone pillars parted at human height into a lace of narrow columns, and as Julia listened, ear pressed against a column, the guide tapped another nearby so that she variously heard the sounds of a tabla drum, a bell, trickling water.

He was creating this last sound with a rapid drumming of his fingers when Julia became aware of another person at an adjoining pillar, listening in and sighing audibly. Looking up, she recognised an Indian woman she had seen reading a hardback book in the cafe at breakfast.

'Beautiful, isn't it.'

'Yes, but sad also,' the woman replied, pointing to a defaced figure on a column. 'They were very thorough, the Muslims. See how they chiselled away the faces of the goddesses, hacked off their breasts, cut out their eyes. They even broke off the trunks of the carved elephants, the beautiful Ganeshas.' Julia ran her hand across the wounds in stone, as if almost expecting still to feel the violation. 'There were so many temples here that the Muslims chained elephants together and charged them right through,' the woman continued. 'Imagine that, herds of elephants charging through fields of temples, levelling them.'

She was tall and graceful in an azure blue sari, with a fineness of shoulder and elegance of bone that extended to the tips of her fingers. Her every word was chosen with the care of fruit by a seasoned picker. That English could be uttered with such clarity, such beauty, Julia marvelled. Where she came from it was humbled to a mumble. The smile was both warm and courteous, but with a hint of wistfulness too, as of something carried within. And noticing a certain roundness in the woman's abdomen, Julia wondered if she was not doing just that. They exchanged a few more words and the woman took her leave, to rejoin a man who waited in the temple courtyard.

That evening Julia ate at an open-air cafe where diners dangled their toes in the cool sandy floor. The Indian woman was also dining there, with the man who turned out to be her husband, and they invited Julia to join them at their table. Dorothy Mukerjee was twenty-nine years old, a lecturer in English literature at a university in Calcutta. Cyril was two years older. He was a compact man in the polo shirt and blue jeans of the Indian middle class, funky retro round-framed spectacles, longish hair oiled and parted, and possessed a curious gaze and bemused lips. Like Dorothy, his speech was impeccably articulated, giving each word the feel of informed candour. The white card he placed before Julia said he was a senior master at an Anglican boys school in Calcutta. Now that Dorothy was expecting their first child, they had decided to take advantage of term holidays for what would probably be their last proper break for some years.

He sipped his beer, and Dorothy picked up the thread. Theirs had been a 'love match'. They came from Christian families – their eyes had met across the pews. Dorothy's family had opposed the marriage, but she had been persistent, refusing all other suits they had attempted to contrive, and saying that unless they wanted her to end up an old maid they had jolly well better let her marry Cyril. She had finally done so in Saint Paul's Cathedral in Calcutta. They had now been married two years.

'And you, Julia. Are you married?'

'Yes. But we're not really together any more.'

The Mukerjees gently inclined their heads. 'I am sorry to hear that,' Cyril said.

'It's alright. I'm quite alright,' Julia said, but a fraction too quickly, then somehow felt compelled to add: 'We're not completely apart either.'

After dinner Dorothy suggested a stroll around the bazaar. 'The village is beautiful at night. The dark alleyways with cows kneeling in the straw asleep. It strikes me as so Biblical.'

The little tour ended with them escorting her to her door. As they parted, Dorothy handed her a book which Julia recognised as the one she had seen her reading that morning.

'I'm sure you would find it of use. It contains all the information one could ever require on Vijayanagar and its history, which was why I had all those little details at my fingertips when I met you out at the temple.'

By the illumination of a candle Julia arranged her mineral water, bottle and torch within easy reach, re-settled her sheet and blankets, and undressed. She was about to blow out the candle when she noticed the book. It was cheaply printed, its typeface rough, the paper yellowed and brittle. The battered cover gave it the careworn appearance of books found at street markets, beaten up and neglected because they were not valued, because what resided between the covers was not considered worthy of respect. Through no fault of its own, it went unloved down the tedium of its unread years, a melancholic old before its time.

The book was an account of a visit to the Kingdom of Vijayanagar by a Portuguese traveller called Domingos Paes, in 1520. It looked intriguing, promising a wealth of detail about the place and its history. And although she was too tired to read, after she extinguished the candle her mind ranged away through the deserted ruins, once a domain of prosperity, order, of love. She wandered through it like an archaelogist, wide-eyed, stunned that something so powerful and beautiful could have been laid waste. Now she was alone in a cell, out where the desert dogs howled. A colossal ruin lay at her feet.

It was past midday, and ordinarily by then Marco would have been well out of the sun, but today he had broken the return journey from the cafe and remained some minutes seated on the concrete sea-wall of the promenade, across the road from the guesthouse.

A girl walked by, a tourist. She looked nothing like Julia, but somehow her age, or something of her carriage, recalled her. Julia walking somewhere, watched by male eyes. It made him feel oddly jealous. He tried to think of another woman, to dispel Julia. That one walking away from him, who was she? Was she staying at the Sea View? Was she French, American, Irish? He attempted to go with her mentally, step by step. But unlike Julia, she didn't sustain. Instead, a random memory came up, of a tower block apartment in Singapore. His wife, Margaret. Her petite waist, draped with a Thai silk. Her penchant for shades of dusk, rainforest, ocean. When she kissed him her lips compressed a little as if whistling, keeping him out. He always wondered why she did that, when in all other ways she was undeniably his. Or was she merely compliant, just as she was compliant with the craven new world, the Singapore of Mr Lee, with her desk job and credit cards, her accounts with the Orchard Road stores. Her only resistance being a phrase she uttered once or twice, in its unexpectedness almost shocking though: *Singapore is the bland face of fascism. And more bland than fascist,* she would add, extending the horizon of the homily. These foolish things, Marco thought, somehow remind me of you, Margaret, as the tourist girl slipped off into the penumbra of midday. What remained of Margaret now but a momentary memory, prompted by the passing of a narrow-waisted girl, the petiteness of a stranger? And the divorce papers he kept in a drawer with all his other paper detritus.

He turned to the face of the Sea View, silhouetted in white midday light behind him. He saw the little sign on the gatepost, the courtyard within, and above it the balcony of his room. He realised that he and Julia had not been out there. They might have stood at the railing, breathed in the sea air together there, but they had not, would not now, ever. How ridiculous, preposterous, that they would not.

He turned irritated from the Sea View, looked north up the wall, and noticed Dwight on his spot not far along, seated on his little magic carpet of tufted spiny grass, transported to who knew where? To oblivion, white noise? Was that all he needed now, nothingness? A refugee from all that was, from all that was something. From a wife he had lost, children he had lost, an existence that had slid from his grasp. Or was he just insane?

Marco tried to imagine Dwight back in Iowa, if indeed the stories were true and he was from Iowa. Marco didn't even know where the story about Dwight had come from. Who had told it to him? Kingston? It must have been Kingston. Who else could it have been? Or had the story just sprouted spontaneously from the walls of the Sea View, spread like mould, or one of those wall-stains that looked so like a map of the moon. *Mare Imbrium. Mare Serenitatis. Mare Tranquilitatis.* Sea of Rain, of Serenity, of Tranquillity. No, it must have been Kingston. But who had told Kingston? Dwight? As far as he knew, Dwight had never spoken to anyone. But he must have spoken to the Manager though, to obtain his room, and to keep it. Was it the Manager himself who had created the legend of Dwight, the refugee of America? But then the Manager hardly spoke to anyone either. It was much a community of silence, or whispers at least, the Sea View.

Marco considered the profile of Dwight, perfectly still, staring out to sea. Etched into the print of the moment against the white sky, the spindly figures of walkers on the promenade, the trundling by of an Ambassador, the beggar, the boy, the wind off the Bay that harried the scraggy trees, Dwight's head was shiny bald, a celestial dome. Inside were stored all the little joys and profound sadnesses that made him what he was, that had led him here. A man who had knotted his tie and belted his pants, drove a car and raised a family, whacked a baseball, voted for presidents; and who now did very close to exactly nothing, give or take Heisenberg.

Marco tried to imagine him otherwise. As the deserted husband, the husk of the man who still worked on at his desk in an office in, where would it be, Des Moines? Was there any other place in Iowa but Des Moines? And if he didn't work at his desk any more, if he'd left town and job, he might be in Chicago by now. Living in a boarding house, perhaps. Men in middle age lived in fear of the boarding house. The cubicle room with bare bulb and iron bed, the lone chair and the bedside table pocked from butt-ends. The piss and ammonia smell of regret. The single room of refuge to which they had repaired with a half-empty suitcase. But in the end, Marco wondered, was it so different to be living in an Indian guesthouse than in a flypaper hotel in Chicago? A drain smelt pretty much the same, wherever it was.

There were three such men in the Sea View, men who might well fear the boarding house. Dwight, Kingston – and himself. All of them well past the time of their wives, of families. All of them doing nothing. The three Magi, drawn to the same star? No, the Three Stooges. Three Blind Mice, in a boarding house made acceptable merely by the mystique of India. Here they were not lonely men of middle age, marooned in rented rooms by elevated railways above bottle-shard alleys. No, here they were foreigners, intriguing misfits living in a hotel in India, and, the casual enquirer might imagine, perhaps engaged in worthy work, or some suitably recondite philosophical inquiry.

Marco could only smile at the disingenuousness of his own rhetoric.

His eyes had all the while remained upon Dwight. The man did not move. What kind of pain must he be in, for it to need to be assuaged by a ceaseless contemplation of the motion of waves? Should he perhaps walk over, speak with him? Or would that upset him, interfere? And what, too, of his little speech to Julia, about the doing of a good deed?

Marco strained to peer more closely. In profile, Dwight's face looked relaxed, no visible hint of pain. Was he crippled with it, or, perhaps, beyond it? He might even be happy. Not probable, but it was possible. The thought struck Marco as near comical. That the goal of Dwight's loop-tape meditation was release from woe – and that his active doing of nothing might in the end actually yield that, bring happiness. If so, as a means of dealing with the fool's mate of existence, doing nothing was demonstrably superior to selling carbon futures, software, or gold taps (which never seemed to make anyone happy). If the relaxation in the face did reflect a peace within, then Dwight had done well. If the mythology was true and what had reputedly happened had happened, then Dwight had made the right choice in fleeing Des Moines after his wife decamped, fleeing America to spend his days here, staring out at the Bay of Bengal.

The thought encouraged Marco, made him feel there was perhaps something he himself could do, that he should. But what, and how? It perplexed him. Then it annoyed. So much wasted, on grand inconsequentialities. How many neurone bulbs were always lighting up one's mental sky without purpose, fatuous as the fluorescent hoardings of a city? So much thought wasted, so much angst, so much energy. He wished it could somehow be otherwise, but knew better.

The sun was strong on his head. It was certainly time to go indoors. The book awaited in his room, but he could not go on reading it forever. Crossing the road, he thought of Julia, somewhere across the unimagined miles of his India.

There was a child of twelve who hung around the cafe, a boy crippled in both legs who would spend his life scampering on his hands like a crab. But despite his disability, Dilip was happy and bright, and amazingly adult. He came from a village to the north of Hampi where his father made glass bangles. But the bangle business had gone bad, and Dilip's was a big family, and so at the age of ten he had taken a bus alone down to Hampi where he lived a beggar's life, cadging rupees in the bazaar. The owner of the cafe took pity on him and let him hang around the place chatting with the tourists through the day, and eating with the staff when they closed up at night. Sometimes the tourists would give him a present when they left. A German couple had left him his prized possession, the Lufthansa travel blanket in which he slept each night in a corner of the cafe's earthen floor.

'Do you ever go to school?' Julia asked at breakfast.

'No school,' he said with defiance. 'The boys laugh. The teacher beat me like this.' He made a whacking action in the air, his features quickened with the anger he was enacting. Then Julia's food arrived, and he excused himself. 'I go now.'

'You're not hungry?'

'I already eat! I'm full.'

'Let me order you something.'

He shook his head. 'You want come catch fish with me today? Down by the river? The big rocks – I meet you there!'

'I don't know how to fish.'

'I show you! It's easy!' Then he scampered off on his hands to another table where a new group had just installed themselves, and was instantly absorbed amusing them.

Dorothy turned up at that moment, and mentioned she was going into Hospet to buy toiletries. Julia realised she had run out of just about everything herself, and they agreed to join up on the expedition.

Over veg cutlets and stuffed *parathas* in Hospet, Julia learned that Dorothy had studied in America, and had enjoyed it. Despite some misgivings, largely to do with over-consumption, Dorothy nonetheless liked the fact that everyone in America was a discrete citizen in a civic state, even if the politicians were constantly putting their hands on their hearts and invoking God. It was liberating after India, which was meant to be a non-sectarian state too, but was more a confluence of sects running side by side, sometimes with tolerance, sometimes in conflict, occasionally even in harmony. But, she said, India's character, no matter what the post-Gandhians might say, was essentially religious sectarian, and this coloured everything.

There was something else she liked a lot about America: the anonymity. In India there was a terrible feeling on the streets that one knew everyone and all knew each other's business. Perhaps it was just the cycle of karma, she said with a smile, but there was a feeling in India that the same faces went round and round, that you saw them coming at you again and again. America was the reverse. On the street there you felt you were seeing faces you had never seen before and never would again, of people who would not remember you or a single detail about you as you passed them by. It was as if America was two immensely long queues rushing by each other, not pausing to take in a single face. Some people found this alienating, but for her it was a refreshing freedom.

They chatted into the afternoon, by which time Julia realised yet another day was passing with her in neglect of her duty (she still had to go fishing with Dilip) and that if she was going to continue on her way in the next day or so she would have to get moving on the fine detail of Hampi.

On the way back out to the village, Julia flicked through some postcards she had bought, garish pictures of gods and Bollywood film stars, 'almost interchangeable in the Indian mind', Dorothy quipped. Julia was choosing which to send to Tim, and which to Marco (she had been intending to write to him ever since leaving Pondicherry) when Dorothy peered over her shoulder and teased: 'A goddess for your husband, a starlet for your beau? Or is it the other way round?'

A hard reflected blue topped the river as she picked her way down the track passing sheep and goats, and the *dhobis* who alternately dipped and pounded laundry at the hewn stone *ghats*. She found Dilip in the crevice of a granite boulder, sheltering from the afternoon sun. His legs were neatly folded beneath his tiny body, and a long stalk of cane with fishing line attached nestled in the crook of his slender arm.

Perspiring from the walk, Julia sat down gratefully in the shade beside him, took off her sun hat and dangled her feet just above the waterline. 'Caught any yet?'

He conjured two stubby black fish from a hessian bag. 'Good fish. Now you.'

He handed over his cane-stalk rod, and watched as she dipped the hook and stone sinker in the water, and the line cut the river's dark current. The afternoon had passed its zenith, and the day felt easier. As they sat side by side, Julia's thoughts drifted up into the sky, down to the river bottom, off into the distant hills, and she delivered herself up to something like contemplative peace.

'You like Hampi?' Dilip spoke up, eyes on the line.

'Very much.'

His eyes followed hers to the blue and orange horizon. 'This is the most beautiful place,' he murmured. 'The most beautiful.'

'Yes,' she said, turning to look at him. 'You're lucky to live here.'

But her words came out sounding not quite right, and as she spoke she glanced involuntarily in the direction of his shrivelled legs.

He took it in with an adult shrug. 'My mother, she did not know about polio. She did not have school. My brothers and sisters, no injection.'

'How many do you have?'

'Nine. But I was the only one sick.'

'Where are the others?'

'With my father and mother. Only me here.'

'Do you see your family much?'

'Sometime. But most time I stay here.'

'Do you miss them?'

'Miss?'

'Wish you could be with them?'

'Not too much.'

But she suspected otherwise, and put her arm around him. He accepted it momentarily, then eased himself free. They sat through the rest of a perfectly lost and found afternoon, line dangled in the water, without a single bite.

Over dinner that night she told Cyril and Dorothy about fishing with Dilip, and what he had told her about his life.

'Overpopulation,' Cyril stated. 'People are still having too many children, and they cannot even take care of those they have.'

'Surely then there must be an enormous crisis coming here,' Julia said.

'With one billion of us, yes of course a crisis is coming. But that is nothing new for us. India is crisis incarnate.'

'But can't the government do anything? Like the Chinese are doing?'

'India is a democracy. And it is not an easy thing to get people to vote against having children.'

'But surely tax incentives, something like that, to discourage people from having so many.'

'A sound idea, but no party proposing it would ever be elected. You see, lack of education, that is the true villain. Out in the villages they don't even know which century it is. Illiteracy. They would have no idea what their having nine or ten children is doing to our country.'

'This is why we are campaigning,' Dorothy interceded, 'for education.'

'Campaigning politically?'

'Yes. At home in Calcutta we organise protests and such, collect petitions and lobby ministers, to try to get the government to raise the standard of education. To spend more of our tax revenues on educating our children instead of blowing them up in silly atom bombs.'

'Do you have much support?'

'Some, yes,' she said. 'But there are still great challenges for us to overcome. It will be a long struggle if we are to achieve our goal.' She paused. When she spoke again, her voice was softened. 'The tragedy of Dilip is the tragedy of our nation. That our children are uneducated. That they are left to fend for themselves, to sleep in the corners of cafes, live in rubbish tips, die in the gutters.'

Dorothy looked away. Julia saw Cyril rest his hand upon hers.

No-one spoke for a few moments.

'Julia,' Cyril resumed, 'we are continuing down to Bangalore and Mysore tomorrow. And we were wondering if you would you like to travel with us, if you are ready to move on?'

Lying in her bed that night, she realised that Dilip, and Dorothy and Cyril, were her first real Indian friends in so many years of travel. Yes, there had been agents, connections, trusted local people. She and Tim had stayed with them. They had dined together, drunk together. But they had remained contacts in the business of travel. They had never been friendships acquired via the simple ease felt with like-minded people, and real affection blossoming from there. Why was that? Because she and Tim had comprised such a close unit they hadn't needed to submit to any real intimacy with others? Or was it deeper than that, to do with their relationship with India itself?

Two nights later they were farewelled by Dilip at the guesthouse gates, where a taxi had drawn up to take them into Hospet for the night train. They took turns bending down before him to allow him to bestow sweet-smelling garlands of pink and white jasmine around their necks. Then they presented him with their own parting gifts, a floppy cricket hat, a toothbrush and toothpaste, and money, before kissing him farewell on his throne of hay scattered on a small rise of dark earth, beside a slowly scratching dog.

Julia and Dorothy lay in the top bunks of the darkened Ladies Only compartment of the train south, speaking softly so as not to wake the other occupants. Words swished from side to side of the carriage, a whispered exchange of small intimacies, until Dorothy said she had to sleep. After she did so, Julia lay awake a little longer, looking out over the dark profile of the land, and at the occasional station flashing by, awash with amber light.

The end of the cigarette lit up cherry red as Josh sucked. He was sitting at a table on the beach drinking beer and watching the world go by. He held it in a half moment and then let it go, the smoke kissing his lips as it went out in a long slow wraith. He wondered if he would smoke when he got back home. No. Smokers in America were lower than lepers in India. But still it might be funny to do it just for a minute, get around in one of those skin-tight T-shirts with a softpack of Marlboro bulged up in the sleeve. Smoking was so absolutely Bad Boy low-life. He enjoyed that. But really, it was just his Indian trip thing. He'd toss the last pack in the trash at the airport on his way out. Unless he was already addicted, he thought, realising how many he was smoking a day. The smoking doctor. The nice young Jewish doctor with his cigarettes in the bottom drawer. The picture perversely amused him. But he knew it wouldn't really happen.

It was happy hour in the bars on the beach, and the whole world was going by his chair. Girls, mostly. Sometimes it felt appropriate just to sit back and realise how many girls there were in the world. Parading by in their twos and threes, giggling at something, in their halter tops and skimpy shorts, their see-through hippie shirts and wraparound skirts, their navel rings and pierced eyebrows and pierced God only knows what else. An endless line of them, passing right by in front of him like it was a fashion parade, or a slave market, and there was the feeling in the palmy air that all he had to do was stick out his finger and touch one of them on her sun-gold shoulder, and she'd be his for the night. But that was the beer's idea: he'd passed the Five mark now and was about to enter the foggy outlands of the Six and Beyond.

Almost on cue the waiter brought him Number Six and uncapped it. He picked it up and sucked the froth from the mouth, tasted the first of its chill sweet bitterness. It tasted so good he thought he could drink another six of them tonight, maybe another six after that. That was the thing about beer, it invited you to drink more because it seemed so benign, a friend more than a drink, a good-natured dog that would never bite. Somehow you always forgot it did.

More girls were coming along now, on their way to the discos and bars further up the beach, girls with such smooth skin and flat brown bellies, girls with long legs and clear eyes. So many girls, petals out and sweet with nectar, waiting for a bee. Then a solo girl came by, with perfect tits in a nothing top and little black lycra something, a tiny young one that made you feel like a paedophile for looking, but that was what she wanted anyway, while pretending she didn't if you looked too hard. He must have been looking hard because she looked back at him, and for a moment he thought she might be about to smile, but she laughed out loud saying something like 'hey, you're really drunk, man', and walked on by.

She was right but he didn't care. Tomorrow he would, but that was tomorrow. For now his thinking was confined to the girl disappearing into the darkness, and if maybe he shouldn't go after her and try some line even though what she'd said was true and he probably was too far gone to make anything of it (beyond a fool of himself). But he kept on thinking about her, and somehow she took him back to Lakshmi, that fleeting moment of his triumph before it all went to shit. If only the stupid girl hadn't left the door open that little bit, they would have made it. But she did, and they hadn't, and what happened happened. And now here he was getting drunk on Kovalum beach, watching the girls go by, wafting away into the darkness. And where was his dream now, the one of being the medical servant of the poor across the blighted continents of the earth? That felt like it had been dreamed by someone else, a former resident of his psyche, long moved on. Had he been serious? The idea made him want to laugh, and he did, spluttering beer and coughing. He was pathetic, weak and stupid and corrupt, he didn't even deserve to dream a dream like that. He was a jerk watching girls from a bar while he got himself drunk. This was where his great Indian mission had ended, at the end of India, the last table on the last stretch of sand, with the last of his illusions oozing away through the cracks in the table.

He felt for another cigarette but they were all gone. Probably just as well. Then he signalled the waiter for a new pack. It came on a tin platter with a box of matches, along with Number Seven. He lit up and inhaled, sucked on the beer and watched the girls. Jesus, he thought, apropos of God only knew what, maybe I'm gay. Or am I just drunk? No, sure as fuck I'm drunk. The rest I'll leave to another day.

The sandalwood-scented taxi was taking them out to the Lalitha Mahal Palace, former residence of the Maharaja of Mysore, now converted into a five star hotel. Julia had treated her hair Indian-style, coconut oil before the wash. She wore a mirrored and sequined Gujarati dress bought back in Bangalore. On her feet were purple satin slingbacks from the Shoe Museum, a tiny shopfront off K.R. Circle in the centre of Mysore. Dorothy had also dressed for the occasion, in her best *salwar kameez*, and Cyril had stretched to a jacket and tie.

They sat together on the back seat as the taxi glided through the balmy night out beyond the lights of Mysore, skirting the dark bluff of Chaumundi Hill, the thousand-step pilgrimage to the summit lit with tiny silver lamps. The palace appeared like a white ocean liner on the dark horizon, its domes and turrets outlined with lights, the gardens draped with fairy lamps, the front entrance a rose red glow.

In the style of everything owned by the Mysore maharajas, the hotel was exquisite to the last detail, from its marble entrance to its breezy hallways, its understated grace and charm. The dining room was immense, blue and white enamel like a giant Wedgwood sea-shell, the ceiling capped with illuminated stained-glass domes. There were few other diners beyond a package tour of Germans in a far corner, and it felt as though they had the palace to themselves. They dined on aromatic fish and turbulent green creamed spinach while a flute and tabla duo played on a podium.

'Come in for tea,' Cyril suggested, as they climbed the stairs back at the hotel. He slipped the key into their lock and opened the door. Dorothy lit a pair of candles and switched on an electric jug while Julia and Cyril settled onto the couch before the window.

The couple's room overlooked a disused mansion, Italianate-looking, gone to seed, its green shutters closed up and faded, walls peeling a shrivelled skin of yellow paint, pavilions collapsing, colonnades crumbled to pillars and rubble. But somehow the grounds remained tended, the grass blackened in patches from recent burning off. There were watered beds of red coleus, and groves of young palms surrounding an ornamental fountain, a miniature Eros, still working. That afternoon from her own window Julia had watched kites drifting, circling over the mansion, swooping now and then on unseen prey while a solitary groundsman trudged through the scene in the sun, head down and hoe over his shoulder.

'This will probably sound funny, but Mysore feels very Australian to me,' Julia said. 'All this lovely dry and dusty green everywhere. I feel quite at home. Almost homesick, in fact.'

Dorothy smiled, and poured steaming water into a teapot and set it down beside three cups while Cyril opened the windows wide. The night outside was deep and solid. The distant beating of wings, of the thousands of bats which nightly traversed the sky over Mysore, reached their ears. Julia felt her head being gently coaxed into Dorothy's lap, and her fingers running through her hair while Cyril sipped his tea and gazed out.

'Do you know,' Dorothy said softly, 'that in Delhi the red traffic lights illuminate the word *Relax*?'

Julia blinked up. 'No!'

'It's true!'

Still smiling, Julia allowed her head to sink back. 'I love my hair being stroked.'

Dorothy's fingers expertly massaged the scalp. 'Rest, rest, that is what we all crave. Life, it is so tiring, and we need to rest so much, but we never do.' Her voice continued on, almost hypnotically, tuneful to Julia's ear, while Cyril remained silent. 'Don't worry about him – he always drifts off at this time, like clockwork.' And looking more closely, Julia saw his eyes were closed, and his chest rose and fell in an even rhythm.

'Did you write to your beau?' Dorothy asked.

'Yes.'

'Will he write back?'

'If I had an address he might.'

'You didn't give him a poste-restante address?'

'No,' Julia said.

'Bio-feedback,' Dorothy chuckled.

'What?'

'By that I mean, sometimes we become so confused in life that we do not know how we feel from our thoughts alone. We can only observe how we act, to know how we feel.'

'And what do you take from that?' Julia sighed, as the fingers rippled across her scalp.

'What do *you* take from it?' Dorothy replied.
'That I still love my husband?'
'Something like that.'

Dorothy's fingers moved down to massage Julia's temples, and they shared a smile: Cyril was softly snoring.

11

The minibus traversed a quilt of green rice, red earth and golden stubble. Julia looked out the window towards the profile of the Nilgiris Mountains. They were leaving the flatlands of Karnataka, climbing away from Mysore towards their destination, the town of Ootacamund, at the summit of those watercolour blue mountains. She had been sat beside a honeymooning couple who crooned love tunes from masala movies to each other. Dorothy and Cyril had been placed in the seats behind. Julia's eyes followed a passing train of bullock carts, strayed to the tufts of aloe and cactus by the roadside, lost focus. She dozed.

As the early morning warmed, the bus stopped at a wayside place for chai, *iddli* and *uttapam*, cooked up on a griddle with chilli and sweet red onions. Then they were moving again, on through the Bandipur Wildlife Reserve, where wild elephants and even the odd tiger were said to survive. But it looked a scrubby and inhospitable place to her. She saw peacocks, a lone spotted deer, and a pair of elephants strolling through the brush, which reminded her of East Africa, and its flat-topped thorn trees. She and Tim had spent a year out there, in Kenya working as tour guides. This was early on, after their London stint. She shuddered to recall the airless grey cubbyhole where she had earned the money to travel, temping off Tottenham Court Road.

She must have dozed, because she was woken by a strange waft reaching her nose. It was the scent of pine, clean and sharp, almost intoxicating to nostrils habituated to the tropics and their ever-ambient spice and dung. Ahead, around the last hairpin bend up the Nilgiris slopes, were groves of pines tall as Norfolks, and at their feet the manicured green hedges of tea. There were also forests of eucalypts, bearing another shocking smell — home. That brought back Dorothy's comments from the night before. What she had said was true. Julia had not given any contact details to Marco. Because in many ways he was just a repetition of the other men she had been with since Tim. And no matter how she might romance the idea of being with them, the bio-feedback of it (as Dorothy would have put it) was that she had made little effort with any of them. Why did she still so clearly see that girl's dropped earring on the floor in Lavender Bay? And why, if she did not still love Tim, could she not love any other man? The truth of it had to be she still loved him. But if she did not want to act upon it, she had to make a break, a complete break, end this half life.

Tim wouldn't do it himself. Men tended to be trouble-avoiders. They would happily let things drift on, tolerating an accumulation of complications rather than making a decisive move. In some ways it might even suit Tim to know in his heart that Julia still loved him more than any other man. There was after all a great security in that love, because now he was free to pursue whichever Emmas and Rebeccas he wished, while knowing that in a crisis Julia would still be there for him. As she had been when he called and pleaded with her to come here, which was why she sat in this bus seat now and thought this thought. It was bad, very bad, and the more she looked at it the worse it got. There was only one thing for it – she would have to be the decisive one. So she made a pact with herself. She would not leave Ooty until things had been decided. She would either plead with Tim for them to get back together, or she would split from him for good.

They passed a cold, slate-coloured lake and skirted a cemetery studded with brightly coloured wooden crosses, the candy hues of Hinduism painted over the asceticism of Christianity. Cyril leaned forward: 'There are many Christians in these mountains. The missionaries preferred cooler climes, you see. Are you a Christian, Julia?'

Julia swivelled in her seat. Dorothy dozed in the window seat by Cyril's side, her head lolling on his shoulder. 'Culturally I suppose I am, yes. But personally, no.'

'Do you believe in reincarnation?'

'I don't know. I think it's impossible to prove either way.'

'On a scientific level, yes of course, what you say is true,' he said. 'But when I meditate, I feel closer to a belief in it. And that conflicts with my Christian beliefs, and with my positivism. Do you ever experience conflicts like that? Things that run counter to your Western positivism?'

The bus breasted the last rise, and motored smoothly towards the town of Ooty.

'Well, there are times when I visit a place and I feel I've been there before. That kind of thing. I often get that feeling here in India. But I don't know if it's just my imagination.'

'Have you ever meditated, or practised yoga?'

'I do yoga, but not near often enough. What about you?'

'Once upon a time I did. But as you can well appreciate, I am very busy these days with my duties at the school. Besides, back at home in Calcutta our campaign work takes up all our free time.'

'You must tell me about that,' she said. 'I'd like to know more.'

The bus pulled up in the main street. It looked chilly outside. Cyril dug into a bag and handed her a blanket. 'Here, Julia, you will be needing this.'

In the rarified blue of afternoon she was in the Ootacamund Botanical Gardens, a meticulous diagram of trees, flower beds, lakes and pergolas. Within its flowered borders a calm abided, not a lorry to be heard, not a single klaxon quack. She sat in the Edwardian conservatory where flowers tumbled ceiling to floor, luscious white cyclamens and pink begonias, cascading chains of hearts and poor man's orchids: a Tamil Sissinghurst of sorts.

Later, she stretched out on the clipped grass and stared up into the sky. What was she doing here? And what would she do when she had finished what she was doing? At least there was refuge in the praxis of the moment. But after that moment, when she left India, returned to Australia, what? She felt cut adrift from everyone, everything. But then, curiously enough, at the same time there was a slowly growing feeling of satisfaction – the germination of something like 'belonging'. Knowing the Mukerjees, she felt a strengthening bond with their country. But what did that mean, really? How could she ever 'belong' here? She was Australian, not Indian. She had almost started to feel she could not belong in any place, only journey through it.

'Go to sleep you weary hobo, let the towns drift slowly by,' she sang, watching the sky film with silken grey cloud. The day was acquiring a frown. 'Can't you hear the steel rail humming? That's the Hobo's Lullaby.'

Because of an unexplained, unseasonal rush on hotel rooms, they had ended up in different places. The guesthouse the rickshaw driver took Julia to that evening was a shabby, yellowing place, the room the Mukerjees occupied cold and bare. The essential fixture it did possess was a fireplace, and when she arrived Cyril was stoking up a pyre of logs and pine cones to hold back the deep chill coming down off the mountain.

Dinner comprised a medley of curries and side-dishes brought in and consumed at a leisurely pace, and the fire was glowing coals and the hour well advanced when the conversation arrived at the work the Mukerjees were involved in, and Julia again expressed an interest in hearing more about it.

Cyril fixed a new log into place, flames shooting up as the frayed hem of bark met red coals, and had just cleared his throat to reply when Julia experienced a momentary giddiness, and had to steady herself on the arm of her chair.

Dorothy saw it happen. 'Are you alright, Julia?'

'I think so,' she said, clutching onto the chair still. Cyril squatted down before her. 'Are you sure?'

'Yes, I'm fine now.'

'Perhaps you could do with some air,' Dorothy said. 'It can get very airless in this room with the fire going.'

'Yes, why don't we take a stroll?' Cyril agreed. 'The town is most picturesque at night, and the air is crisp and clear.'

'But it's very cold out. Won't that bother you, Dorothy?'

'My baby you mean? Don't worry, she is very snug and warm where she is. For a few more months anyway.'

She located Julia's blanket and wrapped it around her shoulders. They walked down the gloomy corridor and out into the night, and started climbing the pine-studded hillside behind the guesthouse, the well-worn pathway illuminated by starlight.

'We always try to walk after supper,' Cyril said. 'It is most beneficial for the blood, and the circulation.'

As they continued up, breathing more heavily as the slope steepened, clouds of condensation issuing from them, Cyril strode a pace or two ahead.

'Feeling better?' Dorothy asked Julia.

'Much, thank you. I don't know what came over me.'

'Lack of oxygen, I would say. So much better to be outside.'

They reached a clearing at the crest of the hill, and stood getting their breath back and surveying the town below. In the icy thin air its lights glimmered up sharply.

'People will always tell you it was once a very pretty town, Ooty,' Cyril said.

'It still is, don't you think?' Julia replied.

'I do. But these same people will tell you it isn't anything like the quaint colonial gem it once was. With its churches and steeples, and its efficient English post office.' He pointed out a darkened section of ground, a kidney-shaped stain in the earth, beside the main commercial area of town. 'That was the racecourse. The British who came up here for their summers brought horses, and they enjoyed racing the poor beasts and gambling on them.'

'And now they are gone, thank God,' Dorothy said. 'Back to that small cold island from which they descended upon us, like the wolf on the fold.'

'A queer people, the British,' Cyril resumed. 'Even today most of them still see us as living in the shadows of their grand imperial past, pygmies scurrying about in their crumbling white masonry.' He took in a breath, exhaled a ponderous cloud. 'Nowadays of course a lot of Indians say exactly the opposite – which I also find a bit hard to take. To them we are Titans, rising up from the imperial dust. And it's true to say the economy is booming nowadays. Big sums are being made – much of it black money of course, untaxed. Now there is a whole generation for whom Michael Jordan is more of a god than Shiva. To them Gandhi is just a name in dusty old books, something to do with spinning thread. But even this brave new India of ours will still not spend enough to teach its poor to read.'

'But isn't education compulsory?'

'Enshrined in law. For all children. But the government will not allocate the money for the teachers, for the classrooms and the equipment. They won't teach people to read a newspaper — but they'll make damn certain they'll get MTV. And that is why I fear for this new India. I fear we will end up much like anywhere else in the world, only with a hint of mystique, a tinge of saffron. And so many of us still unable to read and write.'

When he stopped speaking, a deeper silence seemed to well up out of the cold valley, from the sleeping township below, over which a pale shroud of foggy haze was coalescing. They watched it gather, as if drawn across the streets and rooftops by unseen tiny hands. Cyril whispered something to Dorothy, and walked a few paces off. 'To smoke,' Dorothy said. 'He knows how much the baby and I disapprove.'

'That's at least considerate of him.'

'He is learning,' Dorothy acceded. 'Julia, what Cyril was saying just then, about India disappearing ... personally, I do not agree with him. I don't believe we will lose our identity. I think the opposite will occur, that India will devour all these foreign fast food places, the banks and cars and computers, and make them Indian. That is how India has always behaved. We take in other influences with enthusiasm. And for a while it appears we will be overwhelmed. But in the end it is India who wins out, India who makes things her own.'

'You mean we can expect a McCurry Soyburger to appear one day?' Julia said.

'Soon,' Dorothy said. 'If it already has not.'

'But, if you don't agree with Cyril, why didn't you say it when he was speaking?'

'You mean, that despite any appearances or chat to the contrary, am I really a subservient Indian woman?'

Julia looked down, shuffled in the cold. 'I'm sorry, I didn't mean it quite like that.'

'No, no. It's quite alright. I held my tongue because you are our guest. And you might also feel free to ask me why we are Christians, Anglicans to boot, when we hold such opinions of the British. That is a fair question too. But to be a good Indian nationalist, must one be Hindu, Muslim, Jain? Many people would say yes. But you see, a faith is a faith, and there is no denying it, wherever it originates from. Besides, it doesn't come from Canterbury. It comes from God.'

Julia shuffled again. Her legs were numbing with cold. 'So, you are at four, or five months?'

'Five, only four to go. And do you know, the funny thing is here we are preaching to all and sundry about education and population control, and now we are having a baby of our own. But we are only having one, only one!' she laughed. 'Honestly!'

'I wanted a child myself,' Julia said, 'very much. But now, to tell you the truth ...'

'Five months ago I felt precisely the same way. I didn't care.

Then the news came, and it shocked us both. You see, it was not expected. But now I want it more than anything.'

'And Cyril?'

'He is if anything even more excited than I am,' Dorothy said. She shivered, and called over to him: 'I'm getting cold now Cyril. Let's go back down, please.'

He set down the tuft of broom, took a Limca from the fridge and popped it all in one motion. His brother occupied the wicker throne their uncle had once sat in, straightening banknotes before counting them.

The younger man took a mouthful of the soft drink. 'The thatch in Seven is letting the rain in. And Four is doing it with Eleven.'

His brother raised half an eyebrow, but did not otherwise divert himself from counting the takings.

'And I think Five will check out tomorrow. Better get full payment from that one tonight.' He settled back into the cane armchair, and drank down another mouthful.

'What makes you think Four and Eleven are doing it?'

The younger man's mouth displayed mild distaste. 'I just changed his sheets. And I saw her swimsuit hanging in his bathroom. Like a fucking trophy.'

'Not really such a trophy,' his brother said.

The young man grinned. 'I couldn't see you turning her away from your door, if she ever got desperate enough to knock.'

The elder brother completed the count and noted the figures

into the columns of the ledger on the table. 'I don't like redheads. Especially ones like her. You know she has a drug problem.'

'Know?' the younger man laughed. 'I know who sells to her, I know what she buys and how much she uses, and what she pays.'

The elder brother looked up. 'And the American?'

'No. But if he's with her, maybe he'll get a taste for it too.'

'I think they would both do well to be very careful.'

'You're getting old,' the younger man said, tossing the empty container into the pile of rubbish in the corner, and taking out a cigarette.

'Don't light that in here.'

The younger man scowled, then shrugged, getting to his feet.

'The American with that one,' his brother said. 'I can't see it. I thought she would be too low for him.'

'He's low enough,' the younger man muttered, going out the door to light up. Then he laughed: 'Though soon I think he'll be getting high.'

A few minutes later Josh came into the office. A woman lingered outside the door, waiting for him.

'Yes?' The young manager did not look up from the page.

'Any fax for me?'

'No.'

The American looked somehow hurt at the news.

'If it is word about money you are waiting for,' the manager said, 'the one thing you can be sure of is that it will always take longer to come than you would wish.'

Josh nodded. He didn't like it. The money should have come a week ago. What the hell was wrong? It wasn't like he asked them for money every day. 'Well, thanks anyway.' He went out, and he and the woman walked away.

The manager looked up, watching them go, and made a mental note to stipulate they start paying their rent in advance.

Julia spent the following day in the cafes and hostels of the town. The guesthouse Cyril and Dorothy were in was on her list, but when she called by they were out, so she left a note thanking them for dinner. Continuing on, it struck her she might not even see them again. She had a rail ticket to Kochi for the following day, and they were returning soon to Bangalore, to fly home to Calcutta. If they missed each other at their hotels, they might not even get to say goodbye. But returning to her hotel in the late afternoon she found Dorothy at the front desk, woollen overcoat neatly folded over her arm, leaving a note of her own. Julia saw the full bloom in her cheeks, the curvature beneath the moon-grey silk of her dress.

Having a little time on their hands, they adjourned to the cafe beside the foyer. The day was overcast and cold, and they took a table embraced by the glow of the corner fire, and watched the first intimation of evening haze the windows. Tea was brought on a dented silver tray by a waiter, his white uniform jacket a noble hodgepodge of rips, frays and brass buttons hanging by a thread. Julia opened the note Dorothy had been in the process of leaving, and saw it was a fond farewell from them. They were starting for home that evening. Reading it, she realised their paths were diverging as quickly as they had converged, and felt saddened.

Over tea, Dorothy asked about her work, and soon Julia was confessing how hard she was finding it to do what she was meant to be doing, and her fast-diminishing interest in the publishing house in general. She had never articulated it quite like that before, but as she spoke it made perfect sense.

'I don't know ... my life, career, whatever, hasn't quite turned out as I wanted,' she found herself saying, 'whereas you and Cyril, you *have* something. You're committed to things. To changing your country. The world. Improving things.'

'You could do that too. Anyone can.'

'But it's such a mess, where do you start?'

'With something very finite. Practical.' Dorothy's eyes happened upon her watch. 'Oh, it's getting late.' She briefly reclaimed her note, uncapped a pen and neatly circled the telephone number and address at the bottom. 'Please do feel free to come and stay with us, at any time. We live in Tollygunge, which is quite a pleasant neighbourhood. We have a granny flat for visitors. It is self-contained and quite comfortable. And Calcutta is a lively city, with numerous literary shoulders to rub. Many of them in our movement.'

Julia took back the note, considering the offer. 'If I did come ... perhaps ... I don't know ... perhaps I could help. Assist with your work, somehow.'

'Why not? That is a wonderful idea. As a Western-educated person, a publisher no less, you have skills which would be invaluable to us. In helping to organise rallies, petitions, lobby politicians.'

'Even as an Australian, a foreigner?'

'All the better to embarrass them into action. They hate foreigners knowing how things really are here.'

'What about Cyril, what would he think?'

'Cyril would love it. Just as we would both love to have you stay with us.' She drank down the last of her tea. 'If the idea appeals to you, please do come. I mean it, Julia. And if on consideration it doesn't appeal, please do come and visit us anyway.'

As they embraced and said their farewells, Julia felt Dorothy's stomach contact her own. As they stepped back, she couldn't help but request: 'Dorothy, would you mind if I …?'

Dorothy smiled, and Julia placed her palm onto the grey silk covering her abdomen. She could feel the smooth skin pucker beneath the fabic at her touch. It felt electrically charged in there.

'So warm and round and ripe. Aren't you frightened?'

'Of the birth?' Dorothy laughed. 'No, I'm terrifyingly blasé.'

The vista of life in a foreign country, and of doing something of worth, thieved her sleep that night. She knew Calcutta. She knew Tollygunge, had even stayed at the Tolly, the colonial relic on the fringe of town to which she and Tim had for years dispatched readers for tiffins and suppers. She knew the neighbourhood, easily imagined the Mukerjee bungalow. She could picture herself chatting on the settee with Cyril and Dorothy, just as she could herself being ushered through outer offices into the sanctum of some white-haired, heavy-lensed Minister, taking tea and chatting pleasantries before getting down to business, a proposal to bring basic learning to some bereft quarter of the city. The Minister, a man – she imagined a man – with a lifelong ease in diplomacy and the exercise of power, would listen to her exposition of the scheme, wrinkling his brow while she reckoned the cost in *crores* of rupees, and with an obliging wave of his beringed hand, while admitting it might be difficult to achieve in the short term, in good time, God willing, he could get it through.

It was an agreeable picture. And as Dorothy had intimated, there would be other benefits too. The world she would naturally move within was that of the city's intellectual elite. She would engage in the liveliest of conversations and impassioned debates – the lobbying would of course extend into the social realm – and she would become known as the foreigner who had immersed herself in the political life of the city.

But these details in themselves highlighted the difficulty of egoism. The vision was, strangely enough, like Josh's. Both of them drawn to that great city, Calcutta, with its multitudinous problems, on a mission – but drawn there by their own personal desires, needs, rather than the needs of the people of Calcutta. It brought back comments Marco had made, over lunch at the Aristo: his view that there was no such thing as a 'good deed'. She had cavilled at the time, but now she wasn't so sure. It was an essentially egoistic thing she was imagining, for the good of the doer before anyone else – just as it had been for Josh. Her ego would be fed well, if not over-nourished. People would naturally be intrigued by her, a foreign curio. She would move with ease down social pathways, golf fairways, corridors of power. There was the higher goal, yes, the good and fine things that might be done – but how much, realistically, could a newcomer achieve against the cronyism, fine talk and no action, devious diplomacy and outright corruption which comprised the warp and weft of much of Indian political culture? The temptation then would be to take it all the way, chase the carrot of political office which might be dangled in due course, and attempt to change things by the exercise of executive power from the glass top of a sizeable mahogany desk. And here she saw another picture, a woman in the back of a shiny white Ambassador, sitting with a secretary, dictating a speech. Fanciful? Yes. But worse, it was a patronising image, the white silk saviour of India. The postcolonial clothes horse. But then, why let that thought stop you trying to be of help? That was a prejudice in itself.

As these thoughts circulated, a background soundtrack played – *Bolero* – a piece she did not even like very much, but which had somehow insinuated itself into her consciousness. Now it wouldn't let go. Where had she heard it? From the doorway of a shop? Then she remembered. It had been playing on the hotel muzak, at tea. Now it had bored its way into her consciousness, and would not release her. The music went round and round, evoking, as commentators had suggested, the plateaux of passionate lovemaking, the moving to ever higher planes of engrossment and excitement, until one couldn't bear it any more. But when the climax came it was a mere blaring of brass, vulgar and ugly, and that was that. It disappointed, always left her wondering is that all there is? But on this night the piece did not reach its climax, unsatisfactorily or otherwise, just kept going round and round and would not let her rest.

It was all further complicated, because thinking of the Tolly club, and the section about it in the guidebook extolling its colonial quaintness, deepened her feelings of unease. It was as if all these years of travelling through India, writing about India, playing her part in the tourist industry, had left her with a knowledge little better than superficial of the place and its people. No wonder she had marvelled at India as a grand mystical puzzle. It felt that way because it had been her business to interact with India superficially, oohing and aahing at its colour and movement, its style but not its content. Until now she might have thought she knew something about India (even if one couldn't know 'all'), but now she saw that knowledge as little more than maps and figures, an outline of history and religions, currency values and the prices of things. Learning otherwise was a precious humility. Beneath the cliché of guru, garland and *ganesha* – which she herself had helped foster all these years – was a people striving for a brighter future, crying out for a better education for their children, like people anywhere. Oh so simple and obvious, but somehow realised properly, fully, now. The exoticism with which India and its people had been popularly imbued in the West was borderline racism, if not south of it. At last her travels had brought her into the companionship, the friendship of an Indian couple, and she had found they were like a couple anywhere. Not that she might have expected anything different – how incipient was her own racism? – but spending time with them had dispelled any remnant illusions.

There were more questions to be asked and answered, but one thing at least was clear: she would leave the business. *And then?* She stopped. That remained hard. She didn't know. So what was this all about, really? A Midlife Crisis? Until now she had thought they happened to receding executives of forty-three. Who woke up on the commuter train one morning and realised they had wasted their youth and would soon be dead with nothing to show for it but juggled figures and cooked books. And who suddenly found they wanted a lot more. Now she too strained to decipher something shimmering way up there, handwritten high in the heavens, that read something like *meaning*, or *contentment*. But who could ever find that? And how? It was a fantasy, surely.

'In the midst of life we are in Perth,' she said clearly, out loud. It was Tim's favourite quotation.

Occasionally in the past, speaking up, saying things out loud, had helped break the mental circuit. But this night the circuit refused to be broken. The questioning, and the tune, abided. So around and around that music went, and she felt sick in the stomach, sicker and sicker, and all she had to look forward to was that hideous braying of trumpets at the end. She sniffed back tears as she tossed in bed. There was a climax to *Bolero*, yes, but Ravel certainly didn't come. He'd faked it. The whole thing was pure frustration, frustration orchestrated, frustration venerated. Godawful.

III

She woke late, the tune mercifully gone from her head. She located an ISD booth on Commercial Road and dialled the house in Lavender Bay. Tim's answer machine said he was not at home just then, but was in Sydney, although about to depart for New York. This was trademark Tim. He was forever leaving over-informative outgoing messages on the machine, as if callers were fascinated by his every move. It had been something of a joke between them, and she smiled to hear it now, as she did to hear Tim's voice, blithe self-assurance.

As she dialled the office she calculated it would be late afternoon in Sydney, but if she was lucky she would catch him before Sky left the switchboard and the machine was switched on. As it happened Sky answered, squealing down the line. Julia heard her shout across the big white loft in Surry Hills, 'Tim! Tim! It's Julia on the line, from India!'

A moment later he picked up his telephone, and like the

connection in the departure lounge at Sydney Airport, she could hear him so spookily clearly he might have been in the adjoining booth.

'Darling! How wonderful. How's it going there?'

'Fine, thanks. Except for one thing.'

'What's that?'

'I want to sell my stake in the business.'

There were few things ever to which Tim did not have a ready answer, and that he did not utter a sound for some moments testified to the enormity of what she had just said.

'Why?'

'I've decided it's what I want to do.'

'When?'

'Did I decide? Last night.'

He trod cautiously: 'And you're ... alright, Julia?'

'You mean, physically ... mentally ... emotionally?'

'All of the above.'

'Yes to all three.'

'It's just that it's, you know, a big step. And I know what it can be like when you're out there alone in another country, particularly one as demanding as India.'

'Don't patronise me, Tim.'

'I'm not. It's just that when you're out there things can appear, you know, bigger than they are. Get magnified. Sometimes out of all proportion. And I know you probably have good reasons for suggesting this, very good reasons, but I can't for the life of me imagine why you'd want to sell now when things are going so well. I mean, your stake will probably be worth fifteen per cent more in a year's time, and another fifteen per cent the year after that.'

'And the year after that and the year after that. Tim, I know what my share is worth. And I'd be very happy to sell for that much now and get out. I've realised I've had enough, that's all. The actual business, I mean. I don't want to be in the business any more.'

Mental cogs turned down the line. She heard the squeak of an office chair, something knock against something else. She saw him doodling a theorem of squiggles around her name on his pad.

'So, what do you want to do?'

'I'm in the process of working that out.'

'What?'

'I said, I'm working that out.'

'Oh come on, Julia,' he said, feet finding turf, 'you don't mean to tell me you want to sell up when you don't even know what else you want to do.'

She was very, very tempted to tell him to shut up, that what she wanted to do was her affair. But a memory of how they had shared everything for so long, shared life decisions big and small (with the exception of the child decision), pricked her, and she found herself wanting to sound him out even though she knew he would inevitably disagree, scoff even.

'I have some ideas.'

'Yes?'

'Well ... do some ... volunteer work in Calcutta perhaps. To promote the cause of education. Do you know they don't even have universal education in India, in practical terms?'

'Of course I do. I wrote a boxed piece about it in the current edition.'

'Did you?'

'You might care to read it,' he said pointedly. 'It's a huge problem. And nothing else gets fixed till they fix that.'

His tone made her want to run straight back to the hotel and check her file copy. As usual he was succeeding in making her feel guilty and inadequate at the same time.

'Julia, listen,' he pushed on, infused with all possible reasonableness. 'If you want to sell your part of the business, I understand, that's fine, it's your fifty per cent and your decision. But what I'd like to suggest is that you're only, what, a few weeks from coming back? And nothing could happen until you got back anyway. So why not just keep chewing on it while you're travelling, and let's talk it through over dinner when you get back.'

'Tim, I won't change my mind. I don't want to do this any more.'

Of all things, he laughed. 'Sounds like you're just having a normal Indian experience.'

'It's not India, Tim!'

'Of course it's India,' he answered, now infuriatingly avuncular. 'India's the most wonderful country in the world. But it drives you bloody bonkers while you're there and you always reach rock-bottom somewhere along the way when you hate it, detest it, loathe everything about it, the crowds, the shit, the flies, when they're all you can see and you can't stand it a moment longer.'

'That's not it. You don't understand.'

'Of course that's it.'

'I've never felt that.'

'Yes you have. On every trip.'

'Rubbish!'

'You just don't remember.'

'Don't I?'

'No.'

'Tim, that is just not true, I have never hated India like that. And anyway that really isn't why I'm saying all this.'

'Isn't it? Okay, anyway, how's the work been going?'

It delighted her instantly to derail his maladroit change of subject.

'I haven't been doing it.'

'What?'

The reassurance evaporated from his voice, and she wished there were more things she could say that might have the same instant effect on him. But there weren't. The thing she had just said was one of an elite few, in the league of *I've got cancer*, that had the power to stop him utterly.

'Why the hell not!' he shouted down the phone. 'What the fuck is going on here, Julia! Everyone's depending on you! You know that!'

'No,' she replied quietly. 'You and I are depending on me. Others up to a point, yes. But in the end it's you and I. You, actually.'

'What is this, Julia? Some stupid kind of misplaced revenge?'

'Somebody suggested that to me along the way, and I had to admit it was true. It upset me and even got me going again for a while. But now I don't care what you think or what you call it. I just don't want to do this any more.'

'Why not?'

'Because it started out as something we did together. It was exciting and it was fun. It was part of who we were. But now we're different and it's different. It's just business. And I'd like to think I could have a deeper relationship with India, something like that anyway. Think of me as a deluded hippie if you like, I couldn't care less.'

In the pause which followed she heard something she thought she might never hear, the quiet creep of defeat. The problem was it touched her, at the very moment when she had struggled to ascendancy, and threatened to undermine all yet again.

'Julia,' he said resignedly, 'if you will do this one last time ... please ... then you will never have to do it again, I promise.'

'You don't need to promise. I know it.'

'Okay, okay. But can you just finish it? And then come back and we'll sort everything out. You can sell, whatever you want. But please, just finish the job.'

Her impulse was to toss everything in here and now. But a compromise might save people back home a lot of lost income, while at the same time setting her decision in stone.

'And if I do it you'll put up no impediments to me selling my stake?'

'None.'

'I have your word on that?'

'Absolutely. So, please, will you finish it?'

She considered again. 'Alright. I will.'

'Good. Thank you.'

In many ways it was more of a divorce than the formal one which would no doubt follow later. The publishing company had bound them together more closely than any marital document. Yet right then, for some reason she found she still wanted to ask if he was seeing anyone, but resisted.

'And how's life on the road?' he asked. 'Hard, I take it?'

'No, I'm enjoying that part. Quite a bit has happened.'

'So I gather. Any romantic interludes?'

'India is always romantic.'

'You're not planning to run off to America with some Yank you've met?'

'No. And by the way that's not what this is all about either, just in case you're thinking that.'

'Where are you?'

'Ooty.'

'Ah Ooty, dear Ooty. Charing Cross shops, tiffin at Jenneys … You know I'd love a tin of Nilgiris tea, if you could bring me one back.'

'I'll bring you one back. And then I'm out.'

'And then you're out.'

'I love you,' she said, the words rushing out stupidly, before she could clamp her lips shut.

'I love you too, angel. You know that, don't you.'

She didn't reply, didn't want to linger melodramatically. She murmured a quick 'bye' and dropped the black plastic handset into the cradle. She felt sick, indulgent, vexatious, absurd. But at least she had said it all. Leaving the telephone booth, she realised the only thing she had left to do in Ooty was buy a tin of tea.

At Mettuppalaiyam, she alighted from the bright blue 'toy' train she had ridden down the Nilgiris slopes from Ooty to the coconut-groved flatlands. Julia found herself in total darkness on a crowded platform, children running everywhere, people jostling. No-one seemed in charge, nor was there any indication of what passengers should do next, but the human tide pushed her towards a train drawn up at another platform, which she earnestly hoped was hers.

She was attempting to go overnight to Kochi, a complicated rail manoeuvre involving two changes, a lot of shunting and waiting in intermediate stations. Three times she was directed to the wrong carriage, but finally was ushered into the correct one by a wiry old man who looked like a Greek goatherd, sold mango drinks from an aluminium tray, demanded *baksheesh*, and might just have been an employee of the Indian Railways.

The compartment into which he showed her, a beaten metal box in battleship grey, was to her eyes a miracle, being a coupe, a sleeper reserved for two persons, normally the preserve of politicians, film stars and criminal *goondas*. She happily paid the man *baksheesh* and bolted the door, determined not to re-open it until morning under any circumstances beyond fire or derailment.

Moments later the train crept from the station onto the plain beneath the blue slopes of the Nilgiris, the warm air chirruping with insects, fragrant with woodsmoke, the waysides crowded with the spidery shadows of coconut fronds, and she discovered the true joy of this compartment, into which no other person could now intrude, in being able to lie back and let the fields and villages go by. The compartment itself was a bizarre artefact, its worn, twisted steel plates and fittings like a remnant of a lost civilisation. The metal had a timeless dull grey lustre, its components melded into a cubist collage.

The carriage rocked, gently rolled. She undressed and stretched out on the leather bunk, awaiting sleep. Through the window came the croaking of frogs, the voices of peasants and lowing of cattle, the sounds mingling with the train's clankings and bangings, the clack of the wheels down the track. As she lay alone in the flashing darkness, she found herself experiencing another 'high', but this one was more profound, deeper than before, almost sexual in intensity. She felt herself released, abandoned, floating over the rice fields on the tropical air, unaware of where or even who she was. Only when the moment had passed and she returned to herself, snug and comfortable on her bunk, did the notion of a lover come. He was not necessarily who she might have expected, although on reflection she had probably been expecting Marco for some time. And for these fleeting miles alone in her compartment, he was.

'I didn't expect to see you back so soon,' Marco said.

She slid a cigarette from a Thai silk purse. 'Well I didn't expect to find you here at all.' She gave a little laugh.

'Why not?'

'I don't know. I thought you might go back to Bangkok or Singapore, or Italy, or wherever it is you say you sprang from.'

'*Say?*' It was his turn to laugh. 'Is that in doubt?'

'Everything's always in doubt with a man.' She lit the cigarette. 'Even when it's one like you.'

'Which is like?'

'An outwardly acceptable outline of a man, or an outline of an outwardly acceptable man, even though he's a cynical bastard and very untrustworthy with women.' She inhaled the smoke and perused the night sky. 'Whatever that means.'

The bar was one of the few places in Pondicherry where you could order wine instead of just beer or whisky, and although it came at a price they had settled down over a couple of glasses that had multiplied, as glasses will do, on the table. The evening was still, with occasional rumbles of thunder. The liquid air licked the palm fronds that surrounded them on the rooftop bar. Out to sea the massive cloudbank was bruised purple, riven with bright fissures of lightning.

Anne had turned up at his door first thing that morning. He had asked for tea to be brought up, and they had sat on the green settee and enjoyed it together. Tea had been followed by a morning walk and a pleasant lunch, a lightly tossed salad of shared memories and anecdotes. Through it, and the sunset walk that bookended the day, he attained the growing realisation that there had been good reasons for what had happened the previous year, in that here was a woman he could pass time with. She had a good intensity, but it was nicely understated, and there was wit. In some ways she was rather like Julia, he thought. She spoke thoughtfully and listened well, was blonde and fit and forty, attractive, overwhelmingly alive.

He thought again of Julia. Where was she, and what was she doing now? Thinking of him, by any chance? Had she thought of him at all since she left that note? Perhaps, perhaps not. There hadn't even been a card, not that she might not have written one, the post was unreliable. The idea struck him she might not even be in India, had gone back to Australia, and that unsettled him. There was something strangely comforting in the thought of them sharing the same sub-continent, even if it was as immense and teeming with people as this one. But she really was probably already back in Australia, with her husband, making up. He tried to picture her there, in Sydney, but all he got was a misty Opera House. What did it matter, anyway? It had probably been best for both of them as a one night stand. If it had continued it would have ended up pretty much the way everything else did. But still there was a nagging he couldn't quite free himself from, that with her it might have been different.

'How is London?' he heard himself ask.

Anne smiled. 'Ah, yes, the lost, gentle art of conversation. London is very well, thank you very much. And sends you her fondest. Didn't you receive my telepathic postcards of Eros and Big Ben?'

He smiled back. 'No, I telepathically didn't.'

The waiter came over and told them the bar was closing, and asked if they wanted any more drinks. They looked at each other, shook their heads, and got up to leave.

The train arrived at Ernakulam before dawn. The ferries plying the harbour had not started up for the day, and Julia had to take a long taxi ride out to the old Fort Cochin to find a room. She worked through the day, and at sunset wandered the foreshore where the Chinese fishing nets were drawn up like a row of giant mantises. Men sat in doorways smoking *bidis*. There were no women to be seen. They would be in a back room, cutting coconuts, drying spices, washing clothes, cooing teething infants.

Back at her hotel, bone-tired, more fatigued than she remembered ever being before, she lay on the flat warm concrete roof as the last rosy dusk faded and the great blue dome spiked with bright planets and stars materialised all around her. The first was the Evening Star, the planet Venus, a roughcut quartz just above the horizon. Then a small star (her knowledge of the night sky didn't go much beyond the Southern Cross) winked on beside it. She peered higher in the sky and saw the first traces of one, two, three others as the dusk receded and darkness was confirmed.

In the distance she heard children playing, the squeaky protest of a puppy, the drone of a ship's horn out in the channel. Lolling her head back, on the horizon behind her she saw pinprick stars sailing in a line like celestial clipper ships. Gradually the entire night sky filled with these hard little gems, like dots in a child's colouring-in book, to be joined to create a picture — an animal or a treasure map, a face perhaps. But, whose face? Was it the face of a deity up there, peering down every night, only we just don't join up the dots? They were inconceivably far off, those suns she saw as dots. So far off that the light reaching her eyes had left many of them before Gandhi marched to the sea, before Marx wrote *Kapital*, Jesus gave his sermon on the Mount, Siddhartha renounced the world. Now those distant bodies swung about as if she lay in a hammock pitched between stars, upon the planets of which others doubtless dreamed with their backs against their cooling roofs, eyes fixed on the unjoined dots of a child's treasure map, the face of the sky.

The yellow moon loomed, full above the dark horizon. She was watching it climb higher into the sky, tantalisingly just out of reach, when she remembered with a small jolt that her period had failed to arrive. The full moon. It was four weeks since that night on the esplanade, when she had watched it rise from the chop of the Bay of Bengal. Usually it was over by the full moon. But no muscle cramped, no blood flowed. In a less regular woman this might not have been so disconcerting, but her cycle was as predictable as the moon's. Was it possible she was pregnant? No, it wasn't.

Aboard an antiquated government riverboat two days later, Julia breathed in the wondrous lewd of the wet tropics. She was making the day-long journey south from Allepuzah through the green primaeval backwaters to Quilon, before proceeding on to Trivandrum and down to Kovalum, her southern terminus. Pastel-coloured houses sat on tiny spits of land surrounded by miles of river, swamp and flooded paddies. Children frolicked in weedy shallows, while their mothers walked in pressed saris shaded by black umbrellas. Old men meandered down levees on bicycles, green fields of rice spreading away on either side. All so profuse, these groves of coconuts and papaya, gardens of potato and tomato, these living fields.

Julia sat on a hard wooden bench beside a German girl she had first seen in Ooty, then Kochi, and now on this boat, still reading the same Harold Robbins novel. The girl had just looked up from the page, and appeared about to say something, when the wafting pall of diesel smoke was suddenly too much for Julia, and it was all she could do to scurry back along the deck to the cubicle at the stern, where she vomited her breakfast through the hole cut in the deck, down into the black-green water.

The hotel room the taxi driver took her to from the Quilon quay was squalid, the bathroom stank, the desk clerk was rude. 'You want a better hotel,' the driver said, 'you must go to Kovalum.'

A long trip, but it was where she was going anyway, after a planned night's rest in Quilon. Tired and out of sorts, she was even tempted. She took another look at the foyer, even more seedy as night fell and the fluoro tubes lit up, giving the faces a bilious tinge. She shrugged okay, and the driver, a young turbaned Sikh, grinned with incisors like white sabres. At some unseen cue a friend leapt into the front seat beside him, the old Ambassador was coaxed into gear, and they chugged out of Quilon. As they cleared the town sprawl and darkness deepened, the car picked up speed.

Driving on Indian roads frightened her at the best of times, but she found it truly terrifying at night. Drivers often failed to dip their lights, so that the roads were a white blinding glare with dark shapes glimpsed at the periphery of vision: a cow with blue-painted horn tips led by a boy, two business-suited men hand in hand, a fisherman with his net neatly folded on his head – all of them passed at speed with the merest gasp of air intervening. And there were all the oncoming trucks and buses, also missed by a bare half inch, the front bumpers somehow just failing to contact, both drivers talking to friends and happily ignorant of any jeopardy, or of the heart-clutching terror of the passenger in the back seat.

In an attempt to calm herself, Julia made conversation. 'A pleasant night', she heard herself say. 'Kerala is beautiful', and, 'I am enjoying the journey, but could you go a bit more slowly please?' Each utterance she felt could be her last. How strange, to die with 'a pleasant night' or 'what is your name?' on your lips. Unfamous last words: 'Can you please go a bit more slowly?' But then how strange to be here at all, in a car with two men she had never seen before, possibly pregnant, charging into the unplumbed depths of night down this narrow strip of bitumen between coconut groves.

They were strong-looking young men, particularly the Sikh. They could take her anywhere, she realised, do anything to her. It was easily within their power. But her experience of Indian men was that they were trustworthy (the man on the train from Chennai to Bangalore notwithstanding). She recalled the look he had given her in that compartment, and it made her not want to look at the face of the driver's friend now, as he sat swivelled in his seat, half turned toward her. She did not want to tempt fate and see that same look. She realised just how much the incident on the train had unsettled her. Was she going to panic now? She felt she might, had to fight it.

She forced herself back into the seat cushion and tried to relax. What other choice did she have? She had entrusted her fate to these two men. Unaware of any of this, they chatted on aimiably in their language (about what? politics? cricket? women? her? – she would have loved to know) as the car hurtled on into the darkness. Her fate, she felt, was sealed and delivered. All she could do was accept it.

THE
GOOD
DEED

S he did the rounds in Kovalum in two days, working rapidly so that she could take a little time off before the haul back to Chennai. She felt the need – she was worn out. The hotel was barely three-star, but after the rigours of the road, of rooms in wayside lodges and overnight train trips, it was bliss.

She settled into a restful pattern, occupied a neutral, padded world, one, she knew, of indulgence. She awoke early each morning in clean white sheets, her head on a soft pillow. Brushing her hair, she would go out onto the terrace to look down through the crowns of coconut palms to the sandy cove below. The air was still early on, barely raising a rustle in the fronds, leaving the ocean an unwrinkled skin of blue. Above, anchored in rock, rose the lighthouse, painted in bands of white and red, from which each night a three-pronged light sprang, beaming out beyond the lamps of the inshore fishing smacks, to the sombre brow of the world.

She would swim alone in blue-green swells, gently bumped in the surf, then jog down the beach to the far point where she would execute a few stretching *asanas* before running back to a breakfast of pineapple juice, a fleshy papaya squeezed with lime, and a pancake stuffed with fresh coconut and cashews, spiced with cardamom and cinnamon. She would spend the day reading and dozing. As the sun began to wane she would pull her swimsuit back on and walk down the dirt road for another half hour in the waves as the sun dipped below the horizon, leaving in its wake bands of gold light streaming up through violet clouds. Then the row of nondescript hotels and cafes interleaved with the beachfront palms would transmute into a little world of a thousand tiny lights, of illuminated shopfronts, beach bonfires, tables of diners on the sand, and above it all the slow sweep of the lighthouse. After her evening meal and stroll she would retire early and sleep with no sound but the sea.

The days passed. She swam, ate, read, slept. She watched as all the tiny bumps and bruises of the road clarified back into her skin. She moved silent and alone across the sands just after dawn and as dusk fell, and did not wish to move on from this place. She had scant contact with the the other visitors, the holiday-makers and the hippies, or with the world in general, whose recidivist felonies reached her in dribs and drabs. She might have been retreating from that world, but in reality she was waiting, for blood, which over the course of days she came to concede would not come. So there was another individual forming inside her, another life. Somehow, despite her precautions, despite the odds, two strings of genes had been thrown together, the dice of life.

So what now? Would she carry this child of a man she barely knew, and had slept with only once? She had been pregnant once before, early on with Tim, a mistake, and she had terminated. She felt prepared to do so again. Certainly the poor groaning earth did not require another human being. But she could sense the child already, feel it begin to assert itself, not physically yet of course, but hormonally, chemically, even spiritually perhaps. Seated on the cane chair of her white terrace in this white hotel so like a hospital or asylum, she experienced her body starting to change. She felt a tidal pull, the same force of nature which would flush her body with hormones, which would fatten her and make her glow softly pink. And this force, this pulling tide, evoked such powerful feelings in her. That first time with Tim she had not allowed herself to feel. It had all happened too quickly and confusingly, and she was a decade younger and that much less ready to deal with it. But over the days, this time, the conviction began to grow, almost organically itself, that the being inside her was a wonder, to be held up in the morning sun, to be treasured, a source of joy. It was inconceivable she could harm such a being. Why? Because she would be thirty-six soon enough, forty soon enough after that, and there might not be another opportunity? Because chance had taken a hand and delivered what she had been so desperate to have, but in a way she might have least expected? Was it just that, a matter of selfish convenience? And had she endured all this, started relationships and ended a marriage, flung herself into new things, journeyed far and alone, just to arrive back at the point everyone else seemed to reach without all this angst and care, a centrally heated nursery where children played with safety-approved toys, watched coffee mug in hand, a place of comfortable normality? And how would she feel if she bled now? Relieved, or heart-broken?

On what became the evening of her final decision, on Lighthouse Road she had encountered a young boy proudly holding up a sea turtle he had captured, its flipper arms still flapping, trying pathetically to swim off through the air. The boy laughed at the creature's helplessness. He knew it would be in the cooking pot tonight, and she knew it was only right that it should be, food for his family. Yet she felt an overwhelming urge to take it and comfort it, deliver it back to the sea.

The next morning she visited a doctor in Trivandrum, and the pregnancy was confirmed. Walking down to her afternoon swim she finalised a plan to return to Pondicherry and inform Marco about what had happened. Then she would fly back to Australia, feed her data into the company computer and sell up her share. And Tim, what would he make of her pregnant? What feelings would that evoke in him? Would that be yet another ending to end all endings, or the first grain of sand around which something new (she dared not think *pearl*) might grow?

She ran into Josh walking on the beach that evening. They only saw each other when they drew close and there was no possibility of either avoiding contact. He looked different, thinner. His hair was messy, and somehow a lot longer than she remembered it being, just a few weeks back. He was with a woman in cut-off shorts and singlet, long and skinny with sun-damaged skin and thin, knotty red hair to her shoulders.

Josh greeted Julia as though they had seen each other only the day before and it was perfectly natural they should bump into each other on the beach. His companion's name was Trish, a New Zealander. She looked older. Julia guessed quite a few years so, into her forties maybe. There was something unsettling about her too, a hardness perhaps, which was not to say she entirely lacked physical attractiveness.

They were staying in the alleys behind the seafront, not far back from the Black Cat Cafe, and Josh invited Julia in for a drink. It was getting dark as they entered the grounds of the little guesthouse. Their hut verged on squalid. The palm leaf matting walls sagged, and Julia glimpsed shards of night through the holes in the roof-thatch. Things were everywhere on the concrete floor: tin plates with old dhal encrusted, a bikini top, a sky-blue scatter of Bisleri empties.

'Make yourself comfortable,' Josh said, gesturing to the single chair while grabbing a half-empty gin bottle from a shelf by the bedside. Trish slapped a mosquito and lit a coil, and said she was off to the Black Cat for tonic.

Neither of them spoke for some time after she went. Julia took in the room while Josh settled onto the bed and stretched.

'You can still hear the sea from here,' Julia said.

'Uh-huh. Not as loud as back at the Sea View though. I've

never heard it that loud, not in a hotel anyway. Too loud in some rooms, those front ones.'

Renewed silence followed the attempt at chat. Julia saw a full ashtray, the butts of joints mingled with cigarette ends. A large black cockroach explored a discarded chocolate wrapper.

'It was all a misunderstanding with Lakshmi,' Josh spoke up abruptly.

'Was it?'

'Of course. Why, what did you think?'

'Nobody knew what to think. All we knew was something had happened, and you'd been kicked out.'

'Listen, she came into the room to clean it, we embraced. Then I notice the door's ajar and some other *ayah*'s looking in. And the next thing Lakshmi's screaming her lungs out for help.'

'You embraced.'

'Yes.'

'Nothing else?'

'No!'

'And she was consenting? To the embrace.'

'Yes! I embraced her. She embraced back.'

The room had already darkened perceptibly. Soon his features would fade.

'The really sad thing for me was what happened to her afterwards,' Julia said.

'What do you mean? What happened?'

'They sent her away. Back to her village. She lost her job, so it seems.'

'What? Why would they do that?'

'I don't know. Blaming her somehow. Or perhaps they felt she was, I don't know, sullied.'

'Sullied? Oh, Jesus …'

'The problem is, she'd need the money, badly. So would her family. These girls always send money home.'

'How much do they usually get paid, domestics like her?'

'A pittance,' Julia said. 'Around six or seven hundred rupees, I think.'

'A week?'

'A *month*.'

'That's less than twenty dollars!'

'That's all they pay them in hotels.'

'But how do they live on that?'

'They just do.'

'Jesus …' he said again, sitting up on the old mattress. 'And so … she lost the job.'

'So it seems.'

'Just because of what happened?'

'I think so.'

'But it … it wasn't her fault.'

'Whose fault was it then?'

'It wasn't anybody's fault,' he stated, with schoolboyish defiance. 'Like I said, it was a misunderstanding.' Despite the smoking coil the mosquitoes were persistent and Julia slapped one, spattering bright blood. 'Maybe I could send her some money or something … when I get back home.'

'I'm sure it'd be welcome.'

'Yeah,' he said, 'that's what I'll do. The moment I get back I'll write the manager for her address.' He leaned over and lit a candle. 'I'd send it from here, only, well, money's a little tight right now. Trish's broke and I've sent home for something from my folks, but so far nothing's come.'

He looked up, his request plain. Julia slapped another mosquito. Her silence affirmed the denial, and he let it go. 'So, what about you? How've you been doing?'

'Fine.' She had intended to leave it at that. What more, usefully, was there to say? But then, for some reason, which she never might adequately explain, even to herself, she emitted a low sigh and added: 'I'm pregnant.'

He looked up startled, as she herself felt startled to have spoken those words as a single sentence, for only the second time in her life, and to Josh of all people.

'Who-ah,' he breathed out slowly, as if exhaling a lung of smoke. 'Congratulations, I guess. And who's the lucky guy, if you don't mind me asking?'

She took in a steadying breath, still at odds with herself. Why had she told him at all? She felt, if anything, just as much strangeness to speak the extra word that followed, but did so, almost with resignation. 'Marco.'

'Uh-huh. Well that doesn't come as a total shock. So what're you gonna do?'

'Go back to Pondy and tell him.'

'He doesn't know yet?'

'I've only just confirmed it.'

'All the way back to Pondy. You could always phone.'

'No I couldn't. You can't tell someone that you're pregnant

with them, and that you're going home to Sydney, all in one phone call.'

'No, no, you're right. That wouldn't be right,' he admitted. 'So, you're gonna keep it?'

'Yes,' she said, with finality. Realising the fact of it in the same moment as, so strangely again, telling it.

'Marco, uh? I hardly met him. What's he like?'

She was about to reply when Trish returned with a bottle of tonic, sat straight down on the floor and started pouring tumblers of the oily liquor topped with the mixer. Julia requested tonic neat.

After they clinked glasses and drank, Trish brought out a rolled joint. 'Opiated,' she said. She lit up and passed it over to Josh, who alternated tokes with sips of gin. Trish watched him as he smoked, her hand resting on his bare thigh.

When he offered the joint to Julia, she declined, passing it on to Trish. Some minutes later, pleading tiredness, she found the moment to take her leave. Walking back, she marvelled that she had once found him attractive.

11

Julia boarded feeling rested, made whole again by her days in the white hotel. She had been unable to get a berth in the Ladies Only carriage however, and First Class and Second Class A/Con were booked out for some days. So she had elected to travel in Second Class. She knew it could be tiring, but it was only an overnight trip. You boarded at night in Trivandrum and arrived first thing in Chennai.

The carriage was crowded, every berth taken. Hers was a top bunk, and soon after boarding, as the train left the platform and gathered speed, she climbed up the three tiers of beds to her nook near the ceiling. With a weather eye upon her fellow travellers, all of whom looked innocuous enough, she took up the newspaper and read in her bunk by the night-light. She had not tuned in to the world for weeks, but nothing much had changed. The Middle East was on the brink of war. Murder in Ireland, blood in the Balkans. In New York and Tokyo indices were aflutter. There were strikes in Italy, drugs in Latin

America, famines in Africa, fashions in France. In Britain people bore it all with a stiff upper lip. There was no mention of Australia beyond a stumps score from the MCG.

She put the paper down and closed her eyes. What was she doing? Travelling back to Pondicherry to speak with Marco. To tell him. Was that all she was doing, really? And was she ready for how he might react? It could be incredulity, it could be annoyance. It could even be joy. Was she ready for that, too, if it was? She thought of the life within her. Already at four or five weeks. How big were they then? The size of a tadpole, probably. A tadpole that would grow into a baby, and make its entry into the world in less than eight months time. Such a short time to reorganise your life for ever. The start of the endless haste of parenthood, headlong into incognita. The nappies, the rattles, the tumbles and falls, the first words, the needles and rashes, and all that snot.

Meanwhile, something was brewing below her. Two men, one middle-aged, the other younger and blue-jeaned, were in the middle of a discussion rapidly heating into argument. They were speaking in Tamil, but she did get the gist of what they were arguing about from the words 'cricket in Chennai' and 'Bal Thackeray' being repeated at frequent intervals. The voices hardened as the argument progressed, and although people pleaded with them to be quiet, that they wished to sleep now, it went on like a dog-barked quarrel over back fences, rasping, ever more passionate, and ugly. Finally a scuffle broke out, and the conductor had to be summoned, but even after the men were parted and promised to simmer down, the exchange of harsh words continued through the night, so that no-one in the carriage got much sleep. Julia slept little if at all, and greeted the dawning day muddy-headed and out of sorts.

Chennai was hot and dusky with pollution. There were no taxis to be found, so she took a rickshaw over to the bus station, where she was deposited into a muddy cauldron of blue fumes, blasting horns and shouted chaos. She discovered two ragged boys on either side of her, grabbing, wheedling, shouting 'You go to Pondy? Bus come now, must hurry, bus come, bus come now!'

And a bus was indeed coming, a red snorting beast thrusting its way through a herd of other red, green and blue beasts. She knew the Pondy bus and this looked like it, alright. The boys chorused and pointed and chorused again, running around her in a war dance as the bus heaved closer over potholes.

'You get on now! Now!' cried the boys, hustling her towards the doorway. 'Give me ten rupees!' demanded the elder one.

But as he did, a fierce-looking old woman in a hessian sack, a crone with a Mohawk haircut, lurched their way screaming, apparently claiming Julia as her own, scattering rocks at the boys and shoving them aside. She gave Julia a crazed grin and tried to grab her by the arm. The bus had drawn up now, coasting on as traffic ahead clogged, the driver leaning on the horn. Breaking the woman's grasp, Julia stepped into the open rear doorway, onto the narrow, steeply inclined stairway, but was amazed to find the two boys already there and blocking her path.

'Not this bus!' they chorused. 'Wrong bus!'

'No,' she said firmly. 'This is the bus. I know it is.'

'Wrong bus!' they repeated, as from up front came the gravelly sound of gears being grated.

'Let me past! Let me past,' she shouted, sweating hard in the heat, starting to lose her temper. She fumbled in a pocket and thrust them ten rupees. 'Now just go!'

'Wrong bus!' they cried again, but in retreat, their lithe brown bodies slipping by her and dropping onto the muddy street. All the while the old woman threw stones at them, while appealing up to Julia with rapid movements of hand to mouth for *baksheesh*.

The bus stuttered, lurched again, shuddered away. But as it accelerated the driver abruptly swung the wheel hard, and Julia was thrown back against the steel handrail. Her hip bruising painfully against it, she was seized in the same moment with the almost fevered realisation that the bus was going in the wrong direction, and that it really *was* the wrong bus after all. In the same moment she saw something else, a young man in a white shirt looking down at her – the man from the Chennai–Bangalore train. He was grinning, coming at her, pawing at her, and she saw she had no choice but to jump off before the bus gained speed and it was too late. It seemed the rational thing to do, to release her grip from the handrail and step off into space. As she did, suspended in mid-air, looking back at the wide-eyed young man staring down at her, she realised in that half-instant that she had been wrong, that it was not the same man after all, but simply another young man who looked passingly like him. She also knew in that same half-instant that he had been reaching out for her smiling, not lecherously, but to assist as she was being bumped around in the stairwell. But it was too late. Her hand had released from the railing. She was flying through the air.

Feet striking the ground, she realised the bus had been travelling a lot faster than she had thought, and tumbled over and over. Fortunately her backpack did not drag her beneath the wheels of the bus from which she had leapt. But its momentum did take her into the path of another bus, a blue one which came towards her as she lay half-stunned in the mud. She managed to roll away as it strained to a halt, front wheel just short of her sprawling legs.

A cry went up – she was unsure whether it was from other mouths or her own – as people rushed in, the boys, the Mohawk woman, onlookers all clustering about, all blaming each other for what had so nearly happened and pulling her to her feet. Everyone seemed to be protesting their innocence while at the same time pleading for money, and between bouts of nausea she distributed rupees enough that she might be left alone. Then, with knee, arm, elbow and face all badly grazed and infected with God knows what from the mud, she ran into the streets of Chennai.

When her senses returned she found herself on a street between a broken-down truck and an old white bullock, with people streaming all around her, her abrasions bleeding, exhaust smoke stinging her eyes, beggars pulling at her mouthing *marm, marm*. And here, for the first time, she did detest India, heartily loathed it, everything – the fat rich, the cringing poor, the opiate addiction to religion, the stupid bureaucracy and the political corruption, the traffic way out of control, the sheer numbers of people, and the filth which swirled and spiralled up at you everywhere. She felt sick in the stomach, and was struck with the sudden terror that perhaps she would miscarry, that the fall would trigger a tragedy.

There was another tugging at her elbow, and she sucked in a snarl ready to spit it at whichever unfortunate had chosen this ill-starred moment to beg, tout or pester, when she found herself face to face with a white-haired man in a ragged suitcoat and stained white *lunghi*, who spoke before she could utter a sound.

'I am saddened to see that you are injured, madam.' He handed her a white cotton handkerchief to wipe her abrasions. 'It is an honour to have you as a guest in my country,' he said, his smile showing full false uppers and lowers.

'Th ... thank you,' she stuttered, half expecting him still to launch into *What's your name? What's your country? Come to my shop*. But he said nothing more, melting away into the crowds until he was just a glimpse of white *lunghi*, then nothing. Then she hated India even more, because it didn't even allow you to hate it. The moment you did, a tiny man appeared like a light bulb coming on, a miniature radiance who helped you glimpse, not the madness, dirt and chaos, but the soul of India beneath that grimy garment. She almost laughed at how much she hated India at that moment – and at how much she loved India beyond that momentary indulgence.

She attempted to call after him, 'Sir, sir!', but her words were swamped by an incremental noise in the air just then, a growl, a rant. She saw the source of it, a loudspeaker van draped with placards and twined with tinselly bright decorations. It came closer down the road, shattering the air, and though she knew no Tamil, and could not decipher the placards on the side of the van, she knew it was political – about the forthcoming cricket match. It was then she noticed the soldiers with guns on the street, saw the little sandbag bunker on the corner, the muzzle of a machine-gun poking out.

The loudspeaker van passed very close by her, pushing her back, trapping her against a steel road railing. Inside she saw the driver, a bleak little man, tensed, torsioned, eyes darting over the crowd. The white-shirted man in the passenger seat bellowing into the microphone looked, to her eyes, like a branch-office clerk. Perhaps he was. If so, he was unchained from the visor and ledger now, grinning as he raved the word – which was presumably prejudice, hate – grinning because he was attracting attention: a momentary star, a jowly supernova.

The crowd was thickening – she could not tell whether with supporters or opponents – and the vehicle slowed to inching, to a stop. One of the loudspeakers on top of it was only two or three feet away, and its bellow came straight at her, as if directing the invective at her alone. Faint and fascinated, she stared into the loudspeaker, disembodied now from the man with the microphone who sat a few inches below it. The flow of words leapt from that dull metal cup, pleading, exhorting, furious. She could not decipher a syllable, but she recognised its cadences, of bigotry, of incitement to violence: the tongue of the mob.

And it was having an effect. She witnessed arguments breaking out in sections of the crowd. She saw the stones young men picked up and held, and the lengths to which wiser ones had to go to stop them smashing the windows, overturning the van, wrenching out the two men and beating them with a ruthlessness their message would have so perfectly inspired. She saw the soldiers too, bodies clenched, watching fearfully, and knew how, if fighting erupted, their fire would be just that much more fuel to the flames.

She might well have feared for her own life, panicked, run if she could have, if she had not been pinned in place by the loudspeaker van. But she found herself of all things amused, at how fine is the balance between the conflicting human urges; at the odd chain of circumstance which had got her to this place, and this moment; and amused too that back along the track she had deluded herself that she knew India 'better', that somehow the making of a couple of Indian friends had changed everything. She didn't know India any better. It blared her own incomprehension into her ears as she stood there, and all she could do was grin like an idiot at the dispelling of yet another onion layer of illusion.

There was no trouble. The men with the rocks did not throw them, the men inside the van escaped with their lives, and the men with the guns relaxed their fingers against the triggers. The crowd parted and the van moved on, leaving Julia where she had stood all the while, against the road railing.

She placed a hand on it to steady herself, realised again that she was injured, bleeding, still in need of first aid. She rested in a shopfront to clean her wounds with mineral water, and a man offered to fetch disinfectant. Another brought her a cup of chai. People gathered, speaking quietly as the noise of the loudspeaker van died in the distance.

'Crazy people,' the man who brought the chai said, with a shake of his head. 'Please be assured, madam, their way is not the way of all Indians.'

Julia thanked him, and took out money to pay for the chai, but he refused it. 'No, madam, please,' he said, 'It is my duty to you.'

III

Pondicherry appeared almost grotesquely orderly after Chennai as Julia got down from the bus. The afternoon breeze was stiff and dry, and her hair annoyed her mouth and eyes.

'Madam has injured herself,' the autorickshaw driver said as he loaded her backpack into the slot behind the passenger bench, eyes rheumy with concern. On her arms, knee, her left cheek and temple, the cuts and abrasions were angry red.

'I fell over, in Chennai.'

'Ah, Chennai,' he said, as if that were all the explanation needed. 'Where do you wish to go, madam?'

'Down the esplanade, please.'

The streets were quiet, almost empty but for the occasional stroller beneath an umbrella. The white European blocks of the Ville Blanche exuded solidity.

'Where is everyone?' she called forward over the racket of the engine.

'Sleeping.'

Of course they were, taking their siesta.

'Which hotel, madam?' he called back.

'The Sea View.'

'Madam …?'

'The Sea View,' she repeated, taking from his tone that he might be about to suggest another place, as the *rickshawallahs* so often did to new arrivals. 'I know it and I like it. Just take me there, please.'

'As you wish, madam.'

She settled back, knowing that in a matter of minutes she would be back there, in those familiar surroundings she realised she had so missed. The comfort of the thought was immense. But, passing the Gandhi statue and approaching along the esplanade, she sensed something amiss. There was a gap up ahead, like a missing molar, in the row of buildings where the Sea View should be. She stared, unable quite to comprehend. But, no, she had to admit it, the Sea View was gone. She blinked. It was still gone.

'It was knocked down two days ago, madam,' the driver said, braking to pull up outside. 'I am sorry. It was a first rate hotel, so many people say.'

She stared dumbfounded at the carnage. Massive blocks of whitewashed stone lay where they had fallen before the wrecker's ball. Huge wooden beams were scattered through it, splintered and shattered. In the morass she saw red shards of broken terracotta floor tiles, smashed light fittings and tangled power cables. Women scavenged while an overseer shouted orders and broken masonry was piled up for carting away.

An immense sadness swept through her. A refuge was gone. There were so few of them in the world, places where it was possible to meet like minds and mingle easily, where the traveller could properly rest. Now another was gone and there would be no bringing it back. She stumbled out of the rickshaw onto the pavement, still unable quite to accept the reality. She saw Guru standing on the other side of the street looking across at the ruin, and walked over to him.

'A terrible thing, madam,' he said. 'A most sad time. For us all, and for Pondy. But this is India now. It is changing, always changing.'

'What will they do with the site?'

'Build a new hotel. Multi-storey.'

'And you?' she asked him. 'What about your job?'

'For now I am to be nightwatchman over this place, madam. And when they rebuild, I will work in the new place. But it will not be the same. The Sea View could never be replaced in my heart.'

'May I take you to another hotel, madam?' the driver asked.

'I suppose so, yes. Thank you.' She turned back to Guru. 'Do you know what happened to the guests?'

'Some left. Some went to the Palms, others to the Villa. And one or two to the Shastri.'

'Do you know where Marco went? Mr Manzini?'

'I think he went there.'

'To the Shastri?'

'I believe so, madam. I think that was the one he said. The Hotel Shastri, on Lal Bahadur Shastri Street.'

'I know it,' the driver said. 'It is on the corner with Rue Romain Rolland. If you liked this place, you might like that one. It is an old place too.'

'Alright then, thank you. I'll try it.' She extended her hand to Guru and they shook. 'Good luck.'

'Thank you, madam.' His brow wrinkled. 'And madam, please to have your abrasions attended to expeditiously.'

The Shastri turned out to be a characterless place on the corner of a noisy main road. Lal Bahadur Shastri Street was the only major road that ran unimpeded from the ring road that circled the city all the way down to the esplanade. As such it carried much of the heavy traffic that needed to pass from the highway through the Ville Noire to the Ville Blanche. Big trucks and buses rumbled by the gate day and night.

The front desk looked flimsy, like burnished boxwood, and there was no sign of anyone around. There was a bell on the counter, and she pressed it with the heel of her hand so that it emitted a high-pitched *ding* that echoed off down the hallway. After an interval, a young man emerged from a side room rubbing the siesta from his eyes. He spoke little English, and the only successful communication between them, in rudimentary French, amounted to the fact that the *patron* was out, and that there was only one room left in the hotel, which she could see if she wished. As they walked upstairs, she attempted to find out if Marco, or anyone else she knew from the Sea View, was staying there, but the young man apparently did not understand and kept on insisting '*patron, patron*'.

The room into which she was shown was minuscule by the standards of the Sea View, having just space enough for its complement of single bed, table and chair. Its sole window opened onto Lal Bahadur Shastri Street, and if she decided to stay here she had the sorry choice of traffic noise and fumes, or to close the window and suffocate in the heat. She was in two minds, but the fact that a hotel as basic as this had only one room left indicated accommodation might be at a premium in town just then. And a mid-afternoon arrival tended to reduce one's choices greatly. There was also the chance that Marco was staying here. If not, she could look for him (and a better room) in the morning. As she paid the deposit she asked again, as slowly and clearly as she could, whether Mr Marco Manzini was staying there, but the young man still appeared not to understand. She thought about asking to see the guest register, but a sharp increment in pain made her realise she had other more urgent matters to attend to just then.

The wavering lamplight over her handbasin made the wounds look even worse, red lines of angry lesions. As she undressed she found that beside the cuts and gravel rash to her face, neck, elbows and arms, there were also wounds, mostly shallow but some deeper, inflicted through tears in her clothing, so that all down her left side from chest to hip ran a range of inflamed abrasions. Unseen, and therefore left untreated with first aid back in Chennai, they were breaches for whatever bacteria were at home in those scum-filled puddles into which she had fallen.

She rinsed out the wounds as best she could, disinfected and applied antiseptic cream. Her knee looked particularly sorry. The skin was shredded, and the knee carried dark traces of mud deeply embedded. These fragments she painstakingly extracted, picking, washing, picking again with tweezers, until what remained was a meaty pale impression of a knee.

There was a knock at her door, and for a wild moment she thought it might somehow be Marco. 'Just a minute please!'

'Take your time,' came the reply. It was a woman's voice.

Moments later, wet towel pulled around her, knee hanging in pink flaps, Julia opened the door. A woman she had never seen before stood there barefoot.

'Are you Julia?'

'Yes.'

'I'm Anne. Ravi mentioned you were looking for Marco, and …' Her eyes widened as she saw the knee. 'Oh!'

'It's alright. I fell over. In Chennai.'

She stepped a prompt half-pace forward and bent down to look. 'You've disinfected it?' Julia nodded. 'You'll want to be careful with a wound like that in this climate. Come up to my room and let me help you finish cleaning it. I think you'll be more comfortable there.'

Exhausted, shaky, Julia found herself happy to oblige. 'Thank you.'

Anne's room was larger than her own, though modest still by Sea View standards. The double bed had been made up, and on it lay a rain-crinkled map of the town, in a tangle of green scarf.

'Sit down while I find my first aid kit.'

Eyes accustoming themselves to the interior, Julia saw a pile of newspapers in a corner, along with a scattering of men's clothing, personal effects, books. Then she noticed something else, *The Plague*, on the bedside table.

'Anne, is that your book?'

'No. It's Marco's.'

'Marco Manzini?'

'Yes.'

Julia took in a quick breath. 'You see, I ... I met Marco here in Pondy, a few weeks ago.'

'I know,' Anne said.

Despite her surprise at this, Julia couldn't help but rush on. 'Is he still here?'

'I don't know where he is.'

'But he's still in town.'

'I don't think so, no. That's what I came to your room to tell you, after Ravi told me you were looking for him. Marco's gone.'

'When was this?'

'Yesterday. Just upped and took off. Left nearly everything behind. Clothes, books. Dumped everything on the floor, just as you see it. Wherever he's gone, he's certainly travelling light.' She opened a bottle of disinfectant and applied some to a cotton wool pad. 'Now look, let's just finish patching you up first, shall we?'

Julia sensed it was not the moment for any deeper inquiry.

'Would you mind if I looked at the book?'

'Go ahead. Keep it if you like, I don't want it.'

Julia picked up the book, and saw a bookmark in it, near the end. Just short of the death of Tarrou, she realised, and of the doctor's wife: the end of everything, even the plague itself. She wondered why he hadn't read to the last.

She took out the bookmark and saw it was, of all things, a portrait of Sri Aurobindo, a re-coloured sepia, of him in his twenties or thirties. She had seen the image before, on a wall in the Sea View, very Christ-like. How strange to find it here, in Marco's book. His humorous perversity, or what?

Anne re-sponged the wound before wrapping it in a bandage.

'Thank you so much, again,' Julia said.

'Have you eaten? We can go to the Aristo if you're hungry.'

'The Aristo,' Julia said. 'Yes, please, let's go there.'

The waiter placed a dessert of papaya juice before Julia, bright saffron orange in a parfait glass, with a wedge of lime. She had tiptoed around Marco over the meal, aware of the probable sensitivity there. Anne seemed a relaxed enough person, but she was still wary about broaching the subject again. In the end it was Anne who opened the way, by mentioning what had happened to the other residents of the guesthouse.

'The old Indian couple ... they returned to Delhi two weeks ago. It was when their room wasn't reallocated that we suspected something might be up with the demolition.'

'Kingston? Mildred?' Julia asked.

'I don't know. Things got a bit confused at the end. They just disappeared – but together.'

Julia smiled. 'Britt?'

'She left weeks ago, back to Denmark.'

'Dwight of Iowa?'

'He moved out onto the esplanade. You can see him there every night still. God only knows what he does during the day.'

'Lakshmi?'

Anne's breezy delivery faltered. 'She's gone to Madras.' Then with a sigh, added: 'They sold her, poor girl.'

'What do you mean?'

'Her family sold her. Into prostitution.'

'Oh no ... no ... the poor girl ... Do you know where she is? How she is?'

'Nothing beyond that she's in Madras,' Anne said, 'and sending back money.'

Julia felt ill: what a fate for Lakshmi. And how appallingly ironic, that it had been brought on by the clumsy gropings of a man.

The strengthening breeze rippled the bougainvillea blossoms and furrowed Anne's porphyry red Rajasthani dress. It was embroidered with gold, scarlet and green thread, the latter hue picking out seams of emerald in the blue of her irises. She sat and stared, toyed with her sunglasses. They had been sat upon, or crushed in luggage, and one of the arms was as wonky as a supermarket trolley.

'So that's it,' Anne said at last. 'Everyone gone. And the Sea View itself gone. Demolished.'

'A tragedy in one stupid act,' Julia said. She spooned the last of the papaya into her mouth. It tasted like medicine now, and she set it aside.

Anne lit a cigarette and sat back in her chair. 'In case you're wondering, he talked about you.'

'I wasn't wondering that.'

'Marco seemed to be thinking about you a lot of the time. We rowed about it. I think that was another reason he took off.' She exhaled a sigh of smoke. 'And the Sea View. He said the heart went out of Pondy with it. Wasn't the same, he said. I think he just doesn't like change.'

'And you don't know where he went.'

'No idea. He's probably left the country though. He always said he didn't like India, only Pondy. I think he feels more comfortable in the past, doesn't like the new.' She swished a blonde lock from her cheek. 'I went out to get some things yesterday, and when I came back he'd gone. Just like that. Took virtually nothing. Packed a few things and cleared off.'

'Perhaps he'll come back.'

Anne smiled knowingly, and shook her head.

'He didn't leave you a note?'

She stubbed out the cigarette half-smoked, and pushed the ashtray aside. 'One time when we were rowing he said he wished he'd gone off after you. That what had happened between you was wonderful, but so annoyingly incomplete. That he'd watched you for days, weeks, before you two even spoke, and how special it was when you finally did. What a great connection you two had.'

'He said things like that to you?'

Anne's curt nod came with a bitter-lemon smile. Floating up, buoyed by the bloodwarmth of the breeze, came the clatter of bicycle bells and the clamour of commerce of Rue Nehru.

'How well did you know him?' Anne asked.

'Not very.' Julia found that despite herself it came out as something of an admission.

'But you slept with him.'

'Yes.' And again despite herself, she felt the heat of a blush rushing into her cheeks.

'And now you're back to see him.' She slipped her palm interrogatively beneath her chin. 'Not pregnant or anything, are you?'

'What?' Julia exclaimed. 'Why do you say that?'

'I don't know. Intuition? But you're not denying it.'

Julia looked down into the pulpy dregs of her papaya. 'No.'

'And you know that it's to Marco?' Anne appeared to be marvelling at a spray of bougainvillea newly erupted up onto the roof, cascading down on all sides. The fingers of breeze rippled through the crimson hedge of blooms. 'You know, it might sound funny, but I think he'd have liked it. To be a father. We even talked about it. For us, I mean. Just a few days ago. He even raised it himself.' She clamped the sunglasses over her eyes. 'Still, men often start going that way in their forties. The hand of mortality on their shoulders for the first time, that kind of thing. And there was his family. His father committed suicide here in Pondy, you know. And I think Marco might have wanted to ... you know ... renew life himself. He even said as much. And we had the chance to. But in the end, he ran.'

Julia grimaced. 'Anne. Please don't think I came back here to tell him I wanted the child with him. I didn't. I just thought he should know, that's all.'

Anne cocked an eyebrow. 'Why?'

'I just thought he should.'

Anne nodded, disbelievingly.

Julia fiddled with the stem of her parfait glass. 'How well do you know him?'

'Quite well. We're married after all.'

The blush boiled up again in Julia's cheeks. 'Married. I ... I'm sorry.'

'You don't have to be. He kept it such a close secret I think the two of us hardly knew it ourselves.'

Julia was relieved to smile. 'But he seemed so cynical about love, marriage. Everything.'

'I know. But he still married me.'

'Here in India?'

'In Pondy, with full pomp and circumstance. An Indian wedding, restricted in scale only by our lack of acquaintances. Guru came. So did the Manager, of all people.'

The waiter brought their bill. 'I'll get this,' Anne said, and despite Julia's protestations to the contrary, leafed notes from her purse and placed them on the platter.

'When was this?' Julia asked.

'Last year. I was like you, a traveller. I saw him once or twice in the corridor. Found him intriguing – he kept so much to himself. We finally met, went out to dinner. Within days we were dizzy mad in love, and of all things this man, who kept telling me what a cynic he is, proposes. And we got married, and it was wonderful. For two or three months. Until I realised that Marco wanted his room back, his life alone back, his solitary confinement back. It wasn't so much us as him – the cliché. Only I think it really was in this case. Because in the end he didn't need love. He wanted to be left alone with something bigger.'

'Which was?'

Anne shrugged. 'His emptiness. That lone male kind of emptiness. They get so sad, men. Old dogs burying bones and digging them up again. There's nothing you can do for them. They're lost to any proper female contact, they just want to mooch and moon.' She reflexively drew out another cigarette, held it poised between her fingers. 'In his case it might be something to do with his father, of course. He never really got over that. He loved his father. So the idea that he could take his own life ... it shook up everything Marco believed in. Or in his case, everything he didn't.' She toyed with the unlit cigarette. 'Or else it was something from before that. Because Marco was a man – excuse the past tense – who never seemed to fit in anywhere. More comfortable left alone with his angst. Being with a woman was a nice idea, but an unattainable one. And I can't help thinking he felt more comfortable with it being exactly that, unattainable.' She eased the cigarette between her lips and lit it.

'How did you deal with that?'

'What choice did I have? I left. Went back to London thinking, oh great, yes, that's all you get these days – a couple of months of halfway decent sex and a few nice cuddles, if you're lucky.'

'What brought you back then?'

'I work as a production manager on films. We'd just finished shooting a commercial in Portugal and there was a break, and because I hadn't heard anything from Marco since I left I thought what if I just lob in on his doorstep and say hello? Just wanted to see the look on his face, I suppose.' She chuckled. 'Which turned out to be the same old mask he always wears. He was so polite I might have been a visiting maiden aunt from Cheltenham. Had tea brought up and made pleasant chat. We might never've met for how he acted. Exactly the same as when I got to know him before. I couldn't be sure of anything. But that somehow made him attractive back then, and lo and behold it made him attractive again.'

'Wasn't that what you wanted?'

'I don't know. I didn't really know what I wanted when I got on at Heathrow. I just wanted to see what would happen if I turned up at his door and he happened to be there still.'

'And what did?'

'We talked. I was trying to be clever and a bit cutting with him, because I was angry about him rejecting me, I suppose, and no doubt trying to impress him at the same time. We went out and drank wine that night. And back to his room. And I thought, here I am in bed with my husband – my *husband*, for God's sake. And I hardly know the man. I don't think anyone does.' She inhaled the smoke, exhaled it in a rush of words. 'It was good for a week, two weeks. But then the same thing started again, this gradual retreat of his. And then he told me about you, and how he felt about you. Said he thought he might even be in love with you. And I thought, you shit, if you can't love me here and now, can't give yourself to that when you know in your heart of hearts that it could work if you tried, how will you ever love anyone? He just seemed to be using you against me, as a device. To justify turning his back on me. We had lots of arguments – but it didn't make any difference. He wasn't really there. We were like two grey areas looking for a little bit of black and white, and not finding any. And I realised what I really had to do was get over him, get right over the whole thing, because it wasn't going to happen. Maybe love doesn't happen to anyone any more, except in films, I don't know. Or else it's the sole property of people too young to know better. And I had to admit that I'd come back with some kind of dream still, but I was deluded. I had to get over it.' She stubbed out the half-smoked cigarette, again shoved the ashtray aside. 'And then they knocked down the Sea View and we moved to that awful place, and yesterday Marco made it official. And then you turn up. And there's nothing more to say, really. Except that you were lucky not to miscarry after your fall.'

'Yes I was,' Julia said. 'Very.'

'And to say that I think perhaps he did love you after all, and that was why he went away. Simple as that.'

'He couldn't have loved me. He barely knew me.'

'I think he did anyway. And that shook him up. Enough to get him moving again. Maybe he's out there right now, looking for you.'

Back at the Shastri they said their goodnights. 'More than goodnight, actually,' Anne said. 'I'm taking take the bus up to Chennai tonight. On the early flight out tomorrow, back to London.' She extended her hand to shake. 'It's been super meeting you.'

'I'm sorry it didn't work out for you,' Julia said.

Anne smiled. 'You too.'

After she had gone, Julia found that despite the exhaustion of the day, she did not want to go back to her room just yet. Instead, she walked back to the esplanade, mingling with the twilight crowds on the promenade. She felt so tired, but wondrously light, composed of nothing, if that were possible. She remembered the night on the promenade those few weeks before, when the children had rushed up to greet her and she had wanted to give them *burfi*, but didn't. The time that intervened felt composed of nothing too.

She passed the Cafe Blanc, empty now of its most devoted patron, and by the Gandhi statue, and continued on until she reached the place where the Sea View had stood. She sat on the wall and rested there, facing out to sea, then turned and looked back at the demolished Sea View.

Workers had levelled off much of the site, and carted away the debris. She could see the handsome but derelict-looking colonial building that stood in the alleyway behind it now, and wondered how long it would be before that one came down too. But then, perhaps it was for the best anyway that they pull down the vestiges of this White Town, and Indians put up their own buildings, however modern and concrete, ugly to the eye.

What was that 'taste' anyway, but a colonial romanticism, another postcolonial conceit?

She stared into the hushed grey of the wreckage. Amid the fallen blocks and planks and bits of masonry, were fragments of herself, of Marco, Josh, Lakshmi, and so many others. Now they were all gone.

Poor Lakshmi, sold into a brothel. A life so tragically lost. But then, she realised, almost perversely, life had been created too. Two men so oblivious to the consequences of their actions, lost men: yet fate, or India, or simple existence, had decreed one as a creator, the other as destroyer. Marco, disappeared; Josh probably down in Kovalum still, acquiring a taste for gin, or whatever. The other residents scattered across the earth, the magnet which had held them together smitten. The Manager, the *ayahs*, Guru, and Vishnu the security man – they might be closer by, but they had gone as well.

Peering deeper into the wreckage, she saw other shades too: Dilip in those Biblical laneways of Hampi, and Dorothy and Cyril, back in the megalopolis of Calcutta. Now even Anne was gone, known a mere afternoon. It was as if all these faces had crowded towards her, in a great and garish cavalcade, fluorescent pinks and greens with gold-leaf faces, bright ebony eyes and teeth of mother of pearl, candied Hindu deities; a parade of them that had passed by, and like the Sea View itself, vanished as though they never were.

Julia returned to the blank of the sea. A vault of darkened emptiness, no moon yet, not even a cloud out there. Her thoughts went back to Anne, and what she had implied about her, about why she herself had come back to Pondicherry. The truth was she had come back at least in part for the same reason as Anne — the remnant romantic belief, hope, curiosity at the very least, that it would turn out with Marco. That he would, of all things, be delighted she was pregnant, and they would run off and live happily ever after.

That was the fantasy which, wittingly or unwittingly, had drawn her back. In all truth, she would have been horrified if he had said thanks for telling me and here's the money for the termination, or here's my address for the school fees. No, what had brought her back had been the fantasy, the one she thought she had turned away from by force of will when she had walked past the Cafe Blanc that morning, with him perched over his papers. She had thought she had gone beyond it then, but she hadn't. Its glory-box roots went down so deep that it had turned her round, subtly, and in effect she had gone back into that cafe, had sat at the adjoining table, and conversation had ensued between them, and all that had followed followed. She had not rid herself of it at all. Her return to Pondicherry was just another chapter in a True Life Romance: it could even have been the title.

And still there was Tim. He had been in her thoughts less since the phone call in Ooty, because in the back of her mind, after discovering her pregnancy, she was already subconsciously playing out scenarios with Marco. With him gone, inevitably and infuriatingly, she was already thinking about Tim again, romancing that one too, that scenario, in which she steps off the plane, cheeks pink with pregnancy, and he sweeps her off her feet saying she's never looked so beautiful, and that he wants her more than ever and the three of them will live happily ever after in Lavender Bay. Lavender Bay – even the place names conspired: how dare a city give any place so romantic a name?

She tried not to think about what time it was in Sydney – very late anyway, too late to ring – and how close the nearest ISD booth was, and how quickly they could make the connection for her now that India was up to the minute in all things. She didn't want to think about him at all. She knew he was yet another part of the chimera of love, the illusion in which she had played so willingly, tricking herself with such a masterful sleight of hand that the other hand wished to clap.

Her mind ranged back to Anne, and her bitterness about Marco. Julia didn't feel any bitterness herself, not that she had any cause to. She felt sympathy for him. He was a man with money and freedom for the whole world, who in the end had confined himself to a single room. He was contrary and contradictory, but she liked that too, the humanity, the human failing of him. She recalled his comments about religion, how compassion was its only rightful goal, no matter how unattainable, but how no-one ever did a good deed simply for the sake of another person, that there had to be a selfish component too. As it turned out, Marco had done a good deed. He had helped her get the one thing she so desperately wanted, and she was grateful. True there had been pleasure for him too, but momentary. Her pleasure, no, joy, would last the length of a life. And for that she loved him, as Anne had said he loved her.

She pictured him on an overnight bus, being driven into the

heart of India, as, she felt, he had wished all along. And was there in his possession the only thing he had valued too much to leave behind, that she knew would be missing from the things he had shed onto his hotel room floor, his inheritance, *Views of India*? Well, now at least he was seeking the real thing. Or was that all simply fond imagining?

So now she sat by the sea, trembling on the lip of India, alone and free, or at least with the illusion of freedom, the cavalcade passed on, and no home to go to, only a continent, and a house. She might have wept, for the sharp intermingledness of sadness and joy. Even the ache in her knee felt right in this moment. She was happy just to stay a while.

She looked down the sea wall, and noticed Dwight of Iowa a little further along, gazing out. She walked over and stood by him, and placed her hand onto his shoulder, let it rest there. He might have smiled: she couldn't see.

PUFFIN BOOKS

THE GIFT OF A LAMB

On a cold winter's night, long ago, three shepherds sit on a hill watching their sheep. Young Dan is especially excited, for at midnight it is his birthday and he can pick the first lamb to start his own flock. The little black and white lamb he has chosen also catches the eye of the notorious Thieving Jack, who is creeping nearer and nearer ... Suddenly a light fills the sky and they are all overwhelmed by the sound of angels singing, for this becomes a night which changes them all and in which the gift of a lamb to the baby in Bethlehem becomes very important.

The story of Christmas is told through the three simple shepherds and the rascal Jack as a verse-play for children by Charles Causley, one of our finest modern poets. The stage directions and music for songs are included so that the play can be performed as well as read, and the line drawings by Shirley Felts beautifully decorate the lively little play.

Charles Causley

THE GIFT OF A LAMB

A shepherds' tale of the first Christmas
told as a verse-play

With music by Vera Gray

Illustrations by Shirley Felts

PUFFIN BOOKS

Puffin Books, Penguin Books Ltd, Harmondsworth, Middlesex, England
Penguin Books, 625 Madison Avenue, New York, New York 10022, U.S.A.
Penguin Books Australia Ltd, Ringwood, Victoria, Australia
Penguin Books Canada Ltd, 2801 John Street, Markham, Ontario, Canada L3R 1B4
Penguin Books (N.Z.) Ltd, 182–190 Wairau Road, Auckland 10, New Zealand

First published by Robson Books 1978
Published in Puffin Books 1980

Copyright © Charles Causley, 1978
Music copyright © Vera Gray, 1978
Illustrations copyright © Shirley Felts, 1978
All rights reserved

Typeset, printed and bound in Great Britain by
Hazell Watson & Viney Ltd, Aylesbury, Bucks
Set in Monotype Bembo

Except in the United States of America,
this book is sold subject to the condition
that it shall not, by way of trade or otherwise,
be lent, re-sold, hired out, or otherwise circulated
without the publisher's prior consent in any form of
binding or cover other than that in which it is
published and without a similar condition
including this condition being imposed
on the subsequent purchaser

To
Colin Smith

The first performance of this play was broadcast in the BBC Radio for Schools' series *Let's Join In* on 2 December 1977, with the following cast:

Storyteller	GARY WATSON
Ben	EDWARD KELSEY
John	LEONARD FENTON
Dan	GORDON GARDNER
Thieving Jack	CLIFFORD NORGATE
1st Angel	ROY SPENCER
2nd Angel	ERIC ALLEN
3rd Angel	ROBIN BROWNE
Joseph	HAYDN JONES
Mary	JILL SHILLING

Produced by DAVID LYTTLE

The music was played by ANNE COLLIS (percussion), SARAH FRANCIS (oboe), LIONEL BENTLEY (violin) and GEOFFREY BURFORD (piano).

CHARACTERS

Storyteller

Ben, the grandfather ⎫
John, the son   ⎬ shepherds
Dan, the grandson   ⎭

Thieving Jack

1st Angel

2nd Angel

3rd Angel

Joseph

Mary

The stage directions are given from the point of view of the actors.

[*Music.*]

STORYTELLER: Once on a night
                  Both dark and chill
                  Three shepherds lay
                  Upon a hill;

                  Out in the black
                  And iron air,
                  Guarding their sheep
                  From wolf and bear.

Their watch on sheep and lamb
Ne'er ceased,
Lest they be robbed
By man or beast.

Each in a shepherd's cloak
And hood,
They lit a fire
Of winter wood.

Where grass was thin,
And thick the stones,
They tried to warm
Their bitter bones.

And quiet stars
Burned over them,
Those shepherds three
Of Bethlehem.

[*Lights come up to reveal the summit of a gently-sloping hill. It is winter. On the R. slope are three shepherds:* BEN, *a grizzled grandfather,* JOHN *his son, and* DAN *his grandson, all well-wrapped against the cold. By them are sticks or staves, a pack of food, and one or two leather bottles. They also have, respectively, a fiddle, pipe and a drum at hand.* JOHN'S *whistle-pipe is tucked in his belt. A fire glows. The dim outlines of sheep may be seen.* BEN, *leaning on a shepherd's crook, stands at the lowest level.* DAN *is seated by the fire, on which a pot of broth is being heated.* JOHN, *nearest the top of the hill, peers into the darkness watchfully.*
Music for song:]

BEN: [*sings*] I am a shepherd,
My name is Ben,
I've shepherded
Three-score years and ten.
Spring, summer, autumn,
Winter, too!
The years and the seasons
How they flew!
Now my nose is fire
And my hair is frost,
But never a sheep or lamb
I lost.

JOHN: [*sings*] I am a shepherd,
My name is John,
I work with my father
And my son.
In forty years
Of cold and heat,
I never have lost
A lamb or sheep.
In weather gold,
In weather grey,
No sheep or lamb
Was stolen away.

DAN: [*sings*] I am a shepherd,
My name is Dan,
In seven more years
I'll be a man,
But ever since I
Could stand or run
I've shepherded sheep
In rain and sun.
I've shepherded sheep
On hill and moor
As my father did,
And his before.

BEN: [*speaks*] Ay, that we have, a thousand seasons through.

JOHN: And, if God wills, so may Dan's children too!

BEN: Now feed the fire with sticks!
The night is bleak.
The sharp air pinches
At my hand and cheek.

JOHN: Bestir yourself, young Dan,
And watch the pot
That keeps the good broth
Bubbling and hot.

BEN: And at the stroke of twelve
　　　We'll sit and sup,
　　　And drink Dan's health
　　　And clink a merry cup!
　　　For then, my dearest grandson,
　　　Joy to tell,
　　　Comes in your birthday
　　　With the midnight bell!

JOHN: Though poor we shepherds be
　　　And light our pay,
　　　We have the gifts you chose
　　　To mark the day.
　　　To hold: a shepherd's crook,
　　　To wear: a smock.
　　　Then, that you choose a lamb:
　　　First of *your* flock.

DAN: Father, grandfather, good you are and kind;
　　　I thank you with my heart and with my mind.
　　　And O, the lamb I choose this happy night
　　　Is that with body black and head of white!

BEN: John, take your whistle-pipe...
　　　[JOHN *takes it from his belt and blows a single note.*]
　　　And Dan, your drum...
　　　[DAN *strikes a sharp, double-tap on the drum beside him.*]
　　　I, with my fiddle tucked beneath my chin...

[*He picks it up and plays a quick chord.*]
We'll play a tune,
And with a jig
Welcome Dan's birthday in.
[*They strike up. The lights fade on them.*]

STORYTELLER: But as they played
So sweet and clear,
A stranger crept
Their pasture near;
And even as
The shepherds played,
A stranger crept
From shade to shade.
He did not stand
Beneath the sky
And greet the shepherds
Eye to eye;
He did not sing,
He did not hum –
He wished no man
To hear him come,

But secretly
And without sound
He crawled across
The glimmering ground;
Over the meadow,
Up the hill,
To where the sheep and lambs
Lay still.
His brow and neck
He'd smudged with soot,
And on his face
A mask he'd put.
He carried on his back
A sack,
And the name of the man
Was
Thieving Jack.

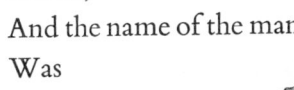

[*Lights come up on the L. slope of the hill. What at first seems to be a rock or boulder slowly begins to move. It is* THIEVING JACK. *The shepherds' music is heard a little distance off, and held behind his voice as he begins to speak.*]

THIEVING JACK: Hark to the silly shepherds
As they sing and as they play –
Though what they've got to sing about
Is more than I can say.
A shepherd's lot is 'eavy,
An' a shepherd's lot is poor
In every kind o' weather you can think of –
An' some more!
They works by night an' day –
Why, it's enough to make yer weep!
If you ask me, a shepherd's
Just as silly as 'is sheep.
But that's 'is silly business,
An' as for mine, my friends,
You won't catch *me* a-workin'
All the hours the good Lord sends.
I likes to eat, I likes to drink,
I likes to lie a-bed;
I calls no man *my* master –
'Ere's what I do instead:
I nicks a little chicken

Or I bags a side o' beef,
So guard yer goods when I'm about
Because I am

    a

      thief!

I robs the rich AND poor –
You never
Met a worse than me:
For anything that's *yours*
Is mine,
And mine's me own,
You see.
No ducks that quack
Are safe from Jack,
Nor any sow that squealed;
Nor any sheep or lamb that's left
Unguarded in the field.
And O, but it's a lamb this night
On which I've got me eye –
I liked the black and white of it
As I went passing by.
An' so among the rocks I creep,
An' opens up me sack . . .
[*Very faint bleat of a lamb.*]
An' slips the lambkin in –
[*Slightly louder bleat.*]

NOW!
It belongs to Thieving Jack!
[*Bleat.* THIEVING JACK *chuckles. Bell begins to sound midnight. Light fades L. and increases R.* SHEPHERDS *play and sing on the hill.*]

BEN: [*sings*] Now the bell at midnight
Chimes to make us glad,
Bringing in the birthday
Of a shepherd lad.

JOHN: [*sings*] He shall have a wooden crook,
A smock as clean as light;
He shall have a lambkin
Whose wool is black and white.

[*Bell ceases striking. Light begins to grow in the sky above the* SHEPHERDS. *The echo of the bell's last note becomes a sustained, metallic sound held behind the following:*]

DAN: [*alarmed*] Good father, and grandfather dear,
    What is that light, I pray,
    That burns above us in the sky
    And turns the night to day?
    Each spike of grass, each stone, is bright
    Upon the midnight hill –
    Yet lamb and sheep they soundly sleep,
    And silent are, and still.

JOHN: [*gazing up, wondering*] Such fire it comes not from the stars,
    Nor comes it from the moon –
    And bolder is it than the sun
    That blazes at the noon.

BEN: My children, kneel;
    My children, pray
    That God may give us grace,
    For none may know when he must go
    To meet him face to face:
    [*Music.*]
    Here is a holy place.

[*Music. More light. Three* ANGELS *appear in the sky above the summit of the hill. Music behind the following:*]

1ST ANGEL: Fear not, shepherds, for I bring
Tidings of a new-born King –
Not in castle, not in keep,
Nor in tower tall and steep;
Not in manor-house or hall,
But a humble ox's stall.

2ND ANGEL: Underneath a standing star
And where sheep and cattle are,
In a bed of straw and hay
God's own Son is born this day.
If to Bethlehem you go,
This the truth you soon shall know.

3RD ANGEL: And as signal and as sign,
Sure as all the stars that shine,
You shall find him, shepherds all,
Swaddled in a baby-shawl;
And the joyful news will share
With good people everywhere.

2ND ANGEL: Therefore, listen as we cry:

THREE ANGELS: Glory be to God on high,
And his gifts of love and peace
To his people never cease.

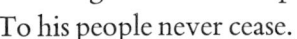

[*Light and music fade on* ANGELS. *A moment of silence. The* SHEPHERDS, *bewildered, exchange glances, shake their heads, rub their eyes.*]

DAN: Grandfather, O tell me clear,
Did *you* see and did *you* hear
Angel-voices, angel-gleam?
Do I wake? Or do I dream?

BEN: [*reassuring*] Why, indeed the angels came . . .

JOHN: [*quickly*] And I heard and saw the same . . .

BEN: So, with swift and fearful tread,

Let us to that cattle-shed.

DAN: But the night is dark and deep.
Who will watch the lambs and sheep?

BEN: Dearest grandson, do not fear;
God will keep them safely here:
Guard the hill and guard the plain
Soundly till we come again.
[*He smiles, and removes the pot from the fire.*]

JOHN: Then let's music play...

DAN: And sing!

BEN: For we go to greet a King!

[*Music.*]

SHEPHERDS: [*sing*] High in the heaven
A gold star burns
Lighting our way
As the great world turns.

            Silver the frost
It shines on the stem
As we now journey
To Bethlehem.

            White is the ice
At our feet as we tread,
Pointing a path
To the manger-bed.

[*They go off R., singing. Their voices fade. Silence. Then, a couple of long moans from* THIEVING JACK. *We see him lying in a heap on the hill-side as though struck by a thunderbolt. The* SHEPHERDS *approach from back L., following a winding path down the hill. Music.*]

SHEPHERDS: [*sing*] High in the heaven
    A gold star burns
    Lighting our way
    As the great world turns . . .

[*They break off.*]

BEN: Why, mercy me, who's this I see
All white and wan and shaking . . .
[THIEVING JACK *gives a loud groan.*]
Flat on his back and with a sack –
And what a noise he's making!
[*More groans.*]

JOHN: Good stranger, own: was it a stone
That sent you downhill clattering?
[*Groans and chattering teeth from* THIEVING JACK.]
And is that why you moaning lie,
And all your teeth a-chattering?
[*Groans and more chattering teeth. The* SHEPHERDS *group themselves about* THIEVING JACK *as he sits up, greatly shaken.*]

THIEVING JACK: My friends, tonight was such a sight
Above me in the 'eavens,
It's blown me wits to bits – I'm all
At sixes and at sevens.
I saw the fire of fifty suns,
The sky was broken wide,
An' all the lights of God shone down –
There was nowhere to hide!
I 'eard the sound of seven seas
Upon the beatin' shore.
The strong earth shuddered at me feet.
I 'eard a mountain roar.
There was a noise of whirrin' wings
About the place I trod,
An' at the 'eart of all, it seemed,
I 'eard the voice of God.
What means that sight, what means that sound
I cannot speak nor say.
Shepherds, pray help me from this place
As you go on your way –
For here Jack cannot stay.

JOHN: Rise up, master, do not fret –
You shall see the morning yet!
Keep you quiet, keep you calm;
Take my hand and take my arm:
For the light that shone around,
Cast you senseless to the ground,
Was a host of angels white

>   Praising Heaven in the height,
>   Praising Heaven on the earth,
>   And a King and Saviour's birth –
>   Long, long promised...

DAN: And, they told,
In a stable, by our fold!

BEN: Come, friend, with us through the wild
To a mother, and her child:
That, among mankind, we be
First of folk God's Son to see.

THIEVING JACK: That I will, and give you thanks.
[*They help him up, and he moves stiffly.*]
Oh, me arms! And oh, me shanks!
[*Groans.*]
Bruised me body! Bent me bones
By the sticks and by the stones!
[*Groans again.*]
Gave each finger such a crack,
I can scarcely hold...
[*Suddenly remembers the theft of the lamb. He gasps out the words:*]
Me sack!
[*The SHEPHERDS remain quite unconscious of the reason for THIEVING JACK's extra uneasiness.*]

BEN: It seems that you journeyed from market, good stranger,

But crossing our hill is no freedom from danger
Of footpad and felon, or thieving attack
From villains who'd empty the pack on your
  back!

(SHEPHERDS *strike up their music, play quietly
and even foot a brief dance while allowing* THIEV
ING JACK *time to pull himself together and rub
away his aches. As he does so, he delivers the follow
ing aside:*]

THIEVING JACK: My eye! I'd forgotten – I've 'ad such a shock –
The black and white lamb as I stole from their
  flock!
And not only that: I'm afeared and afraid
I've robbed and I've bobbed 'em what's come to
  me aid.

Me 'ead fairly whizzes, I'm in such a jam!
To own I'm a thief it's ashamed that I am.
I'll bear the sack gentle and easy and neat,
An' 'ope that there lambkin won't let out a bleat.
My goodness! My badness! There's never a doubt,
If I does a wrong, someone's bound to find out.
But I've learned me lesson – I've 'ad such a fright;
When we gets to the stable, I'll put it all right.
[*He joins the others, who move off L., singing.*]

SHEPHERDS: [*sing*] High in the heaven
A gold star burns
Lighting our way
As the great world turns.

Silver the frost
It shines on the stem
As we now journey
To Bethlehem.

[*They are gone. Lights come up C., as in a cave under the hill.* MARY *is seated, holding the Infant Jesus.* JOSEPH *stands a little to her L. Music.*]

MARY: [*sings*] Sleep, King Jesus,
Your royal bed
Is made of hay
In a cattle-shed.
Sleep, King Jesus,
Do not fear,
Joseph is watching
And waiting near.

Warm in the wintry air
You lie,
The ox and the donkey
Standing by,
With summer eyes
They seem to say:
Welcome, Jesus,
On Christmas Day!

Sleep, King Jesus:
Your diamond crown
High in the sky
Where the stars look down.
Let your reign
Of love begin,
That all the world
May enter in.

[*Music of the* SHEPHERDS *is heard as they approach.* JOSEPH *stands at the entrance to the stable to greet them as they appear round the foot of the hill from R.*]

JOSEPH: I bid you enter, shepherds, as you come
From the world's dark with fiddle, pipe and drum,
And nipping fingers, and white-smoking breath!
My name is Joseph.
Out of Nazareth
I journeyed far with gentle Mary here,
And who, this night, a son has borne so dear.
Therefore, good shepherds from the mountain steep,
Draw near to where the infant lies asleep
That you may tell to all, and tell it true,
The tale of wonder now made known to you.

BEN: [*shaking him by the hand*] Joseph, we thank you for your welcome warm
As we step in from out the weather's harm.

Angels, Archangels in the sky looked down
And bade us leave our flocks, and to the town:
And this we did with joy, and with hearts light
That Jesus Christ, God's Son, is born tonight –
And by God's grace is given human birth
To live, with sinful man, upon the earth.
So, Mary, lady, on my knees I fall
To worship him who comes to save us all.
[*He kneels.*]
No gift have I to bring the Heavenly King
Save my poor fiddle, and a fiddle-string.
[*He plucks it.*]
But this, that is my comfort and my joy,
I freely offer to the Holy Boy.

JOHN: And I, sweet mother, as the babe I scan,
And see God's gift to woman and to man,
Give him my whistle-pipe.
[*He kneels and offers it to* MARY.]
Now, haste the day
As a good shepherd, *he* will pipe and play.

DAN: [*steps forward*] Jesus, I bring a greeting fair and fine,
Proud that your birth day is the same as mine.
Alas, no gift have I in either hand,
I've neither gear nor goods at my command:
Only this drum.
[*He kneels.*]

But with the crowing cock
I'll have a shepherd's crook, a shepherd's smock;
Yet these I will not bring, but with the light,
My dearest gift – a lambkin black and white.
This I am promised. This is to be mine –
And mine to give: and of my love, a sign.
The lamb I'll offer, for your keep and care,
On bended knee, to mark the day we share.
[THIEVING JACK *is now standing on his own.*]

THIEVING JACK: [*aside*] Great blocks and bricks,
Now 'ere's a fix –
An' all of me own makin'!
If truth I tell,
To prison-cell
A journey I'll be takin'!
For 'ere I am,
That little lamb
Snug in me thievin' sack . . .
[*Pause. Then he comes to a decision.*]
BUT
I'll be strong
An' shame the wrong,
An' dare to give it back.
This Infant King
Of whom they sing
Is merciful and good;
So, from this day,

As best I may,
I'll do things as I should!
[*He clears his throat loudly and turns towards th*
SHEPHERDS.]
Kind shepherds three, who freely gave me aid
When on the 'ill I lay, and was afraid –
Blinded by 'eaven's light, struck by its sound,
Stiff as a stone upon the quakin' ground –
Shepherds, who raised me up and spoke me fair
Comforted me, an' took me in your care:
[*A deep breath.*]
I was no peaceful traveller on the 'ill,
For on your sheepfold I'd long gazed my fill,
And as you watched about your
   furze-fire bright
I crept, *a robber*, to your flock last night.
The lamb that's black an' white, *I'd* fancied too,
An' thought, 'Why, Jack, that's just the one for
   you!'
An' so I popped it in the very sack
I bears, so careful-like, upon me back.
See, as I opens it . . .
[*Faint bleat.*]
The 'ead appear . . .
[*Louder bleat.*]
Its Jacob-coloured coat . . .
[*Bleat.*]

        The eye, the ear.
        [*Bleat.*]
        And see, my cheek is red,
        My shame is sore;
        I vows I'll go a-thievin' nevermore,
        An' give you back the lamb; though well I know
        For this night's work to prison I should go.
        This price I'll gladly pay; but one thing lack.
        Humbly I beg of you – forgive old Jack.
        [*He hands the lamb over to* DAN.]

DAN: [*warmly*] That, willingly –

JOHN: And I –

BEN: And I as well.
        As for the stolen lamb, we'll no man tell.

DAN:	And thanks to Jack, my gift I *now* can make.
	Take it, my lady, for your Son's own sake:
	This trusting lamb that on my arm now lies,
	As rests on yours the God-child, pure and wise
	[DAN *presents the lamb to* MARY.]
THIEVING JACK:	[*kneels*] Mother – a gift *I'd* give him if I could.
MARY:	And that you have: a heart that's turned to good.
	Likewise, in Jesu's name, to all I say:
	Receive our thanks for these your gifts today.
JOSEPH:	Thank you for whistle-pipe, and fiddle true –
	When they are played, masters, we'll think on you!
MARY:	And thank you for the lamb: of sin and stain
	As innocent as him who comes to reign;
	And ere you rise, and ere your ways you take,
	A gift, from Jesus Christ, to *you* I make.
	This goodly lamb I give to you again
	As sign of God's own gift from Heaven to men
	[MARY *returns the lamb to* DAN. *Faint bleat.*]
	Go, tell to all the angel-story bright:
	And how you saw the word made flesh tonight
BEN:	That we will, lady, each with joyful heart:
	And wish God's family well. And so, depart.

[*Music for song.* SHEPHERDS *and* THIEVING JACK *sing a line of each verse solo, in turn, and mime the way in which the various instruments mentioned are played.*]

SHEPHERDS AND
THIEVING JACK: [*sing*] Fiddle, play!
        (Zim, zim, zim)
    Strike the drum!
        (Dum, dum, dum)
    Blow the pipe!
        (Toot, toot, toot)
    For Christmas come!
        (Clap, clap, clap)

Chorus: Merrily!
      Cheerily!
        Let the music say –
    Christ was born in Bethlehem,
    And is born today!

Verse 2:   Beat the gong!
        (Dong, dong, dong)
    Blow the horn!
        (Ta, ta, ta)
    Sound the flute!
        (Tee, tee, tee)
    For Christ is born!
        (Clap, clap, clap)

Chorus: Merrily!
      Cheerily!
        Let the music say –
    Christ was born in Bethlehem,
    And is born today!

Verse 3:	Cymbals, clash!
	    (Clash, clash, clash)
	Church-bells ring!
	    (Ding, ding, ding)
	Play the harp!
	    (Ting, ting, ting)
	For Christ is King!
	    (Clap, clap, clap)

Chorus:	Merrily!
	  Cheerily!
	    Let the music say –
	Christ was born in Bethlehem,
	And is born today!

[*They are dancing at the play's end.*]

The Opening Music. This should be played by two people at one piano, and although the top part looks rather daunting it is merely octaves for most of the piece. The chords in both parts lie easily under the hands.

The Shepherds' Song and High in the Heaven (same tune)

The Shepherds' Song

I am a shepherd,
My name is Ben,
I've shepherded
Three-score years and ten.
Spring, summer, autumn,
Winter, too!
The years and the seasons
How they flew!
Now my nose is fire
And my hair is frost,
But never a sheep or lamb
I lost.

I am a shepherd,
My name is John,
I work with my father
And my son.
In forty years
Of cold and heat,
I never have lost
A lamb or sheep.
In weather gold,
In weather grey,
No sheep or lamb
Was stolen away.

I am a shepherd,
My name is Dan,
In seven more years
I'll be a man,
But ever since I
Could stand or run
I've shepherded sheep
In rain and sun.
I've shepherded sheep
On hill and moor
As my father did,
And his before.

High in the Heaven

High in the heaven
A gold star burns
Lighting our way
As the great world turns.

Silver the frost
It shines on the stem
As we now journey
To Bethlehem.

White is the ice
At our feet as we tread,
Pointing a path
To the manger-bed.

The Shepherds' Jig. An oboe, recorder, flute and drum can all join in the jig, taking different phrases of the melody – the drum keeping a constant rhythmic pattern.

Now the Bell at Midnight. A glockenspiel can play the note 'C' in crotchet rhythm all the way through this song. Xylophones could also join in if the soft sticks are used.

Now the bell at midnight
Chimes to make us glad,
Bringing in the birthday
Of a shepherd lad.

He shall have a wooden crook,
A smock as clean as light;
He shall have a lambkin
Whose wool is black and white.

The Angels' Music

SECONDO
Ethereally (♩ = 60)

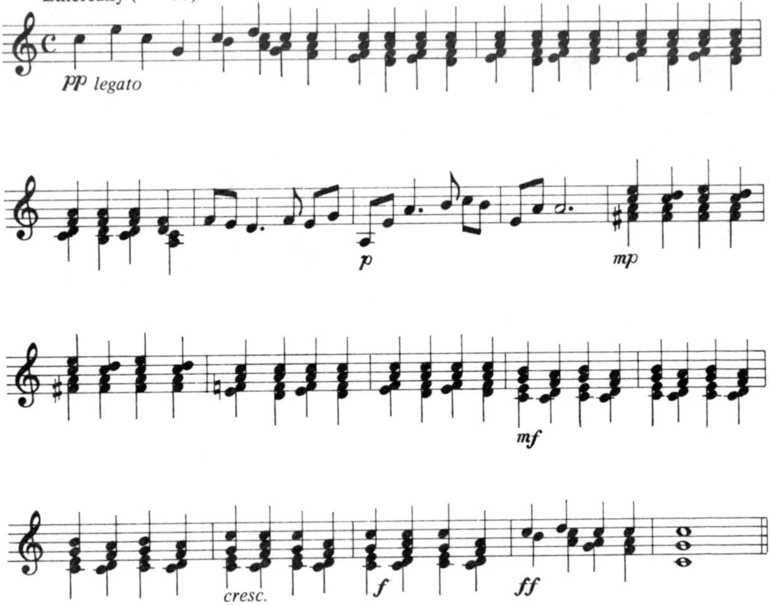

pp legato

p   *mp*

mf

cresc.   *f*   *ff*

Mary's Lullaby. This song could also be used as a two-part song with the under part of the treble line being either hummed or sung to words such as 'lull-a' or 'hush-a'.

Sleep, King Jesus,
Your royal bed
Is made of hay
In a cattle-shed.
Sleep, King Jesus,
Do not fear,
Joseph is watching
And waiting near.

Warm in the wintry air
You lie,
The ox and the donkey
Standing by,
With summer eyes
They seem to say:
Welcome, Jesus,
On Christmas Day!

Sleep, King Jesus:
Your diamond crown
High in the sky
Where the stars look down.
Let your reign
Of love begin,
That all the world
May enter in.

Fiddle Play

Fiddle Play (music on opposite page). All the instruments mentioned in the verses can feature in this song. If they are pitched instruments the notes of the song can be played. The song can be sung in two parts, the voices dividing in the verses in every alternate bar.

The author suggests that the audience might learn this song before the performance in order to join in at the end.

Fiddle, play!
   (Zim, zim, zim)
Strike the drum!
   (Dum, dum, dum)
Blow the pipe!
   (Toot, toot, toot)
For Christmas come!
   (Clap, clap, clap)

Merrily!
  Cheerily!
    Let the music say –
Christ was born in Bethlehem,
And is born today!

Beat the gong!
   (Dong, dong, dong)
Blow the horn!
   (Ta, ta, ta)
Sound the flute!
   (Tee, tee, tee)
For Christ is born!
   (Clap, clap, clap)

Merrily!
  Cheerily!
    Let the music say –
Christ was born in Bethlehem,
And is born today!

Cymbals, clash!
   (Clash, clash, clash)
Church-bells ring!
   (Ding, ding, ding)
Play the harp!
   (Ting, ting, ting)
For Christ is King!
   (Clap, clap, clap)

Merrily!
  Cheerily!
    Let the music say–
Christ was born in Bethlehem,
And is born today!

ABOUT THE AUTHOR

CHARLES CAUSLEY, one of Britain's finest contemporary poets, is a holder of the Queen's Gold Medal for Poetry, and in 1977 the University of Exeter conferred on him the Honorary Degree of Doctor of Letters. He was for many years a teacher in his native Cornwall, but is now a full-time writer. His famous collection of poems for children, *Figgie Hobbin*, is available in Puffin, and he is also editor of *The Puffin Book of Magic Verse* and *The Puffin Book of Salt-Sea Verse*.

OTHER PUFFINS BY CHARLES CAUSLEY

Figgie Hobbin

One of the most popular and well-loved collections of poems for children to have been published in the last decade, *Figgie Hobbin* is firmly Cornish in flavour, sometimes savoury and sometimes sweet.

The Puffin Book of Salt-Sea Verse

Here are poems about sailors, fish and fisherfolk, ships, storms, dreams and treasures, and above all about 'the wild and wasteful ocean' itself. Gathered together by Charles Causley, who has spent all his life on or near the sea.

The Puffin Book of Magic Verse

'Incantations, curses, elves, changelings, wizards, ghosts, mermaids and the like are plain enough subjects in an anthology of magic verse. But I have also included poems of the mystery and magic many poets see in the day-to-day events in the natural world and of everyday life.'

OTHER PUFFINS YOU MIGHT ENJOY

Charlie and the Chocolate Factory:
A Play adapted by Richard George

It's always fun reading plays, and almost everyone who has read *Charlie and the Chocolate Factory*, by Roald Dahl, has wanted to join in Charlie's adventures. Now, with the help of this dramatization, any bunch of enthusiastic actors could put on a performance of this play, either at home or at school.

A Book of Bosh
Edward Lear [chosen by Brian Alderson]

Here is a new and unusual collection of Learical Lyrics and Puffles of Prose, put together by a devoted admirer and aimed to display a wide range of Bosh both known and lesser known. As well as limericks and nonsense songs, there are *eggstrax* from his letters and a dictionary of his *wurbl inwentions*.

Heard about the Puffin Club?

... it's a way of finding out more about Puffin books and authors, of winning prizes (in competitions), sharing jokes, a secret code and perhaps seeing your name in print! When you join you get a copy of our magazine *Puffin Post*, sent to you four times a year, a badge and membership book.

For details of subscription and an application form, send a stamped addressed envelope to:

The Puffin Club Dept A
Penguin Books Limited
Bath Road
Harmondsworth
Middlesex UB7 ODA

and if you live in Australia, please write to:

The Australian Puffin Club
Penguin Books Australia Limited
P.O. Box 257
Ringwood
Victoria 3134